Incidentals

ALSO BY SHEILA YASMIN MARIKAR

The Goddess Effect

Friends in Napa

Incidentals

a novel

Sheila Yasmin Marikar

Little
a

Published by Little A, New York
www.apub.com

EU product safety contact:
Amazon Media EU S. à r.l.
38, avenue John F. Kennedy, L-1855 Luxembourg
amazonpublishing-gpsr@amazon.com

ISBN-13: 9781662527692 (hardcover)
ISBN-13: 9781662527685 (paperback)
ISBN-13: 9781662527678 (digital)

Cover design by Lucy Kim
Cover image: © Maksim Toome, © Daria Proskuryakova, © popout, © icemanphotos / Shutterstock

Printed in the United States of America

First edition

To all the incidentals I've met along the way.

ONE

"Your boarding pass, please?"

Sarah blinks up at the woman behind the reception desk of the Emirates Lounge at Los Angeles International Airport. Her boarding pass? Doesn't Sam have it? Sam holds on to all of their documents when they travel together, a vestige from their first trip abroad, so long ago now that her memory of the trip itself has grown mold. But when she turns to her husband, he gives her a look of barely concealed exasperation.

That's when she remembers. She insisted on holding on to her own boarding pass and passport. "We're not having a repeat of London," she'd said, before they left home. "Not after what happened last time."

Last time. As if Sam needed reminding of what had happened the last time they'd embarked on a big international flight, London to Los Angeles, when he had gotten so drunk in the Virgin Atlantic lounge that he had been denied boarding. You have to be *really drunk* to be denied boarding a flight out of London. It was beyond embarrassing. And he had had the folio with both of their passports, embossed with their initials, an engagement gift from his uncle, so when he was carted off to the Heathrow holding cell—he'd resisted arrest—Sarah was left to languish at the gate.

She had to bring it up. She knew how much he hated to be reminded of that incident. He'd apologized until the word "sorry" lost meaning, devolved to a sludge of syllables. What could he do? The cops were racist.

"They have a thing against us, babe, you know that, it's baked in," he'd told her pleadingly, in the airport Hilton that he'd checked them into upon his release eight hours later. He had thought that they could get a bottle of Champagne and toast to twenty-four more hours in their favorite city on the planet—well, his, anyway—albeit in a suburb an hour outside of London and not London proper. A minor aberration, nothing a little bubbly couldn't wash away. There had to be good chicken tikka masala by the airport. They loved chicken tikka masala.

But no. She'd paced a semicircle around the bed with the too-starched sheets, refusing to look him in the eye, let alone drink the Perrier-Jouët sloshing around the cheap plastic ice bucket, sweating all over the laminate hutch.

Now, in front of the receptionist guarding access to the Emirates Lounge, Sarah presses her lips together in apology and rifles through her nylon carryall. It has been specifically designed for travel, has eighteen compartments with which to organize your laptop, chargers, identification, and personal items, and she uses exactly none of them. At the bottom of the bag, boarding passes from trips past overlap with one another, mottled by time and spilled liquids, like leaves on a forest floor.

Coming up empty, she pats herself down. It's not in the pockets of her cargo pants (there are seven). Not in the side pockets of her oversized denim jacket. Finally, she finds the boarding pass in the right breast pocket, crumpled up, the long ends seemingly stuck together.

As she attempts to uncrumple it, a wad of gum reveals itself, yawning wide.

The receptionist turns down her mouth. Sam puts his head in his hand.

"Sorry," Sarah says, picking the gum off, rolling it into a ball, and shoving it into yet another pocket. She's not normally a gum chewer, but the Uber driver offered. She tells herself that she'll remember to throw it out, she won't forget.

She presents the sullied boarding pass to the receptionist, who holds a barcode scanner a good foot above the offending document and waves them toward the long entrance corridor with a flap of her hand. Sarah can feel Sam's eyes on her as they wheel their suitcases down the hall.

"Can you not?" she says, not looking in his direction. She knows she ought to do better. Be more of an adult. She's almost forty, she's too old to act like this, in theory. But gum on a boarding pass is nothing compared to the way that he made a fool of them both at Heathrow. The way he continues to make a fool of them, if she's being honest.

Sam knows he should pick his battles, their couples counselor has said as much. "It just might be easier, if you were a *little* more organized—"

"I said, *can you not?*"

Sam exhales roughly and fixes his gaze on a white podium up ahead. There's a plastic bucket of Champagne on top of it, Krug Grande Cuvée, sublime stuff by airport lounge standards. The uniformed woman behind it is smiling at him, smiling in a way his wife never smiles anymore.

She holds out a glass. Sam thanks her as he accepts it. He can feel Sarah's side-eye.

"You haven't eaten anything," she says.

"We're on vacation," he says. "Besides, you know that I never eat before noon." Why does he feel the need to justify himself, he wonders. He paid for their tickets. Well—credit card points and airline miles paid for their tickets. Their combined points and miles. But he knows how to catalog, monetize, and deploy them to make the most of their value. Sarah can't be bothered, Sarah with her journalist boondoggles and free hotel stays and la-di-da, everything-will-work-out-because-the-universe-decrees-it attitude.

Well. Sarah *used* to have that attitude. For the past year, it's like a black cloud has swallowed her up, turned her into *Sad*-rah, a nickname Sam uses in his head and his head alone, because if his wife ever heard it, she would rip him to shreds like a notice from the IRS.

He knows that he has played a part in her depression—if that is, indeed, what it is; she refuses to see a therapist despite his suggestions (which have been gentle, maybe overly so). He feels, frankly, awful. He wants them to be further along. In a house instead of a condominium in the not-so-glamorous part of Hollywood, on a side street a stone's throw away from the Walk of Fame and its attendant tourists and vagrants. With a family on the horizon. With the sort of discretionary income that would allow them to *not* liquidate all their points and miles to take a last-ditch, if-we-can't-make-it-here, we-can't-make-it-anywhere trip to save their marriage.

He has never been to the Maldives, but from what he understands, it's tough to be mad when you're surrounded by a bathwater-warm lagoon the color of a midsummer sky. Tough but not impossible, and he is not confident that they won't argue during the seven nights to come, nine if you count the travel there and back.

Which is why he sprung for business-class tickets on Emirates. The business-class cabin of Emirates has a bar, a semicircular, gleaming (according to the photos he's clicked through online more times than he'd care to count) mahogany bar staffed with chignoned flight attendants who, in acknowledgment of the fact that you've paid upward of $10,000—or the equivalent in points and miles—for access to the cabin, will happily shake you one, three, five, however many martinis you'd like over the course of the sixteen-hour flight to Dubai and the four-hour connection from Dubai to Malé. He knows he can easily take down seven (martinis, not flight attendants, he stopped playing that game when he and Sarah got serious), but he also knows that Sarah will be watching and judging, and that he should probably use some of the in-flight hours to sleep, because there will be a resplendent bar at the lounge in Dubai, where they have a layover, and he'd like to avail himself of that, too.

Is he an alcoholic? Define "alcoholic."

He surveys the lounge, looking for two of the Eames-ish chairs with ottomans, ideally overlooking the terminal. Sarah charges ahead of him, toward the buffet and the cafeteria-style seating that surrounds it. He watches as she brings her suitcase to a stop at a two-top that is spitting distance from a family with a toddler. The toddler is banging an iPad on the table. He wonders if the iPad's yellow silicone cover is strong enough to ward off the damage inflictable by a two-year-old in the throes of a tantrum; he doubts it.

He does not want to sit there. In the absence of an Eames-ish chair to kick back on while enjoying another pre-meal glass of Champagne—an aperitif, if you will, the French consider Champagne food, it's not alcohol, not *really*—he'd prefer to post up in the lounge's invitation-only dining room, where you can order à la carte. The menu is three pages long. He pulled strings to get invitations; his wine supplier knows a guy who knows a guy.

He approaches his wife, who is scowling at her phone.

"Guess what?"

Her eyes flick up in a way that suggests she wants nothing he can offer. But who knows what will make her happy? The least he can do is try. He reaches into his duffel and unfurls two laminated cards that the receptionist handed him while Sarah was rummaging around for her boarding pass.

"Invites to the private dining room," he says. "Had to call in a favor. Pulling out all the stops for my best babe." He taps her playfully on the arm with one of the cards; she recoils.

"I'd rather do the buffet," she says.

Who would choose sneeze guards over must-be-on-the-guest-list à la carte? Surely not his wife.

"Did I mention," he says, brandishing the cards, "that it's *invitation only*?"

"I know. I've been, remember? Their menu sucks. Deep-fried calamari and whatnot. I'm trying to be healthy."

That's right, boondoggle Sarah has been to the invitation-only lounge, back when Emirates flew her to Dubai to write about why it was the new Las Vegas. She spent a week at Atlantis The Royal, eating Nobu, going to nightclubs, and getting Gulf Sea salt scrubs in a thirty-thousand-square-foot spa. One of the most frustrating things about being married to Sarah is how little he can do for her, how much she has already done for herself.

It wasn't always this way. In the beginning, she *liked* deep-fried calamari, especially when he made it Kerala-style. In the beginning, she *liked* Champagne, especially the bottles of Salon that he got at a discount thanks to the wine supplier of Tiffin, the restaurant for which he works. Not that Tiffin serves Salon. Or Champagne. Much to Sam's chagrin, Tiffin is a Kim Crawford and Josh kind of place, middle-of-the-road, red vinyl banquettes so slick that you'd slide off of them were it not for the errant rips in the fabric, sloppily camouflaged by duct tape that may just adhere to the back of your jeans if you're lucky.

"Well, *I've* never been, so I'm going to go," he says, mustering more authority than he feels. If she wants to be "healthy"—as if the à la carte menu contains only deep-fried calamari, as if there isn't a whole plethora of high-fiber, high-protein, produce-forward options on offer, but who knows—who is he to guess what she means by "healthy"? Maybe for his wife, being healthy means not being around him.

She finally looks up, and it's not a good look at all.

"Seriously?" An abbreviated roll of the eyes, a brief shrug of the shoulders. "Fine. Enjoy. See you at the gate."

Sarah turns back to her phone. She half expects Sam to relent and slide into the seat across from her.

Out of the corner of her eye, she sees him stride away.

She knows that she's being irrational but can find no way of acting otherwise. She hates that à la carte dining room, the stuffiness of it, the lack of windows, the fact that you can't dress your salad the way you like.

Yeah, she likes salad. With a hefty squeeze of lemon, a dash of olive oil, and a pinch of sea salt—*actual* sea salt, the flaky sort harvested from European shores, not the grainy stuff that comes in those tiny, perforated packets that she can never open. And why should she have to justify her predilection for salad? Was it a crime to want roughage before a sixteen-hour flight during which even the classiest of premium classes would parcel out servings of mixed greens like gruel in *Oliver Twist*?

Sam always said he wanted to be healthy but, when given the choice, ran toward hedonism like it was his long-lost brother. Maybe it was in his DNA. His father acted the same way. Sarah was not puritanical by any means—she loved Champagne, she relished a party, a raucous 4:00 a.m., cap-it-off-with-In-N-Out type of night. But there was a time and a place.

When she felt confident. When she felt like peacocking, strutting her stuff. Which she had not, of late.

Perhaps she can't blame Sam for wanting to drink. If she were married to her, she would want to escape, too. Numb her senses, speed into oblivion.

She needs a distraction. Anything to stop her from thinking about her own problems. She opens the app, the most used one, the one on which she routinely spends several hours per day, losing track of what is real and what amounts to an elaborate illusion. She pulls up Alana's account and starts tapping. She's already seen many of these posts, from a child's birthday party in Laurel Canyon, but here is something new, the cake, and what a cake it is. Three-tiered pink ombré with a pink sailboat affixed to the top. It's followed by a fit check: Alana's four-year-old daughter in a sailor-style dress, per the party's theme, and Alana herself in a bikini-and-caftan ensemble. "Saint-Tropez tropes," reads the overlaid text, which is in the sans serif font that all the women who got invited to all the events had recently started using.

The caption doesn't quite make sense, but Alana's language doesn't need to. Her beauty and station in life do all the talking. Alana is the head of brand at a lifestyle company founded by a Grammy-winning singer, a company that, while initially laughable, became the sort of trendsetting juggernaut that earned the establishment's respect as well as millions of dollars. In Sarah's mind, Alana has it all: money, power, respect, good looks, a husband who appears to adore her, and—here is the rub—a daughter adorable enough to be a model in mainstream television commercials, not just sponsored social media ads, but who would not actually model because Alana would never "do that" to her child. Her child would go to Yale because the multihyphenate Alana works for would write her a recommendation. (Yale or Brown. Probably Brown.)

Where Sarah lacks information, she fills in details befitting the narrative ossified in her mind, itself a hodgepodge of assumptions spackled on top of facts.

Alana and Sarah had moved from New York to Los Angeles around the same time, knew the same people, had lunched together at the Sunset Tower Hotel twice, had run into each other at parties and events more times than Sarah could count. Like Sarah, Alana was of South Asian descent, and when they were both new to LA, people occasionally mistook one of them for the other, which Sarah never minded. Alana was a better dresser, a better schmoozer, and, given the charitable organizations to which she belonged, presumably a better person than she was. She was flattered to be mistaken for Alana.

They had also worked together, in Sarah's previous life as a journalist. Sarah had interviewed Alana's boss, the singer/founder, and while Sarah and her editors thought that the resultant story had been fair and balanced, Alana and her boss did not agree. Alana called Sarah and dressed her down over the phone: "What were you *thinking*? Were you trying to be cute? Because this is not cute—this is how you make enemies, and I thought you'd be smart enough to know that."

Sarah wasn't trying to be cute. Sarah just thought it was kind of *funny* that a lauded singer and wellness entrepreneur couldn't seem to stop puffing from a banana-shaped vape that engulfed her (and everyone around her) in a sickly sweet cloud. ("That Magnolia Bakery banana pudding was going to be the death of me," the singer had said, "until I found this.")

No way could Sarah have left out that observation, that line. She had thought Alana would get it, Alana had a sense of humor, but she couldn't say she was entirely surprised by Alana's blowup, which was presumably predicated by her boss. This happened. Some people didn't like it when a mirror was held up to them. They preferred to hold the mirror themselves, angle it so that the reflection cast them in the best light. Alana was just doing her job. Brand gatekeepers and journalists did not always see eye to eye. She had assumed things would smooth over in time.

They never quite did. Sarah can't remember the last time she saw Alana in real life. And in the intervening years, Alana's star rose as Sarah's fell. Journalists hardly had a place in Los Angeles if they weren't chronicling the ins and outs of Hollywood. Especially journalists who worked for New York–based publications, which none of the LA publicists or brand managers could ever seem to wrap their heads around. "You write for *The New York Times* but you live in LA? You can do that?"

As if there were some referee determining who you could write for based on your zip code. As if you couldn't leave the place from whence you came to reinvent yourself, to start anew. As if people in New York only cared about things that happened in New York.

Well, the last one was kind of true.

She could scoff all she wanted, but there was no denying that she was a fish out of water, and by the way? The water was evaporating, fast. The media industry was shrinking, even her friends in New York were having a tough time landing freelance gigs and holding down full-time jobs, layoffs never not looming.

So she put journalism on the back burner and poured herself into writing a novel. On spec, because that's how it works unless you're as famous as Alana's boss, the Grammy-winning singer/founder. On the assumption that Sam's career, Sam's family, would keep them afloat until she sold it, which, she was certain, would only be a matter of months.

That was three years ago. The novel is now in virtual tatters, cut and pasted and grafted to oblivion, irrelevant, languishing in the cloud, taking up space and not in a good way. It is the thing that Sarah claims to be working on when she loses untold hours to social media, comparing herself to everyone who seems to be living larger than her.

And Alana is living. Thriving. Alana is everything Sarah wants to be, and more. Alana occupies the penthouse of Sarah's mind, is always up there, clomping about in her on-trend heels, reminding Sarah of what she doesn't have, of who she is not.

Sarah has other Alanas in her life, populating her social media feed—the influencer she interviewed, who has become markedly more influential since Sarah's piece on her ran; the jewelry brand founder; the pajama brand founder; this woman who makes really lovely arrangements with plants that she forages from the side of Los Angeles thoroughfares. Most of them are mothers. Most of them know each other, are friends in real life, gather for dinner and book club and coolly pose for selfies in elevators hung with burnished mirrors.

Sarah feels out of the loop because she *is* out of the loop, and she can't figure out whether the problem is her, Sam, Los Angeles, or all of it.

"Miss, may I interest you in a drink?"

She stops spiraling and regards the uniformed server bent over in front of her. Right. While they didn't take food orders in this part of the lounge, they did offer to fetch your beverages.

"Sure," she says, stalling. What she wants is a Negroni. But what if Sam emerges from the à la carte dining room and sees her with her hand around a frosty cocktail, thereby forcing her off her high horse? She can't chastise him for drinking if she's drinking, too. "I'll have a Pellegrino with lime." She says this with more confidence than she feels.

The server furrows his eyebrows. "Is that all? Our resident mixologist this month is from one of the World's 50 Best Bars." He gestures behind him at a placard that states as much. She recognizes this bar. She went to this bar, one of London's finest, on a long-ago work trip to profile a modern-day Emily Post who disseminated etiquette lessons through TikTok. This bar makes a killer Negroni. One that would normally cost twenty-four dollars but, in accordance with airplane lounge laws, will, in this vicinity, be free.

"Hm," she says, stalling once more. So what if Sam sees her drinking? She can do whatever she wants. She's a modern woman. One who can handle her alcohol. One who knows when to stop. Wouldn't it be anti-feminist to curb her desires because of what he might think or say? Emphasis on *might*. There's still a while before boarding, and from what she remembers, there are restrooms attached to the private dining room. Sam has no reason to come out here, besides seeing her. Ha. As if. "Okay, sure, twist my arm," she says, wiggling in a self-deprecating way that makes her hate herself for a moment. She doesn't need to act this way. She's allowed to change her mind! "I'll have a Negroni, please."

"Excellent choice," the server says, gliding away, seemingly satisfied. She wonders if he gets paid on commission or if he's compelled to push the cocktails because the temporary occupants of airports tend to be slightly less annoying once they've had a drink. Key word being "a."

Having breached her definition of healthy, she figures she'll head to the buffet and go whole hog. A few slices of mortadella, unctuous and redolent of barnyard, will nicely offset the Negroni's sweetness, as will a cube or three of Roquefort. Castelvetrano olives? Don't mind if I do, she thinks, filling a little bowl with the glossy green orbs and making room for it on her meat-and-cheese plate. A half scoop of Marcona almonds and she's off to the races, back at her designated table, where her cocktail has been placed atop a leather coaster. They don't have the ice she likes—the big block, the better to evenly melt—but beggars can't be choosers, and *hot damn*, she thinks, taking a sip, the Negroni is so good that she would, in fact, beg for it. Not sure what she was thinking earlier, denying herself this.

The fact is that her press trip days are over. Unless she swallows what shred of pride she has left, grows a new personality, and reinvents herself as a perimenopausal influencer, she will have to make like the rest of the world and pay for access to the good life, which is a problem, seeing as how she has a dwindling sum of money in her bank account and a negligible amount coming in. Her most steady gig: writing copy for a members-only restaurant reservations app. Every time she blurbs another new restaurant in another far-flung location she'll probably never get to try, a little piece of her dies.

So she would do best to drink this cocktail quickly and order another before the one-quarter-left mark because you never knew how long it would take them to make the next cocktail—a crush of people could come into the lounge, as often happened—and she wanted to be able to enjoy *at least* two cocktails before switching to wine, which would go better with the mains and sides arrayed at the buffet, the lamb tagine and the couscous and the pomegranate-seed-adorned baba ghanoush that she'd stud with cucumber and carrot sticks, which would make it kind of like a salad. Baba ghanoush was eggplant, after all. She *was* being healthy. Health came in so many forms.

~

Sarah has finished her second cocktail and her second cheese, meat, and olive plate, and is loading up for a third time with the cuisine of the Middle East when she feels her husband appear at her side. Feels or sees. It's hard to miss his purple Nike Air Maxes, eyesore that they are.

"Enjoying yourself?" he asks, not unkindly.

She exhales, pictures her demons exiting her body, spinning circles above the buffet. "I mean, I guess." She tells herself to be nice. She will do herself no favors if she blows him off. But she will also do herself no favors if she feigns joy, so she brings up what's been on her mind, the thing that they've discussed but that she still can't quite parse.

"I guess I just don't know why we're doing this," she says, turning to face him. They're close enough to the buffet that her jean-jacketed elbow momentarily grazes the sneeze guard.

"Eating before the flight?" he replies, playing dumb. He knows what she's asking, but they've been over it so many times. He does not want to get into it again. Not here. Not now. Not in the lounge, in front of all these strangers.

"You know what I mean," she says, gesticulating to such a degree that the lamb tagine veers to the edge of her plate, as if it, too, is loath to take part in whatever's going on here. "It's obscene, how much we're spending on this trip. I know it's points and miles, but shouldn't we be saving that for other things, for a rainy day?" She can see his face darkening, but she feels that she has to keep going, make herself heard. He steamrollered her with this trip, bringing it up when she was knee-deep in the umpteenth revision of her novel and unable to concentrate on anything besides the dreaded blinking cursor on her computer screen. She blurred her vision, reading the email confirmations, as if they were meant for someone else, someone carefree and eager to get away with their husband, someone who would be able to slip on a sunny attitude as easily as a sarong (she has no idea how to tie a sarong). She chose not to think about the fact that they were actually going until the last minute, as in, two days ago, when she began packing only because he kept stomping around the condo, dramatically unboxing tropical-print shirts and holding them up for her assessment, each one more garish than the last. If avoidance were a sport, she'd be an Olympic athlete.

Sam talked about add-ons to their agenda, massages, snorkeling, tasting menu dinners. Each time, she sort of hmm-ed and changed the topic. Massages she had no problem with, but there was the issue of cost (surely, they couldn't pay for their treatments with points). Same with tasting menus, which never failed to test her patience. As far as breathing through a tube to meet sea creatures that would see her as fresh meat? She'd rather not.

But those are excuses. The truth: She is afraid. She is afraid of what will happen when she and Sam are alone on an island together, devoid of distractions and the routines that hold their tenuous union together. Tropical vacations are meant for couples that are in love. Sam and Sarah are something else.

They are lost.

"Should we just." She pauses. "Is it too late to, I don't know . . . cancel?"

He abhors when she does this. When they've already set off down a path, literally or figuratively, and she proposes turning back. Most of the time, she doesn't even want to turn back. Most of the time, he suspects, she does it to make herself feel better, to be able to say, if only to herself, I didn't *want* to go, it was all *him*, he *made* me do it. Such a child, his wife.

If she genuinely feels this way, she could've voiced her opinion two months ago, before he booked the trip. About which he asked her thrice. "Hey, is it okay if I," et cetera. Her replies: "Whatever you want." "Sure, I guess." "You're the points guy, you figure it out. I have to go, I'm trying to write."

She could've done it when he relayed the plans he'd made on their behalf—a morning snorkeling trip where they might catch sight of the rare rose-veiled fairy wrasse, a newly discovered fish with sunset-colored scales. A tasting menu meal at the on-site Japanese restaurant, complete with wine pairings. A four-hand Ayurvedic massage—eight hands in total, four hands for each of them.

Who wouldn't be excited about a four-hand Ayurvedic massage?

In the pocket of his joggers, Sam's phone starts buzzing. Saved by the bell. He looks at the number. Tiffin. The West Hollywood location. The one that would be his crown jewel if only his father would give him the crown as he previously promised. Surely some crisis on the other end.

He looks up at his wife. "We can't cancel," he says. "We'd lose everything. You know that." He holds up his phone. "I have to take this."

He fixes his gaze on a wall and starts striding toward it so that he doesn't have to see Sarah roll her eyes or otherwise express her dissatisfaction. Baffling, her attitude. People would *kill* to go to the Maldives, especially Jala, the seven-star resort where they're staying for seven nights.

"Talk to me," he says, holding the phone to his ear and feeling immediately idiotic. Who does he think he is, Ari Gold? (He would die to be Ari Gold.)

"Boss, it's Anand," Tiffin West Hollywood's manager, Steve, tells Sam. "He called out sick again."

Sam presses his thumb and middle finger to his temples. Anand is supposed to be a head chef, but that would require him to spend more hours in the kitchen than he does at the bars in Santa Monica, and Anand seems to have a problem understanding that. Sam knew this would happen. Ninety-nine percent of the folks his father hires fail to launch, impress the old man in some way or another, and then, paycheck secured, reveal themselves to be the con men (or women) they always were.

"This is what, the fourth time this month?" Sam says.

"Fifth," says Steve.

Sam once talked to his father about instituting a three-strikes-you're-out rule. "Wha?" his father said, flapping his hand as if to shoo away a mosquito. "No way, man. You manage properly, you don't have to do these strikes and outs and whatnots."

Maybe that worked if you had a team of all-stars. Sam was managing the wack pack.

"Can Edwin pick up the slack?" Sam asks. His longtime line cook is one of the good guys.

"Sure, but he's getting frustrated," says Steve. "It's a lot."

"I know," says Sam. "I know. Look. Anand's gotta go. You know that, I know that, I just have to—"

"Talk to the big boss," Steve says, underlining what Sam has long known to be true. He has no agency. All major decisions regarding Tiffin come from the top, a.k.a. Balraj Gupta, better known simply as B., the man who made him, the man who makes him absolutely insane.

"I've gotta go," Sam says, suddenly eager to end this call. "I'll have internet for the next hour or so. Text me if anything comes up."

"Don't worry, boss, we've got this," Steve says. Sam suspects that Steve will motivate the staff with a combination of old-school hip-hop and tequila, one disseminated by a Bluetooth speaker, the other by a Don Julio bottle, and while it'll make for a rowdier environment than he or his father likes, it might serve Balraj right, to see what happens when Sam's not there.

"Have a blast," Steve says. "Maldives, right? Trip of a lifetime."

Sam mumbles something to the effect of thanks and hangs up. It is the trip of a lifetime. With a woman he wants to spend the rest of his life with. If she'll let him.

He turns around and sees her back at her table, half-eaten meal pushed to the side, a goblet of red wine in one hand, phone in the other.

Scrolling yet again. He knows those apps are bad for her, but when he says as much, she lashes out at him, says he doesn't understand how her job works, that she *needs* to be on social media, that she will render herself irrelevant if she quits or even takes a prolonged break.

She is an adult, and she is preternaturally good at presenting herself—this afternoon's display at the airline lounge reception desk aside—as intelligent, capable, and curious. It's one of the things that made him fall in love with her, back in New York, back when they were just friends.

But he also knows that she is exceedingly hard on herself, that she hates asking for help, and that she gets into her head to the degree that—well, he doesn't know what goes on in there, what jungles and caves exist in the dark, uncharted terrain of his wife's mind. Where she goes when she retreats from him.

He wants to get them back to where they once were, but he has no idea how. He thought this trip might help. Thus far, it's only made things worse.

Two tones sound from the speakers in the lounge; an announcement in a robotic voice with a British lilt follows: "Passengers of Emirates flight 11 to Dubai are now invited to board."

Shit, he thinks, watching a fleet of suitcases assemble and move toward the exit. He likes to be at the gate when boarding starts. He hates having to elbow his way through the crowd, all "excuse me" and "sorry," the cross looks from the other passengers. Sarah is the opposite. Left to her own devices, Sarah would like to be the last person on the plane. Sarah has already expressed her desire to not board this particular flight at all, and he would like to prevent that from happening, if only because it would be a criminal waste of points and miles, and he does not want to go to one of the world's most romantic resorts (according to all the glossy travel magazines) alone.

He jogs back to the à la carte dining room, where his carry-on and duffel are resting against a tan banquette. He grabs them and rolls up to Sarah's table. "Babe, time to go."

"I have to refill my water bottle," she says, not looking up. She's mad at him for the way he was curt with her earlier, he can tell.

"They'll have water on the plane," he says.

"You know I never board without a full water bottle."

"Fine, just *hurry up*."

"Boarding takes, like, an hour," she says, finally meeting his gaze. "They're not leaving anytime soon."

"I just want to get on and get settled," he says.

"Then fucking *go*," she says, vehemently enough that the tables around them turn to look. He widens his eyes at her. She looks chastened, like she's about to apologize. He doesn't want to give her the satisfaction.

He whips around and strides toward the exit.

~

By the time Sarah reaches the gate, they're boarding group C. Far from last call. Sam can be such a control freak. She figures it stems from the fact that he doesn't have any meaningful control over his own life, Daddy's little helper, forever longing for something of his own.

She can be such a bitch sometimes.

She was not always this person. She doesn't know how to describe it. It's like one day she woke up and all the parts of her that had been tender had hardened, dried up like orange rinds on a counter. She's not sure what happened. Part of why she moved to Los Angeles was so that this *would not* happen. She knew that if she stayed in New York long enough it would. But maybe it's always lived inside her, this cynic, this coldhearted, selfish individual who can't see beyond herself. Maybe it's the truest version of herself, and she's been hiding it all these years.

She might've saved herself if they had had children. A dismal prospect at this late stage. Beyond the fact of biology—she imagines the inside of her ovaries as a senior citizens home, the remaining stragglers playing bridge and popping wine coolers—and beyond her doubts about whether she would be good enough as a mother, whether she could hack it, there is the issue of how. The fact is that it is hard to have sex with your partner when you are barely on speaking terms and he is drunk all the time. Fine—maybe not *all* the time. What *is* true is that she feels sexy exactly none of the time, does not want to be seen, and has taken to clothing herself in oversized sweatpants so old they have holes in the crotch, and not in a kinky, Frederick's of Hollywood kind of way.

She has a feeling, though, that if she *were* a mom, she would not be this hard, uncompassionate person. The baby would bring out the best in her, make her awestruck and loving anew. If she were a *professionally formidable* mom, a mom like Alana, she would be an even *better* person. She would know how to use her time and use it wisely, she would have a team around her to help her run her family and her life, and she would be overflowing with joy, cooing and oohing and bursting with gratitude. She would be at sailor-themed birthday parties in Laurel Canyon and in elevators with burnished mirrors, selfie-ing with the rest of the cool moms. She would be part of the group chats and book clubs and wine nights and tennis foursomes that are currently out of her reach, off-limits, not just because she isn't a mom—other non-moms got invited, she knew—but because . . .

Well, let's face it, she's wronged enough members of that crew that, child or no child, they will likely never admit her into their inner circle again. But that's not why she wants to be a mother. She wants to be a mother because, after many years of assuming that a child would hinder her from being her best self, she's begun to think that motherhood might open her up to a self that could be better than she ever imagined. Maybe for her—certainly not for every woman, she's only talking about herself here—motherhood would be the ultimate unlock. Maybe.

The thought of a tiny person to love, to nurture, to show the world to—the good parts, the sunsets and the soft-serve and the bud break that signals the coming of spring—it makes her heart swell.

Now, in the scrum of boarding group C, she lacks the vigor to elbow her way to the front, even though her business-class boarding pass affords her that right. Instead, she queues up behind a couple of backpackers. They're wearing identical rucksacks and what appear to be his-and-hers versions of Crocs. Gross, she thinks. Then she sees one turn to the other and share that look that couples share, a moment of intimacy, an inside joke, a reference to something only these two people would get, and their faces both alight, the woman squeals with glee, and the man wraps his arm tighter around her shoulders.

They are the dictionary definition of "in love," this couple. She realizes that she's not grossed out at all. What she feels is envy. She longs to be them. She and Sam used to have that, that kind of chemistry. Now, even the memory of it feels as hard to grasp as steam from a kettle.

"Is it just you in your party?" the gate agent asks, as Sarah steps up to the boarding pass scanner. Maybe she's reading into it, but it sounds like a premonition. Sarah Shetty, party of one.

She vows to do better. Drop the bullshit and commit to this trip and her marriage the way that she and Sam said they would in their last therapy session. She owes it to herself, to them. If they don't make it in the end, if this ends up their last trip as a married couple, at least they can say they gave it their all.

"My husband's already on board," she says to the gate agent jauntily, overdoing it in an attempt to mask her sadness. "He's saving me a seat." She laughs at her own joke. Idiotic.

"Celebrating something?" the gate agent asks, as if he doesn't want to know the answer. He hands her back her boarding pass.

"Five years of marriage," she says. "We couldn't be happier."

TWO

Sam is putting $200 on a three-team parlay—if the Dodgers beat the Mets and the Chargers beat the Giants and the Lakers beat the Knicks, he wins $2,000—when he sees Sarah coming down the aisle. Though from that distance she has no way of knowing what he's doing with his phone, he reflexively puts it face down on the shelf beside his seat and busies himself, rearranging the essentials he's already arrayed there: noise-canceling headphones, device chargers, eyeglasses, eye mask.

While he does not want to get out of his seat and help her put her carry-on suitcase in the overhead compartment—her hostility toward him knows seemingly no bounds, and she's liable to scream at him for lending a hand ("You think I can't do it myself?" et cetera), call him anti-feminist or a misogynist or who knows what—once she's in front of him, some chivalrous impulse takes over. Some chivalrous impulse combined with low-grade guilt over what he was doing with his phone. He can't not help.

"Oh, thanks, babe," she says, offering a conciliatory smile as he slides her suitcase into the compartment and closes the bin with a satisfying click. She gestures at the window seat in front of his own. "Is this me?"

"Yeah, is that okay?" Not that there are any other options. He booked the tickets so (relatively) last-minute that there were no "suites" to be claimed, those two seats in the middle of the cabin that could turn into a veritable bedroom if you pushed down the adjustable wall between them.

"Of course," she says. "You can poke me whenever you need me." Perhaps as a show of good faith, she reaches out her pointer finger and pokes him gently on the shoulder.

He regards her, bemused, before sliding back into his seat. "Will do."

He flips his phone over, checks to make sure his wager went through, then closes the gambling app. Then opens it again, scrolls, sees what else people are wagering on, what boxing matches and golf tournaments and foreign elections—you can bet on pretty much anything—are popular among his peers. He tells himself it's okay. He probably won't be able to access the app in the Maldives, where gambling is illegal. He could still text his new bookie—a referral he got through Steve, he can never contact his old bookie again—but he told the new bookie that he'll be unreachable. Not that the bookie asked. Or said anything at all. Steve had merely linked them on a text, and Sam felt the need to say he would be out of town. A preventative method, maybe. But bookies know that if you really want to get in touch with them, you'll find a way. Or if they want to get in touch with you, they can easily elicit a response with a message teasing a bet: "You can't lose," "It's a no-brainer," "You don't want to regret missing out on this."

The thrill of those texts. Almost as acute as the crash that came when they all but invariably did not pan out.

He doesn't think it's a problem, his gambling. Sarah feels differently. Especially after what happened six months ago. But that is how it works—you win some, you lose some. There is always another potential payday up ahead. And Sarah doesn't get it. When your line of work has been preordained, you need to find other ways to manifest your own destiny, to exert control, and he can very much control his bets.

Well. He can control the volume. The outcomes, alas, are out of his hands.

In front of him, Sarah stands, readjusting the cushions of her seat. He quickly puts his phone face down and picks up the in-flight menu. A major highlight of flying Emirates, the in-flight menu. This month's selection includes dishes from Hawker Stand, "the Michelin-lauded Los Angeles hot spot," per the italicized description on the menu. Sam sneers but feels something else. Envy. He knows the chef-owner of Hawker Stand, Ronny Lee. They worked together at Per Se in New York. Malaysian guy. Good dude, if a bit smarmy. Little full of himself. Though Sam figures he would be, too, if his first restaurant got a Michelin star and the cover of *Food & Wine*.

He's thinking about the interview that he'd do with *Food & Wine* about Tiffin's in-flight menu—mind you, there is not a chance in hell that Tiffin is on the radar of anyone at Emirates, or *Food & Wine*, or Michelin—when he hears a familiar voice from overhead. A fat finger plants itself on a bowl of brothy noodles pictured on the entrée section of his open menu.

"Bro, heard the laksa's *banging*."

Sam looks up, sees Ronny's shit-eating grin, and wonders if he conjured him.

They slap hands and ask each other what they're doing there.

"Dude, it's sick," Ronny says, leaning in. "They're flying me out to develop a new menu for Q2. They've never repeated a featured chef before, but they said the feedback's been so bomb they're making an exception. Seven days in Dubai, all expenses paid, plus the lump sum. I'm looking at beach houses in Mexico, man. This corporate shit is *beyond*. You've gotta get in on it. But wait, you didn't tell me what you're doing. You going to Dubai? Dubai's nuts, man. Pros for days. I got this chick's number if you want it. Kinda crazy, but you get what you pay for, you know?"

"Ronny, meet Sarah, my wife," Sam says loudly, giving Ronny a look as he gestures at the seat in front of him, the one directly below Ronny's extramarital overshare.

Sarah turns around, says hi, plays nice, turns back.

"Sorry, bro," Ronny stage-whispers. "Had no idea you got hitched."

"Five years ago," Sam says. "We're actually headed to the Maldives for our anniversary."

"Finally found a gal to make an honest man out of you," Ronny says, nodding proudly. "You're a better man than me. I can't quit these pros. Don't tell the Mrs., though, you know?" He guffaws and jabs Sam's shoulder.

Sam had forgotten Ronny was married. Borderline arranged, if he remembers correctly. Poor woman.

"Don't get me wrong, she's my *wife*, the mother of my *boys*, but, you know, when the dog's away." He guffaws again.

The only redeemable thing about this conversation is that it reveals Ronny to be the asshole Sam always suspected he was, and it makes him feel better about not being quite as successful as him. Well—more than not quite. Sam manages a place that was once great but now lives and dies by to-go orders. Ronny's restaurant has a three-month-long waiting list for reservations. Apples and oranges. Saran-wrapped, waxy Red Delicious apples and succulent, tree-ripe Cara Cara oranges.

Sam hopes Sarah is eavesdropping, because the other redeemable thing about this conversation is that it might give them something to laugh about later. They need more to laugh about.

"Sir, may I help you find your seat?"

A comely flight attendant is peering over Ronny's shoulder, and Sam silently thanks her for the intervention. She glances at Ronny's boarding pass.

"Oh, Chef Lee, what a pleasure to have you on board," she says. "You're actually in our first-class cabin. Please follow me."

Ronny mimes grabbing two cantaloupes as he follows the flight attendant up the aisle and turns around to throw Sam one last guffaw.

Sarah whips around.

"*That's* Ronny Lee?"

"A real piece of work," Sam says. The irony of that philanderer bringing him and Sarah closer together.

"Uh, yeah," she says. "Though, getting featured on an airline like this, not once but twice? Nice work if you can get it."

That's all he needs to feel, once again, like a failure. Never mind that the guy just admitted, repeatedly, that he cheats on his wife, the mother of his children, with prostitutes, that he "can't quit" them. All *Sam's* wife cares about is that this guy is more gainfully employed than her husband. Well, breaking news, Sarah—every man on the Michelin list is like Ronny, in some way or another. Egomaniacs, narcissists, dudes who believe they can take a bite out of whatever they like. Is that who she wants him to be? A serial cheater who gets off on all-expenses-paid trips to Dubai, who appraises flight attendants with his tongue hanging out of his mouth, who saves the numbers of prostitutes under she'll-never-figure-it-out aliases like Lawn Supply Guy and Plumber George? (He's guessing.)

A sad marriage that would be, her content with his line of credit, him flitting all over the globe, in search of yet another notch to punch in his belt.

In any case, he can't get that work because he works at a restaurant whose chief claim to fame is a 4.4 rating on DoorDash, which is pretty good for an Indian restaurant in Los Angeles, no small feat, especially given the E. coli scandal from however long ago that they were still recovering from. But, it goes without saying, a 4.4 rating on DoorDash is nothing compared to a Michelin star.

He would kill for a Michelin star. He would kill for a Michelin . . . tire. At this point, if they threw anything with their name on it in his direction, he'd consider it a win.

An announcement on the PA: "The boarding door is now closed." The comely flight attendant is coming down the aisle once more, this time taking orders for the entrées that will be served soon after the plane departs.

The worst part is that, in spite of everything, he wants the laksa.

No, the worst part is that, in spite of everything, he will never leave Tiffin and launch his own restaurant, which is the only surefire way to establish himself as a culinary force to be reckoned with. But he simply can't do that to his father, abandon the business that old Balraj built so that Sam could one day take it over, something his father has been telling him for as long as he can remember. The problem is that old Balraj is not ready to hand it over. They've been engaged in a tug-of-war, two dogs with a rope, for years. Could Sam forcibly rip it from B.'s teeth? Maybe. But it would break Sam's heart. He can't picture himself doing it.

The flight attendant is smiling down at Sarah, who, he overhears, has ordered the laksa. Naturally. The flight attendant greets him, pen over pad, expectant.

"I'll have the short rib," he says.

~

Sarah downloaded a stack of books to read—classics, Edith Wharton and Virginia Woolf, as well as instructional tomes, Stephen King's *On Writing* and Jami Attenberg's *1000 Words*—in the hopes that they might excavate her and her novel from the rut in which they wallow. All of the anthropological observations about Los Angeles that once struck her as clever now seem bitter, thinly veiled digs from a novice author unable to separate herself from her protagonist, an influencer who gets canceled after live streaming a mushroom-fueled trip to Joshua Tree. But the written word is powerless against the "award-winning" Emirates in-flight entertainment system—who gives out awards for in-flight entertainment systems?—replete as it is with hundreds, perhaps thousands, of movies and television shows.

It would take a good chunk of the flight to scroll through them all, and while Sarah generally likes to make a decision only after assessing all the available options, once she's favorited a dozen different rom-coms and TV series she's already either sampled or watched in their entirety, she decides to commit. *The Devil Wears Prada*. You can't go wrong with *The Devil Wears Prada*.

Or, she realizes shortly after takeoff, her welcome glass of rosé Champagne long ago metabolized, you *can* go wrong with *The Devil Wears Prada* when you're down in the dumps and it reminds you of your New York City glory days when you were all hope and promise and unmet potential. Fucking Andy Sachs and her glow-up. As if an executive assistant at *Vogue* could afford that job without a trust fund.

Instead of switching to something else, she glowers at the movie, rubs salt into the wound, tells herself to loll about in the depths of her uselessness. This is it, babe, she thinks. You had your moment. Now you get your kicks by watching fictional people have their moments on-screen. You made your bed, now lie in it, loser.

She's curled into the side of her reclined seat, picking at her chapped lips, when her husband appears in her peripheral vision, saying something.

"What was that?" she asks, pushing her headphones back. This was marriage, in a nutshell—repeating yourself and asking the other person to repeat themselves until the end of time.

"I said, do you want to go check out the bar?"

She frowns. "You know you can order a cocktail from your seat." She is planning on another Negroni, having breached the barrier of healthy eons ago, at sea level.

"I know," he says, "but the bar is kind of the whole point. How many planes have a full-fledged cocktail bar?"

She registers his frustration, remembers that she's supposed to try. Fine, sure, whatever, she'll go to the bar.

She flings her headphones on her seat, slides her socked feet into the amenity-kit slippers, and follows her husband down the aisle. Along with the amenity kits, the flight attendants handed out pajamas, cultish-looking sets of seafoam modal. A perk, for sure, but it strikes her as unnecessary and unhygienic, changing clothes in an airplane bathroom, even if the stall is marginally bigger in business class than economy and supposedly cleaned every hour. She'll stay in her cargo pants, thank you very much.

She sees, as they walk toward the bar at the back of the cabin, that several passengers have thrown sanitary caution to the wind and changed into the Emirates pajamas.

The lounge at the rear of the cabin isn't large, it could fit maybe a dozen people comfortably. There are two glossy tables on either side with hinges so that they can fold flat when not in use, and between them is the pièce de résistance, a semicircular bar that appears to be made of mahogany but is very clearly, judging by its plasticky sheen, not. Sam leans his elbows against the edge.

"We'll be ready to take your order in just a moment," says a flight attendant with a bouncy blowout. She's behind the bar, emptying a bag of ice into a bucket.

"Cool beans," Sam says, which annoys Sarah, this juvenile turn of phrase, though, again, she's supposed to be trying, not judging. Her judgmental muscle seems to be in a permanent state of flex.

Two other passengers saunter in, clad in pajamas. The woman has long, thick strawberry blond waves that could be extensions or could be real, Sarah can never quite tell. The man's got a swoop of chestnut hair streaked with gray. They're jovial in a way that belies their age, which Sarah guesses to be between fifty and sixty. Most of the fiftysomethings she knows—granted, she doesn't know that many—are sarcastic and joyless, the realities of their limited time on earth and dwindling prospects of dramatically increasing their income finally sinking in. But these two. These two are giggling like schoolchildren. She wonders if they're having an affair, if their actual spouses are at home, none the wiser.

"Should we change?" Sam asks her. He's also watching the couple, perhaps chalking up their conviviality to their clothing. It is easier to be carefree when you're not worried about errant spills and stains.

"Ew, no," she says, wrinkling her nose, though her conviction is faltering.

"All right," the bouffanted flight attendant says, tying on an apron. Her name tag says Lucy, and she speaks in a singsongy British lilt. Her lips are lacquered the color of fruit punch. "What can I get you?"

"I'll have a 50/50 dirty martini," Sam says, and Sarah wills herself to tune out the explanation she has heard so many times, she knows it by heart. "Half Beefeater, half dry vermouth, with a splash of olive juice and three olives as a garnish."

"I've never heard of a 50/50," Lucy gushes, reaching behind her for the gin. "How did you come up with it?"

"Oh, it wasn't my idea, it's how martinis used to be made, back in the day," Sam says, pressing himself into the bar, closer to Lucy, who, Sarah realizes, would probably make a great nanny or secretary-turned-office-slut-type porn star. Or both.

Lately, she turns every woman who interacts with Sam into a potential foe. Something about seeing him be nice to them irritates her to her core. Makes her think about how he must've been with that woman. How they must've celebrated when he won. Though he swears it was never "like that," that it was "strictly professional," but she can't shake the specter of what she doesn't know.

"An extra-dry martini is really just a cup of gin or vodka, if you think about it," Sam continues. *She doesn't care, you moron*, Sarah thinks.

"I never considered that," Lucy says, securing the cap of the stainless steel shaker, "but you're right! No wonder I feel as if I've been hit by a train when I have a couple of those."

To Sarah's horror, as Lucy's shaking the 50/50, the blond woman in pajamas sidles up to the bar, next to Sam, and starts in. "I couldn't help but overhear," she says. "I'm normally a tequila gal, but I've *got* to try one of these martinis."

"Look at you, starting a trend," coos Lucy, pouring the contents of the shaker into a frosted glass.

Sam's cheeks flush with delight. Now Sarah has to admit that she was wrong, if only to herself. The bartender and the blond are curious about 50/50s. They do want to engage with Sam. But it's not fair. The bartender and the blond don't spend every night with Sam, didn't uproot their lives to be with Sam, didn't leave the only city they'd ever really thought of as *their* city to be, like Ariel in *The Little Mermaid*, part of his world.

Granted, she *wanted* to do all of these things when she did them. Did them of her own volition, did them despite Sam's reticence about her moving across the country for him, did them, perhaps, because of his reticence. The easiest way to get her to do something is to tell her not to do it.

"And what can I get for you, my dear?" Lucy asks, once she's poured out another 50/50 for the blond woman, who is now making small talk with Sam.

Sarah wants to ask for a lobotomy. Instead, she orders a Negroni.

~

"So you're a chef? The chef of—what was the name again—Tiffin? How *sexy*," the blond woman says, giving him a coquettish look. She fingers a gold heart pendant at the center of her sunspotted chest. It's engraved with two *K*s.

Sam hastens to correct the record, imagines Ronny Lee, the real chef in first class, ogling this woman like a piece of prized Wagyu. "I mean, that's not really what I do day to day," he says. "I'm more the managing partner. I direct the chefs, handle staffing, come up with menu concepts, ideas for new restaurants. It's a mixed bag." It's also something of a lie. Most of what he does is put out fires, sometimes literally, as happened the time Anand almost burned down the Tiffin West Hollywood kitchen by dropping his phone into a boiling-hot vat of *vadas* and knocking over the vat in an attempted rescue.

"Why do I feel like you're downplaying it?" the blond says, appraising him. Sam wonders if she's flirting, but then she casts a hand about for the guy she came in with. He's leaning against the bar, talking to Sarah. "Babe, what's the name of that Indian place we went to the other night? The one in West Hollywood. Was it Tiffin?"

The guy turns to them, furrows his eyebrows. They're hefty, caterpillar-like.

"You mean Raffi's?" he says. "That was Lebanese, darling. And it's in Glendale." He throws Sam a bashfully apologetic look while gently chastising his wife: "They're not all the same!"

"I know they're not *all the same*," the blond says, though she's laughing, too. "I wasn't talking about *Raffi's*, it was the other place, I thought it was in West Hollywood, although wait, maybe it was downtown . . ." She trails off, shaking her head in bewilderment; Caterpillar Eyebrows shrugs amiably and resumes his conversation with Sarah.

"I used to pride myself on my memory, but these days? I can hardly remember my own name. Which is Krista, by the way." She raises her martini glass and clinks it against Sam's, which is his cue to introduce himself.

"Sam?" she repeats, quizzically. "Is that your full name? Oh gosh—can I even ask that? I'm so sorry. I'm a walking human resources violation. My kids refuse to be seen with me in public."

Sam laughs, wanting to put her at ease. He does not think she's flirting with him, but there is something undeniably charming about this woman. Maybe it's the mere fact that she seems to enjoy talking to him, which is more than he can say of his wife these days.

"It's short for Samir," he says. "But I went by Sam growing up, and it just kind of stuck."

"Well, Sam, pleasure to meet you, and thank you for the tip on this cocktail, you might just convert me to martinis after all. Now where are you and your—wife, girlfriend? Where are you off to?"

"Wife," Sam says, glancing over at Sarah, who's nodding along to something Caterpillar Eyebrows is saying about tax rates. "And the Maldives. What about you two?"

"No way," she says, reaching out, digging the tips of her French-manicured fingernails into his forearm in a not unappealing way. "Babe, get this, they're also going to the Maldives!"

Caterpillar Eyebrows whips around again, this time with his whole body, eyes wide. "Of all the islands in all the towns in all the world," he says, and Sam recognizes this as a riff on Humphrey Bogart's iconic line in *Casablanca*, despite the fact that he couldn't pick Humphrey Bogart out of a lineup and he's never seen *Casablanca*. He's pretty sure the only reason he knows that line is because of some meme. "Where are you lovebirds staying?"

"This place called Jala," Sam says.

Krista looks as if a record has scratched in her brain.

"SHUT. UP," she says, digging her nails into his flesh again. She exchanges a look with Caterpillar Eyebrows. "What are the odds?"

"You're going to Jala, too?" Sarah ventures. Sam can see the trepidation in her eyes, a sort of oh-fuck-are-we-going-to-have-to-spend-our-vacation-with-these-strangers malaise.

"Indeed we are. By the way, my name is Kevin." He extends his hand to shake Sam's, and Sam's gaze fixes on the watch on Kevin's wrist, a Patek

Philippe that catches the fluorescent lights overhead. It's a watch collector's watch, the kind you only spring for if you've got several million in the bank and a fleet of lesser Rolexes and Cartiers in your dresser drawer.

"That's a heck of a watch," Sam tells Kevin, after introducing himself.

"Oh, this old thing?" Kevin says, shaking his wrist. "Kidding, of course. It was a retirement gift to myself. Except that I didn't actually retire. That's the problem with buying nice things—they make you want more nice things! And then you've got to go back to work so you can afford them!" He chortles and claps Sam on the back.

Krista glances between them, seemingly clocking their camaraderie. "Shall we sit?" she says, gesturing at one of the tables alongside the bar. "I don't know about you, but I could die for some truffle popcorn. Emirates makes the best."

Kevin nods genially and moves toward the table. Sam locks eyes with Sarah. The look she's giving him says, I don't want to do this, but I don't have much of a choice, do I? At least, that's what he thinks it says. He used to be able to divine her mood from the other end of the house, based on her footfalls, the cute humming noises that she'd make when she was happy, the ughs of frustration she would grunt when she was not.

Now, it's like playing poker. Or roulette. Russian roulette. Guess wrong and you're a goner.

~

Sarah does not want to fraternize with these people. Despite the fact that talking up strangers was once integral to her profession—not only talking, seducing, that's what journalists did, really, with their subjects, seduced them until they cracked open like overripe pomegranates—she dislikes making friends in this way. It feels fake. How well would they all get to know each other, really? Even if they are staying at the same resort for one week. And if that's the case, why not wait to fraternize until they absolutely have to, like if they happen to find themselves parked on pool loungers next to each other? Why start now?

On the surface, Krista appears to be your average Orange County mom, the type of woman who had an abortion when she was twenty-two but votes Republican for tax reasons. Not that there's anything *wrong* with your average Orange County mom, but that's not Sarah's type of person. Sarah's type of person is Alana, someone with social power and influence, someone she can put on a pedestal and want to be. She often imagines Alana and the legions of other people she knows mainly through her phone judging her as she moves through her day. What would they say about Krista? Would they want to sit with her?

Krista, on the other hand, shows no hint of ambivalence at all. She keeps touching Sarah, resting her fingertips on Sarah's right shoulder blade as Sarah attempts to explain how she spends her days.

"Well, I was a journalist, but now I'm working on a novel."

"Okay, Joan Didion!"

Sarah did not expect Orange County Mom to name-check Joan Didion.

"Who do you write for? What's your novel about?"

Perhaps there are writers who surge with pride when confronted with these questions. Sarah has never been one of them. She drops the names of the New York publications that relied on her before she proved herself unreliable, and Krista makes the appropriate sounds of awe, which makes Sarah feel worse, because it reminds her that she should have taken her role as a journalist more seriously. Awash anew in regret, the last thing she wants to do is describe her novel—even in the best of circumstances, she can't do that succinctly, she never nails the elevator pitch—so when Krista asks what kinds of articles she likes to write, Sarah takes that topic and runs with it.

"I once profiled the founder of Megaformer Pilates—"

"No way, I *love* Megaformer Pilates." Krista grabs Sarah's forearm.

"And logged a day in the prep kitchen of Erewhon."

"Shut. Up. I'm at Erewhon *all* the time!"

"But maybe my favorite piece of all time was the time I got to spend a week with the *Vanderpump Rules* cast."

"You have *got* to be kidding me, I used to *live* at Sur! Are we sisters? Are we sure we're not related?"

Well, yeah, Krista, given that you're blond and blue-eyed and I'm brown all the way through, I'm gonna venture a guess that we're not related, Sarah thinks but does not say. Beyond that, Sarah doesn't want to point out that the things she writes about are exactly the sorts of things that monied women living in Southern California would be into. Monied white women, mainly. She doesn't want to point this out because she's not sure what it says about her. She can attempt to convince other people that she is critiquing the trappings of pseudo-progressive coastal elites from an anthropological perspective, but she can't kid herself—she writes about the life she wants to live. A life that's always felt foreign to her, despite the countless lunges she's done on spongy Megaformers, despite the troughs of Erewhon buffalo cauliflower that she's consumed.

And yet, as they continue chatting, Krista's enthusiasm rubs off on her, or maybe it's the second round of drinks that makes Sarah's walls lower further, retreat underground. It *was* uncanny that they lived less than ten miles from each other—Krista and Kevin were residents of Beverly Hills, not the OC—and happened to be heading to the same private island resort some ten thousand miles away from Los Angeles. Clichés aside, it was, in fact, a small world.

"So what do you—" Sarah finds herself saying, then rephrases. "How do you spend your days?" She silently thanks herself for remembering that, in polite society, you never ask a woman what she does for a living. She might simply maintain appearances, which, in certain circles—Krista's, for sure—could be as time-consuming a job as any.

"Well, I was an unpaid Uber driver for twenty-something years," Krista says, "carting my kids to soccer and ballet and God knows what. But our youngest went off to Stanford in September, so now I'm . . . what *am I*, even?" She grabs Sarah's arm again and lets out a little sputter of disbelief. "Sorry, I didn't mean to get so *existential* so quickly." She laughs it off. "Must be the altitude. You know what they say about how easy it is to get emotional on planes."

First the Didion drop, now a Kierkegaard reference. Perhaps Sarah has judged Krista all wrong.

"There are the charity boards, of course, and tennis, and book club, but the thing I'm really into these days," Krista says, "is needlepointing. Check it out."

Krista swipes at her phone—it's encased in gems and slung across her body on a lanyard of pearls—and pulls up a social media account called Point Being. There are only nine permanent posts, all photos of cushions with irreverent, needlepointed sayings across their canvas covers: "A woman's place is in the C-suite." "Hate you, mean it." "Bitch, please."

"Did you make these?" Sarah asks.

Krista trills in assent. "It's actually really easy, once you get the hang of it. Meditative, too. I have an Etsy shop and everything. I started it a few months ago, I've only had a couple of orders. Mostly from mom friends who probably pity me. But it's exciting, to have something of my own, you know? A creative outlet, even if I'm barely breaking even."

Oh, does Sarah know. Sarah once had a creative outlet that she enjoyed, but the memory of enjoying it feels out of her grasp, a piece of fruit on a branch that she can't quite reach.

Of course, needlepointing is not the same as writing. Writing is a craft, an art. Needlepointing is . . . well, also a craft, in the Michael's/Hobby Lobby kind of sense, but . . . it's not *analogous* to what Sarah is doing, was doing, wants to do.

Is it?

"Check out this one, it's kind of a departure for me," Krista says, turning her phone screen to Sarah.

It's a needlepointed coaster in the shape of a vulva. There's nothing else it could be.

"Interesting," says Sarah, blinking at the photo. She recognizes a name among the 107 likes. Natalie Nguyen.

"Do you know Natalie?" Sarah can't help but ask.

"She just started following me," Krista says, sliding her phone back down to her side. "Love her podcast, *huge* fan. I'd do anything to be featured in one of her gift guides."

Who wouldn't? Natalie Nguyen is the influencer Sarah interviewed, the influencer who has become markedly more influential since Sarah's first piece on her ran. The influencer who once called Sarah her friend, who asked Sarah to be her plus one to a Cult Gaia store opening, to a Sweetgreen seated dinner, to a soiree at Flamingo Estate. The influencer who, after all those dates and more, invited Sarah over to her home in the Hollywood Hills, where they split a bottle of orange wine and talked about boys and business and hopes and dreams.

The influencer who, in no uncertain terms, disavowed Sarah, blocked her on social media as well as every other form of communication after Sarah went and made a mess of things.

"Do you know her?" Krista asks.

"Sort of," Sarah says. Natalie's endorsement—she doesn't follow many people—means that Point Being, and thereby Krista, might be worth paying attention to.

A kernel of hope heats up in Sarah's mind, begins to sizzle. What if—*big* what-if—what if she and Krista become friends and post photos together, and Natalie sees them and realizes that Sarah is okay after all, that she just made a mistake, she's only human, but she's learned, she's rehabilitated herself, and now she's safe to invite back into the circle, and what if Natalie tells Alana, too, and Sarah returns from the Maldives with a whole inbox of invitations to this and that, which will lead to story ideas that will capture the attention of the editors who refuse to respond to her emails, which will lead to assignments, which will mean she can back-burner her novel or attack it from the new perspective of being on top, where she once was?

Again, big what-if.

But it's a possibility worth exploring. What else does she have to do on this sixteen-hour flight, on this vacation in the Maldives?

All she has to do is befriend Krista. Seduce her, as it were.

"But wait, back up," Sarah says, curling her body so that there's a distance the width of a martini glass between her and Krista. "Tell me about yourself. Start from the beginning. I want to know *everything*."

THREE

Sam awakens to the gentle prodding of Lucy, who, having shut down the bar shortly before the plane began its initial descent, has resumed her normal flight attendant duties. "I'm so sorry," she says, "I just need you to bring your seat back up. We're about to land."

Sam, bleary-eyed, fumbling, mumbles an apology of his own. Damn. He missed breakfast. He was looking forward to the foul medames, wanted to see what array of alliums and spices they'd offer as toppings for aromatically stewed fava beans at thirty-five thousand feet. Alas.

But he must've needed the sleep. He can't quite remember when he turned in, has vague memories of stumbling back toward 10F, knocking into a sleeping uncle along the way who hit him with a rolled-up newspaper. "Just like home," he said, before dissolving into snickers. Too loud for 4:00 a.m. or whatever time it was in that pressurized vessel in the sky. Had Lucy shushed him, escorted him the rest of the way, laid out the down-filled mattress pad, and tucked him in? Or was that a dream?

Better not to recall, he figures, twisting the top off the bottle of Acqua Panna at his side. He has brought tools to help with hangovers. Pills that South Koreans swear by. Electrolyte supplements that biohackers swear by (the bad biohackers, the ones who still occasionally drink). But these are all squirreled away in his duffel bag in the overhead compartment, along with his Advil, his life-saving, life-*giving* Advil, and owing to the fact that he's pretty sure the Burj Khalifa is not far below his window, he cannot get out of his seat to retrieve them.

He feels nervy, ruffled. In need of a warm body to lend him comfort. He leans forward, tiptoes his fingertips across the top of Sarah's head.

She jerks away from her headrest, slaps his hand, and whips around.

Because of the seat configuration, he can only see one of her eyes. It looks mad. "I thought that was a bug."

"Just me," he says, smiling. "Good morning."

Her expression softens. "Morning. Or—whatever time it is. I barely slept. You were *out*."

"Like a light," he says. He bends his elbows into his torso and shimmies in his seat. "Slept through the flight—"

"*Stop*, it's too early to go 'Sicko Mode,'" Sarah says, shaking her head, though he can see her trying, and failing, to tamp down the corners of her mouth. Making a fool of himself has always been his love language, and it's quite easy to make a fool of yourself when you're imitating Drake.

He is relieved to see that she is not mad at him for overdoing it at the bar. They ended up having dinner there, splitting a bottle of Sonoma Coast pinot and then a Bordeaux while tucking into their twin bowls of laksa, which he finally relented and ordered after the short rib arrived dry and inedible. Perhaps she'd been so engrossed in her conversation with Krista that she didn't even notice how many glasses he had. (He certainly didn't.)

In any case, it's a pleasant turn of events. He's thrilled to have a break from the interrogation lamp, to feel, if only for a moment, the warmth of her sun.

"Did you have a good time?" he asks.

She shrugs noncommittally, but it appears that the answer is yes. "There's more to her than I thought," Sarah says, voice low. "We can talk about it later."

Yet another reason to be thrilled, the promise of a future conversation in which his wife (presumably) won't be yelling at him. The trip, in Sam's mind, is off to a smashing start.

He broaches the topic of their long layover. "We land in Terminal C," he says, "and we depart out of there, too, so it's probably best that we find the lounge and hunker down." While he knows the Terminal A lounge is better—it features a full-service spa and a duty-free, luxury shopping mall within the lounge—the Dubai airport is huge, and he doesn't want to spend their layover roaming the halls, dragging along their carry-ons. Besides, you have to pay to use the spa. They are not going to pay to use the spa.

"Krista actually invited us to the first-class lounge in Terminal A," Sarah says.

Sam is taken aback. The first-class lounge in Terminal A is the granddaddy of lounges, one that Sam hadn't even considered given that business-class passengers can't access it. From what he's read on Miles & More and *Robb Report* and other outlets that chronicle travel far beyond his reach and means, it is quieter, sleeker, and more holistically luxurious than any airport lounge on earth. "She and Kevin upgraded their tickets to first class for the Malé leg, and they each get to bring a guest. She also wants to treat us to massages."

Sam is not normally one to turn down a freebie. And he wouldn't mind going to the granddaddy of lounges, the one that serves Dom Pérignon and has its own dedicated suite of duty-free boutiques and assigns every party of passengers a personal butler (more than one, if there are more than four people in your party). But this seems like a little much from a couple they met mere hours ago.

Sarah reads his face. "Why not?" she says, shrugging. "When are we going to be in Dubai again?"

The plane touches down, the wheels bouncing twice as the aircraft screeches along the asphalt.

"I mean," Sam says, stalling. On the one hand, he's happy to see his wife finally invested in this trip, eager to participate. On the other, he can't shake the feeling that Kevin and Krista must want something from them if they're being this nice. He and Kevin had a fine enough conversation, picking apart the Dodgers and the Los Angeles real estate market, in which Kevin was apparently a linchpin, but they didn't hit it off quite as fabulously as Krista and Sarah, who you'd think were long-lost sisters, the way that Sarah is treating Krista's invitation.

"It just seems weird," he says. "What do they want from us?"

"What do they *want*? Why do they have to want something? Maybe they're just nice people. You were the one who started it with Krista, going on about your 50/50."

"'Going on'? She asked what it was. What was I supposed to do, not answer?"

Sarah throws her hands in the air, her way of saying "whatever," and whips back around to face forward. They'll pick this up again soon enough, he is sure.

The plane slows to a stop, and he busies himself with tying his shoelaces and making sure he has all of his things. (How many phone chargers has he left behind on past flights? He hopes they're happy, wherever they've ended up.) He hauls their belongings down from the overhead, unprompted. He slides her duffel over the handle of her rolling suitcase, which she accepts with a tacit look of truce.

"I just think we should make the most of this," she says, once he's arranged his bag on top of his carry-on. "Didn't we tell Margaret we'd do that?"

Margaret is their couples counselor. Sarah only invokes Margaret when it serves her, which, he supposes, he can't blame her for. He does the same thing. (Doesn't everyone in couples counseling?)

"Don't you think there's something off about them, though?" says Sam, leaning on the handle of his carry-on, which brings him physically closer to his wife. Through a haze of stale coffee and burnt croissant, the last traces of breakfast wafting from the galley, he catches a whiff of her rose-scented shampoo, a scent so homey that it disorients him, sensing it in this carpeted tube nine thousand miles away from everything he holds close.

"Off how?"

He doesn't relish pointing it out, but he can't not.

"Swinger vibes," he says, lowering his voice. "All that PDA. And the wife's so touchy-feely."

Sarah rolls her eyes dramatically. "Oh, come on. Do you really think she'd be into you? Or me? She's gorgeous. They're so in love. And beyond well off. Kevin owns the Park, for Christ's sake."

The Park is an outdoor shopping mall in West Hollywood that might as well be LA's answer to Central Park. A ring of multinational clothing conglomerates instead of a jogging track, a four-tier fountain named after nothing instead of a reservoir named after a former First Lady. A tribute to consumerism that might see more foot traffic on any given Sunday than every other attraction in Los Angeles combined. (Sam thought a Tiffin there would do swift business. Balraj did not agree.)

"So, because they're rich, they can't be swingers?"

Sarah hisses his name in an admonishing tone, but it's clear that she's amused.

"I just can't imagine that they'd be into us, not in that way."

Sam doesn't think Krista is into him, necessarily, but he resents the implication that he is as appealing as some sort of Gilded Age street urchin because his take-home salary doesn't hold a candle to Kevin's. Sam has money coming his way, *would have* more money in his pocket at this *very moment* if his father had done the thing he said he would and handed him the keys to the kingdom nine years ago, when Balraj unceremoniously summoned his son back home, ripping him from the very nice life he was erecting in New York as carefully and methodically as a house of cards.

A fine way to put it, seeing as how, with a tug from across the country, that life came crashing down.

The only piece of it that survived, the thing that ended up making his LA life worth living, was Sarah. The fact that she had joined him in Los Angeles, moved even when he thought there was no way she'd actually make the jump, even after he actively advised her against making the jump. He was scared. Scared he wouldn't measure up. Scared they wouldn't make it. Scared she would eventually see him for the imposter he feared he was, a boy playing dress-up with Daddy's loafers.

Against all odds, the opposite happened. Sarah took to Runyon like an influencer in Alo. She got along so well with his family, they liked her better than him (they would never admit this, but he'd seen enough evidence to know the truth). She was not the *best* driver, not even a very good one, if he was being honest, but she did it, she conquered her fear of the 101, took his 2011 Audi two-door coupe and made it her own.

Most of all, she loved him for him. She never made him feel small or stupid or less than for doing right by his father instead of following his own dreams, instead of taking the time and space to dream those dreams. The problem with a family business, in his experience, is that you're born into it. He was earmarked for the throne before he even had ears. What chance did any dream of his stand?

At least, she never used to make him feel small or stupid. In the past year, the barometer has swung the other way, and a black cloud has settled over her very being. Everything he thought he knew to be true about Sarah has been turned upside down. Does she love LA? Does she love his family? Does she love him?

He is no longer sure.

The queue of passengers in front of Sarah begins moving. Whatever effervescence he felt earlier has flattened, like it never existed at all. He nudges his carry-on forward and follows his wife down the long and winding jetway to the air-conditioned terminal beyond, all too-high ceilings and too-bright lights. There are a handful of Emirates employees holding signs for various connecting flights and offering to help direct the disoriented passengers stepping off.

"May I point you in the right direction?" one of them asks Sarah.

"How do we get to the first-class lounge at Terminal A?"

The Emirates employee asks to see her boarding pass, correctly assuming that Sarah does not, in fact, have access to that lounge. Sarah shows it to him and explains, in her news anchor voice—the voice Sam knows too well, the voice she uses when she wants to be taken seriously, slightly snooty and prone to over-enunciation—that she and Sam are guests of Kevin and Krista King.

"They were ahead of us," Sarah says. She cranes her neck, casts her gaze about. "Maybe they're still here."

"Babe, let's just go to the business-class lounge in this terminal," Sam says. "It's easier."

Sarah shoots him a look that makes him think of one way to kill a lobster. The humane way, or so they say.

She turns back to the terminal, lifts a hand. "There she is." She starts waving frantically. "That woman over there." She shouts Krista's name.

Krista spins around and comes over to them, beaming, apologizing, something about how Kevin had to run to the restroom, middle-aged bladders or prostates, details that far exceed the upper limit of what Sam cares to know.

"They're with me," Krista tells the Emirates employee, flapping her Dubai to Malé boarding pass uncomfortably close to his face. "Are you guys ready?" Her head is bobbing like one of those desk toys. Sarah nods. Sam feigns a smile. What choice does he have? Better this than his wife sullen and unspeaking, right?

Right?

"*So* exciting," Krista squeals. "Get ready for the best layover of your *life*." She turns to the Emirates employee, who, Sam now sees, is named Shreekanth. One of his people, no doubt. Just another brown man trying to survive.

"Sir, sir?" Krista is asking. "Can we get a buggy to Terminal A? Time is of the es-*sence*. Mommy needs a massage, stat."

Shreekanth glances at Sam, and Sam averts his gaze, pretends to be engrossed in the pattern of the linoleum floor. He does not want to see what he's pretty sure is in Shreekanth's eyes, what should not be in Shreekanth's eyes with regard to Sam. Sam is American and therefore mighty and in control of his destiny, and ought to be regarded as such.

Except that he is neither mighty nor in control of his destiny, and it doesn't matter what he is or where he's from, because the look in Shreekanth's eyes transcends national boundaries and makes Sam feel even more guilty for thinking that politically incorrect thought at all.

What's in his eyes is pity.

~

"Wait, are those Celine?"

Krista has curled herself toward Sarah in the rear-facing seat of the buggy, is appraising Sarah's sunglasses from a distance of perhaps five inches.

"They are," Sarah says. Gift from some direct-to-consumer makeup brand, back when direct-to-consumer makeup brands wanted her to write about them.

"No way," Krista says. "I think I have the same ones." She commences rifling through her Louis Vuitton Neverfull, on the hunt. It's not exactly a surprise—a million girls have the black Wayfarer-style Celines, they go with everything—but it pleases Sarah to have something in common with Krista. A little feather in her cap. While Sarah initially judged Krista as vapid and unambitious, a stay-at-home mom content to whittle away her husband's money, Krista is not that at all. Krista is so much more.

Beyond her needlepointing—intriguing in and of itself, the notion of this Beverly Hills mom making vulva coasters—Krista has a degree from Stanford. "Psychology," she told Sarah at the in-flight bar over a pot of fresh mint tea, after the boys had stumbled back to their seats. "Not that I ever got to use it, given that we got married at twenty-two and I got pregnant with Connor on our honeymoon."

"Where did you go?" Sarah asked.

"Hawaii," Krista said. "The Hilton Waikiki, to be specific. Tacky beyond belief. But cute-tacky—too-sweet drinks and over-the-top luaus that would probably be considered culturally insensitive now. But it was all we could afford back then, back when Kevin was working in sales at his dad's hardware shop."

By that point in the evening, Sarah understood from whence the Kings' fortune came. The Park, the National, the Shoppes at Santa Monica—every Los Angeles mall worth going to was built on land owned by Kevin King and leased to the respective developers. "I lucked into a deal in the nineties," he had been quoted as saying, "after the riots and the quake, when no one wanted to invest in LA."

Sarah had googled him when she availed herself of the complimentary thirty-minute Wi-Fi pass that Emirates gave to business-class passengers. She'd found his LinkedIn page, which was blank but for his current title, founder and CEO, King Real Estate Holdings. He had recently shared a profile of himself from a real estate news website she had never heard of, but there were so many niche news sites these days, you could hardly keep track of them.

She had thought that the Park was owned by the real estate magnate who developed it, but that wasn't mentioned in the profile, and at that point, ten hours into the flight and months since they'd been put to professional use, her search faculties were nowhere to be found. Maybe Kevin had partners, who knew. What stuck out to her, when Krista mentioned the hardware store, was that they had not been to the manner born. (Krista made a point of mentioning that she'd gotten a full ride to Stanford, that there was no way her single mother, then a high school teacher in Santa Clarita, could've afforded it.) More than that—Kevin had been an indentured servant in a family business, too, like Sam. But he had broken away and made his own name, his own fortune.

Krista and Kevin didn't scream new money. Her accoutrements hinted at her wealth instead of hitting you over the head, Van Cleef studs downplayed by scuffed leather sneakers, a base-model Cartier Tank that rubbed up against a cashmere sweater as soft as a cloud. Krista moved like she floated through life on a bed of feathers, which Sarah figured was pretty close to the truth.

In the hushed cabin, dawn creeping at the horizon, Sarah considered what she knew. She wondered if Krista could teach her a thing or two.

So now, as the buggy screeches to a halt at the entrance to the first-class lounge of Terminal A, Sarah slides off in time with Krista, comes around to Krista's side, and links her arm through her new friend's elbow, held out akimbo, as if in anticipation.

"You do know that you're never getting rid of us now," Sarah says, as they march through the automatic doors. She finds self-effacing humor helpful in these situations, underlining the gap between her and her subject even as she tries to act like she's one of them, like she can be trusted.

"Fine by me," says Krista. "The kids never want to go anywhere with us anymore, we could use new vacation friends. Ooh, Kevin, what did we used to call them, the couples that we would make friends with at resorts, back in the day?"

"Incidentals," Kevin says from behind. He and Sam have been wordlessly charged with organizing and keeping track of the luggage.

"That's right, incidentals, don't you just love that?" Krista says, slapping Sarah's arm and looking pleased with herself. "You and Sam can be our new incidentals. It's been *ages* since we've met anyone fun."

Sarah detects a wink. Sam's reticence echoes in her mind—"swinger vibes." She hopes that's not what this is. She does not want to hook up with Kevin or Krista; the thought of it gives her the ick.

Does she, however, want to *be* Krista? Inhabit her body, her skin, her brain space, her Beverly Hills mansion, her privilege so palpable it seeps from her pores?

There's something attractive about this prospect, yes.

It's not that Sarah hates herself. Well—she doesn't feel *great* about herself, that part is true. It's that, when she meets a woman like Krista—or Alana, or Natalie—a woman eminently comfortable in her own skin, she seethes with envy. She wants to absorb everything they do with the goal of becoming like them, as if through osmosis, as if that will cure all that ails her.

Krista slaps her passport and boarding pass down on the creamy marble counter of the reception desk. She gives the woman behind it her and Kevin's names. "We called ahead for guest passes for our friends," she says, and briefly, Sarah wonders how that could be the case, given that they were on the ground for all of ten minutes before reuniting in the terminal and Sarah had eyes on Krista and Kevin, in the middle "suite" seats in row four, ahead of her and Sam. She doesn't recall seeing Krista make a phone call. She couldn't have done it in flight, and it always takes Sarah's phone a few minutes to find a signal when she lands in a foreign country. Is Krista, like, an international calling ninja? Or did she maybe text an unseen assistant from the air and put them on the job?

But why is she wondering these things? Who cares? Why does her brain go to this place, trying to figure out how things add up? Krista said that she and Kevin each got a guest pass. Maybe that's what Krista is referring to? Maybe she didn't make a phone call at all?

It's true that Sarah's brain generally starts whirring in this way when things aren't adding up. But her brain is also tired. Her brain doesn't know up from down.

"Yes, of course, Mrs. King," the woman behind the reception desk says. She's wearing a beige skirt suit and a red pillbox hat draped with a cream chiffon scarf. "I also see that you made spa reservations. Two sixty-minute couples massages, correct?"

"That's right," says Krista, "one for me and that old lug, and one for our new friends." She leans over the desk, conspiratorial. "It's their wedding anniversary."

"Well then, we must offer an extra add-on, on us," the receptionist says, keying something into her computer.

"Oh, it's not actually our anniversary until next week," Sarah says. While she rarely turns down a freebie—something she and Sam have in common—she does worry about being greedy, wonders if the universe will pull the rug out from under her if she takes too many treats.

Though the universe hasn't been all that kind to her of late. The universe might owe her one, come to think of it.

"Nonsense," Krista says, slapping Sarah's arm again. "It's your anniversary every day of this trip. Marriage isn't easy. You deserve a party for every mile marker."

"By the way," Sarah says, "I never asked—how'd you end up deciding to go to the Maldives? Special occasion?"

"Kevin's retirement," Krista says. He was finally handing the keys to King Holdings to his second-in-command. "I'm happy for him, but"—she leans in and lowers her voice—"frankly, terrified for myself. Him, puttering around the house all day? Kill me now."

~

Another skirt-suit-and-pillbox-hat-wearing employee—their assigned butler, her name is Habiba, one facet of women's empowerment in this part of the world is that women can be butlers, too—leads them through a grand set of double doors to the spa. The men are directed to one locker room; Habiba leads Krista and Sarah to another. Sarah has seen more than her fair share of over-the-top enclaves to which she would not have been invited if she was not a reporter, but she's never been in an airport lounge like this, and she can't help but marvel at the fact that the locker room boasts more amenities than even the nicest Equinox—seven kinds of infused water, a hammam in addition to a steam room, sauna, and a cold-plunge pool.

"There's even cryotherapy," Krista says, correctly reading Sarah's silence as reverence. "It's the best for combatting jet lag. Actually—why don't we do a round? It'll only take three minutes, max. I rarely make it more than ninety seconds."

Sarah has never done cryotherapy. Does she want to pop her cryotherapy cherry with this relative stranger? But then, when else is she going to get to do it? Cryo costs upward of sixty dollars per session in LA. The thought of driving and parking to freeze in a glorified meat locker for mere minutes—not her cup of tea. But to do it here, in the most lavish airline lounge in the world, with a fabulous new friend who could very well hold the keys to getting her life back on track?

"Should we let the guys know?" Sarah asks.

"I'm already texting Kevin," Krista says, tapping away at her phone. "Maybe he and Sam can do it, too. They should! Kevin's hungover, and I can't stand when he's hungover, he gets so needy and annoying." She flags down Habiba, who is pulling two fluffy robes out of a stack, and informs her of the new plan. Sarah pats herself down—they've checked their bags at the reception desk—certain she's got a credit card in one of her pockets.

She finds it, a Chase Sapphire that's so heavily used the plastic cover around the corner of the metal interior has chipped. She proffers it to Habiba.

"Absolutely not," Krista says, slapping it out of her hand. It lands with a clink on the floor.

"This is too much," Sarah says.

"It's *fine*," Krista says, discreetly sliding her American Express to Habiba, who scurries away, clearly discomfited by this exchange. "You can buy me a drink or something at Jala. We've got a whole week together, don't forget. You're our guest here, at this lounge, it's 100 percent our treat."

Sarah relents. They change into the disposable undergarments that have been placed on the blond wood bench between them. Sarah tries to not feel weird about disrobing in front of someone she's barely met—she's done this in gym locker rooms a thousand times—but "swinger vibes" keeps ringing in her head. She turns her back to Krista and attempts to shuck off her cargo pants, jean jacket, and T-shirt as quickly as possible, which results in her banging her knee against the open door of her locker. She yelps.

"Oh *no*," Krista says, in a way that makes Sarah whip around. Krista is naked save for the engraved gold heart pendant around her neck, a necklace Sarah recognizes from Goop, the necklace all the bougie moms have, that they layer with diamond-encrusted plates of their children's names. (How she longs for one of those nameplates, for the purpose it signifies.)

"Don't worry, I'm fine," Sarah says, flustered, rubbing her knee, not sure where to look. She reaches out for a robe, seeking warmth and also wanting to shield her body, newly clad in disposable underwear and a matching bralette made of mesh so fine, it might disintegrate in a cloud of steam.

But Krista is peering into her Neverfull, apparently oblivious to Sarah's clumsiness. "I just realized I didn't bring a change of clothes. I had a pair of joggers and sweatpants set aside in my carry-on, and I forgot to take them out." She shrugs, still naked. "Oh well. I guess I can go out in my robe after the massage. I just don't want to put on those gross plane clothes again."

"Right," Sarah says. She hadn't thought that far ahead, and why should she have, she didn't know she was going to meet Krista, get access to this otherworldly lounge. Did she pack a change of clothes in her carry-on? She should have. If she were in her right mind, she would have. But given that she avoided thinking about this trip for so long, that she left packing until the very last minute, she's pretty sure that all of her plane-appropriate attire is in her checked luggage, her carry-on contains mainly the stuff that wouldn't fit. A pair of high heels. A hair straightener. A notebook she believes will imbue her with inspiration anew, that contains special powers that her electronic devices lack. This means she will have to put on her rumpled plane clothes again, which does seem gross. She should pocket a pair of disposable underwear.

All of these are ancillary thoughts. What she's really thinking is, how the fuck does Krista look like a *Sports Illustrated* swimsuit model at fifty-two, after two kids? Krista volunteered the number while they were bonding at the bar, in the context of detailing the battery of supplements she swore by, and why shouldn't she wear it like a badge of honor? She's got a Pilates body, all lean and lithe. The only suggestions of her age are the faint fans of wrinkles at the corners of her eyes, wrinkles that, Sarah thinks, humanize her, make her a teensy bit relatable.

There is also, on Krista's left knee, a scar the size of a small island. Relatively recent, by the shine on it. It's the one aberration marring an otherwise perfect exterior.

Krista, still naked, appraises her pair of disposable underwear, holding it out in front of her. "I hate that we have to wear these," she says. "You think they'll yell at me if I don't?"

"No, but I think your bits might freeze off if you don't," Sarah says.

"You're *funny*," Krista says, ripping open the underwear's plastic wrapper. "I'm going to like having you around."

Eager to talk about something other than Krista's nakedness, Sarah says, "So does Kevin get hungover a lot?"

"Huh?" Krista says.

"You said he should do cryo because he's super hungover."

"Oh. Oh yeah, well, no, not so much anymore," Krista says. "We had a talk a long time ago. Well—I had to have a talk with him. His drinking was out of control."

"Really?" Sarah says, interest piqued anew.

"Drinking, gambling," Krista says, tugging on the black bandeau. "Too many golf trips and poker runs that got out of control. He would say he was going out to dinner with the boys and not come home until 6:00 a.m. And this was after Connor was born, when I was postpartum and on the verge. Don't get me wrong, I understood the need for a night out—I wanted a night out, I wanted a *week* out—but he took it too far too many times."

"So what did you do?" Sarah asks, fingering the tie of her robe.

"Laid down the law," Krista says, shrugging, like the solution was entirely obvious. "Packed up a bag for Connor and me and told Kevin we were going to my mom's house. We actually checked in to the Montage in Laguna Beach. But by the time he figured that out, when his credit card statement arrived, he was in AA and in no position to point fingers."

"Wow" is all that Sarah can think to say.

"He stuck with it for two years," says Krista. "Longer than I thought he would, frankly. But then the business started picking up, and he got sick of developers looking at him like he had three heads every time he said he didn't drink. Mind you, this was back in the early two thousands, before Cali sober or sober curious or whatever the kids call it these days. He promised to keep it under control. And for the most part, he has. But every now and then, the person he used to be comes back, that reckless little boy who needs another drink to feel like a man, who doesn't know when to stop. There is nothing more unattractive to me."

"I hear you," says Sarah. How many times has she seen Sam reach for the bottle when he's clearly had too much? How many times has she caught him on that betting app? He thinks she doesn't know, but the way he flips his phone face down gives him away.

Krista tugs the sash around her robe tight and gives Sarah a tentative look. "Does Sam have a problem?"

Sarah lets out a hefty sigh. "Define 'problem.'"

Krista scrunches her mouth in sympathy. "You have to help him. You can set him on a better path."

"I don't *want* to have to, though," says Sarah. "Why does it fall on me? Why can't he be an adult and just figure it out, how to behave, how to be?"

"Oh, honey," Krista says, giving her a bless-your-heart kind of look. "Men have no idea how to be."

~

Cryotherapy proves not as torturous as Sarah thought. She and Krista put on mittens and socks and slide their feet into shower shoes. They shuffle over to the chamber and are given an iPad with which they can choose some music to stream for the session, which has a maximum run time of three minutes, lest their bits actually freeze off.

"Upbeat is best," says Habiba, "something to keep you motivated." Krista defers to Sarah, who chooses a YouTube playlist titled "Ibiza Sunset Sound Mix Summer 2023." "Good choice," says Habiba. "You've got this." She gives them a bicep flex of faith and lets them into the chamber, barely bigger than an airplane bathroom, where they stamp around to melodic electronic beats for 115 seconds, squealing about how cold it is, marveling at the little clouds that come out of their mouths.

Afterward, Sarah is, as promised, invigorated, far less fuzzy than she previously felt. The cotton mouth of jet lag is gone, vanished in the frost. She and Krista exchange a hug—their first—after putting their robes back on, before they go their separate ways.

"Don't worry about Sam," Krista says. "We've got a whole week to strategize." She winks and gives Sarah a little slap on the back before another attendant leads her to her treatment room.

Sarah follows Habiba to the room where she and Sam will have their massage. She smiles to herself as she thinks about serendipity. What are the odds of her meeting a woman who not only is going to the same resort as her but has also dealt with the same problems as her? Some of the same problems, anyway.

Perhaps it's not as rare as she thinks it is. Perhaps half the men in Los Angeles are addicts in one way or another. Half of men in general? For sure, every marriage has its issues. Nice to have a mentor to guide her. She can't imagine being this open with her friends. The real ones are few and far between, generally occupied by the children they had when they were still spry, children whose baby pictures she cooed over in the WhatsApp chat, whose school portraits now make her feel ancient by comparison. She's afraid of opening up to these friends about how far back she is in the grand scheme of things. How she can't even control her husband, let alone an actual child. Her mother, Veena, in her sarees; Sam's mother, Chandini, in her salwar sets? Forget about it. Old-school Indian aunties, they would tell her to adjust.

Habiba opens the door to a treatment room done up in blond wood. Bars of warm light emanate from the perimeter of the floor.

There are two massage tables, and Sam is sitting on top of one of them, in a robe, swinging his legs, looking annoyed.

"Where were you?" he asks.

"Krista wanted to do cryotherapy," she says. "Didn't you guys do it, too?"

"Fuck no," says Sam, and Sarah draws back in shock. Consider Habiba, you heathen, she thinks. Poor woman must be scandalized, surely did not sign up for this, probably wants to be at home watching Bollywood movies or online shopping or whatever it is she does when she's not attending to entitled jet-setters with carbon footprints the size of the moon.

"I'm not jumping around naked in one of those things with a dude I just met," Sam says.

"Did Kevin do it?"

"He said, 'Happy wife, happy life.'"

"Might be some truth to that," she says.

Sam rolls his eyes. "Can we please get this show on the road? I want to check out the cellar. They supposedly have super-rare bottles of Bordeaux that you can't get anywhere else outside of France."

Of course he wants to check out the cellar. Sarah stifles her annoyance, bites her tongue to keep from saying something cutting. Can't he just have a cup of coffee? Try some of the much-hyped Dubai chocolate, given that they're in Dubai? It often seems to her that Sam willfully dismisses the problematic nature of his drinking because of his profession, thinks that consuming high-end wines is part of his job, or some sort of passion that elevates him from an average alcoholic. Like if the wine you're drinking is super rare, it would be rude *not* to finish the bottle.

Habiba instructs them to disrobe and lie face down on the tables, beneath the top sheet, while she fetches their therapists. The door closes with a soft click.

They wordlessly do as they're told, Sarah using her elbows and forearms to shield her breasts and midsection as best she can. It was one thing to disrobe in front of Krista—women know how bodies differ and age—and even then, Sarah was quick to cover up, as she always is. The protocol with Sam is different. She does not want Sam to see her naked. It's not about him, really, she just kind of hates her body right now, soft in places where it used to be hard, lumpy rather than limber. He met her at her physical peak, and aside from their wedding, it's been a downhill road since.

She judges like her life depends on it, but the thought of being judged, especially by her husband? It's too much.

Has she ever loved her body? There have been moments, glimpses in mirrors and windowed storefronts. Besides that, it's always been a could-be-better-type situation. There were always inches to lose, things to tighten up, and pounds—forget the pounds. She hasn't weighed herself in years, loath to go down that rabbit hole again.

Head pressed against the massage table's cushioned cradle, Sarah closes her eyes. The fact that she'll soon have a plan makes her feel a modicum better. Krista is going to help. As Krista said, they have a whole week to strategize. Maybe she'll come back through Dubai, following their vacation, with a new and improved husband, a new and improved life, camera rolls of seaside selfies and suntanned limbs. Maybe she'll even like her body! Anything is possible.

The door swooshes open as two therapists enter the room. A woman who introduces herself as Katrina quickly gets to work on the knots beneath Sarah's shoulders, not bothering with the standard questioning about ailments and allergies. She seems to know what she's doing, because Sarah feels herself drifting off, nonsensical movies about Krista and over-the-top premium-class cabins unspooling in her half-conscious mind.

~

Sam twists the cloth napkin in his lap, wrings it one way and then the other. He can't understand it, why Sarah has hitched herself to the wagon of these strangers. Swingers, he is sure. Not that there is anything wrong with swingers, he just doesn't want to give them the impression that he and Sarah are into that sort of thing.

At least he isn't. Is she? He has no idea anymore.

What if that was what it would take for her to be happy, an open relationship, polyamory, swapping spouses, one of these new age arrangements? Perish the thought. He doesn't think he could handle it. He understands that Sarah is not his possession. He is not his father, he's not stuck in the ways of the motherland. But they took vows, and he cannot imagine sharing her with another person. Not in that way. How would it even work? Would they have code words for when they wanted to hook up with other people? Like, "I'm going to get my oil changed?" What if he actually had to get his oil changed?

It seems like a slippery slope, opening the door so that one member of the marriage can venture out, meet someone new, perhaps never return.

In any case, he has no evidence to prove that Krista and Kevin are swingers. Mostly, he just can't fathom why these rich Gen X white people are into them. Krista and Kevin seem to have it all. What could Sarah and Sam possibly have to offer?

He presses himself further against the side of their booth in the wine cellar, which, owing to the structural stipulations of an airport, is not actually underground but in a dimly lit, cushily furnished room within the first-class lounge. Squint and you might think you're subterranean. In any case, it doesn't matter. He tells himself to stop stressing out. He is not here for the vibes, in any sense of the word, or to decode why these people have taken him and Sarah under their wing, he's here for the Château Lafite. And the Château Margaux, if they'll allow him to taste both. If his wife is going to drag him against his will to a first-class lounge to get a massage—he realizes how ridiculous this sounds as he thinks it, but still, he would've rather hunkered down in the other lounge with her, just *her*—he's going to drink all the ultra-exclusive, normally-goes-for-hundreds-of-dollars-a-bottle wine they will serve him, all the wine he can handle, sobriety and general health be damned.

Though, he'll admit—the vibes are immaculate. He would die to have this kind of wine bar in Los Angeles. In Tiffin West Hollywood, speakeasy style, it might actually work, downstairs, in the space they currently use to store twenty-pound bags of besan flour and basmati rice.

He wishes he could flesh out this idea, but he cannot ignore the nagging thought that logically follows. He would have to ask his dad, and if he did that, his dad would poke so many holes in Sam's idea, it would come out looking like a colander. "Where would the money come from to make this speakeasy, huh? My pocket? Yours?" Scoff of laughter. "Where are the customers? Who wants this? No one." His father would answer his own rhetorical question. "Get back to basics, stop with this nonsense."

"Sam?" Sarah is looking at him from across the glossy smoked-glass table, as if he just drooled on it. Has he? In the jet-lagged oblivion of an international layover, anything is possible. He glances down at his shirt to check.

"Do you know what you want to order?" Sarah asks.

Sam realizes that a server is standing beside their table, notepad in hand, pen tentatively poised. "Sorry," he says. "May I have a taste of the Château Lafite and the Château Margaux? I'll decide between those."

The server nods and glides off. Sarah continues burning the side of his face off with her eyes, likely because he asked to sample two wines instead of ordering a glass straightaway. Well, sorry, Sarah, that's what you do at a wine bar that serves two of the most prized bottles from France—you ask for both. If Sarah could opt for cryotherapy, he could opt for this.

"Shall we get something to nibble on?" Krista says, turning over the menu. "Ooh, how about this tandoori popcorn chicken?" She pronounces it "tan-DOO-ree," which is how most white people pronounce it, and while it normally doesn't get on Sam's nerves, coming out of Krista's mouth, it does, her inability to perform the dental plosive "t" as "th" that comes as naturally to people of the South Asian persuasion as breathing. He has tried to teach white people to do it, almost always in vain. What can you do?

He will never be able to tie a bow tie without watching a YouTube tutorial no fewer than seven times; they will never be able to say "thun-duree." Call it even.

"Sounds great," he says.

"Tell us, Sam," Krista says, putting down the menu. "What's your favorite dish to cook? What's your specialty?"

"He makes a pretty amazing fish curry," Sarah says.

Sam is pleasantly surprised by this. Maybe Sarah wasn't glaring at him earlier. Maybe, in his woozy state, he misread her cues.

"It's nothing too fancy," he demurs. "But lately, I've been into Indo-Chinese. Have you ever had it?"

"Didn't know it was a thing," says Kevin. He's spinning a coaster fashioned out of cork on its edge like a poker chip. Poker. That would be an excellent addition to this lounge. Or blackjack.

"It's really popular in India," Sam says, "but it doesn't have much of a presence in Los Angeles. I've been testing out some dishes to work into our menu—Manchurian chicken, Bombay chili prawns."

"Isn't it Mumbai?" Krista asks, looking confused.

"No Indian person calls it Mumbai," Sam says.

The server returns with his samples and the rest of the table's drinks; Sam summarily sniffs, swirls, and swishes. He chooses the Château Lafite, a five-ounce pour, the smaller of two options. The server nods and turns to go. "Actually," Sam calls after him, "make it nine."

Why not? They've still got an hour to kill, and it'll pair nicely with the popcorn chicken. Of course, anything would pair nicely with Château Lafite, even a parboiled shoe.

He sees Sarah exchange a look with Krista. Huh. So they've had that conversation, the one about his drinking. The gambling, too? He wonders how much Krista knows about their relationship, what conclusions she's come to having heard only one side of the story. *Their* story. A story she should not even be privy to, given that they all met less than twenty-four hours ago.

This is the problem with Sarah: She opens up to random strangers and remains closed off to those who know and love her, wary of being vulnerable around people who might, *quelle horreur*, remember her moment of weakness later and throw it in her face. Sam knows this is a vestige of Sarah's father—long passed—who didn't tolerate vulnerability, who taunted her when she came up short, as every child does when they're finding their way. It was something Sarah confessed to him, in their early days of dating, when he asked what her father had been like.

But he wishes she would *talk* to him or, heck, a therapist—maybe her own therapist, not Margaret, the couples counselor who always takes her side—talk to someone with a vested interest in helping her and a certified ability to do so, not this Pilates mom who will probably forget her name at some point in the next seven days and will surely erase her from the record after they return to Los Angeles. If Sarah thinks Kevin and Krista are ever seeing them again once they get home, she's even less tethered to reality than Sam thought.

The server reappears with a nine-ounce pour of Château Lafite and a shallow bowl of popcorn tandoori chicken. The popcorn chicken comes with a fenugreek ranch dipping sauce, which, Sam is pleased to find, is an improvement on the standard-issue Hidden Valley varietal, at least when paired with an Indian-spiced dish. He ought to replicate it at Tiffin. (He hears his father's retort in his head: "To serve with what? Who wants ranch? This is an *In*-jih-unn restaurant. Stick to raita, don't overcomplicate.")

"It's just been so hard, since our youngest started at Dartmouth," Krista is saying. "He never wants to come home. Insisted on spending Thanksgiving in the city, with his 'friends.'" Here, she uses dramatic air quotes, the tips of her fingers bright with turmeric. "I thought I'd bred a good Southern California boy, but I guess I'm nothing compared to Manhattan."

"I thought your youngest went to Stanford," Sam says. He overheard Krista saying as much to Sarah at the on-board bar.

Krista blinks at him. There's a look in her eyes. A how-dare-you-question-me type of look.

"Did I? How strange. Maybe I mixed them up—our eldest, our daughter Alexa, just graduated from Stanford. My little protégé. Majored in psychology and served as the president of Kappa Alpha Theta, just like her mother."

Not having children himself, Sam is admittedly in no position to judge, but he finds it kind of strange that a parent would mix up their children in this way. A mom especially. Call him biased, but mothers tend to remember the little details better than fathers. And which kid went to which school is not exactly a little detail. Surely, someone signed the tuition checks.

Though, given how much money Krista and Kevin have, the checks probably came from the offices of King Holdings and were signed by some accountant several degrees removed. Maybe rich people had the privilege of forgetting the little details. Even the moms. Didn't Krista say that Connor was their eldest?

"What's she going to do now?" Sam ventures. Under the table, Sarah kicks his foot. What? Is it uncouth to ask after the career prospects of Krista's newly graduated protégé? Presumably, after her parents spent all that money on Stanford, she's going to do *something*.

"Excellent question, Sam," Kevin says, tenting his fingers. "I've been asking Alexa and her mother the same thing."

Krista rolls her eyes. "Let our girl have her gap year," she says. "She has her whole life to work and be serious." She turns her attention to Sam. "She's in Europe waitressing, believe it or not." Krista takes a sip of her cocktail, something with pomegranate, saffron, and Serrano pepper that, from Sam's reading of the menu, sounds like a Mideast version of a spicy margarita, salted rim and all. "Honestly, I think she's mostly hooking up with tortured artists and hot buskers, all the bad boys her father would never let her date."

"Krista," Kevin says, apparently dying inside.

"Oh, come on, Kevin, you remember what it was like to be twenty-two. *You* weren't the one who was knocked up. I'm sure you batted your eyes at plenty of 'waitresses' in your day."

"Still do," Kevin says, throwing Sam a wink.

Krista reaches across the table and slaps him playfully. "I think it's for the best," she says to Sam and Sarah. "Let her get her artist-slash-musician phase out of the way, apply to Columbia, get her master's, start her practice in New York, meet a nice man in finance, get married, get pregnant, and move back to Beverly Hills when the time is right."

"You've got it all figured out, huh?" says Sam. Frankly, he's impressed.

"He doesn't *have* to be in finance," Krista says. "Corporate real estate would be fine. Just like her dad! Maybe a tech guy, but"—she screws up one side of her mouth—"they can be kind of weird. Biohacker-y. No one wants their daughter to marry a guy who'll pump their son for plasma.

"I've already put the call out," she continues. "Alerted friends and friends of friends with sons of marrying or, okay, *serious relationship* age. I heard it's hard out there, for the single girls especially. All these porn-addicted boys wanting them to stick lampshades up their asses and whatnot."

"Krista," Kevin says, placing his hands over his eyes. Sam can't help but laugh.

"It's true!" says Krista. "God forbid Alexa ever has to deal with someone like that, not that I would find out—we're close, but we're not *that* close. I just want to do what I can to set her up for the brilliant future she deserves. Of course, it's ultimately up to her. You can only control your kids so much."

"I get that," says Sam, and truly, he does. He wishes his father was as magnanimous toward him as Krista appears to be toward her kids. He'd like to think he'd take the same approach if he ever became a father, if Sarah could ever forgive him, if they ever ended up on the same page.

"Seeing as how this guy"—Krista cocks her head toward Kevin—"was never the type to sit by the door with a rifle, I have to do whatever it takes. Anything for my children." She takes another sip of her cocktail and locks eyes with Sam. "Anything at all."

FOUR

By the time they deplane at Velana International Airport, the premier point of entry into the Maldives, Sarah gravely regrets not having packed a change of clothes in her carry-on. The disposable underwear she filched from the lounge has proven disposable for a reason, getting stuck in places it shouldn't, forcing her to readjust in a manner that is becoming increasingly less subtle. After twenty-six hours of travel, one has few fucks to give.

She gets up from a concave rattan chair, plucks the fabric of her cargo pants from her inner thighs. She needs to walk. To move, to sweat. You'd think they'd have a gym in this arrivals lounge, considering how much time Jala's guests must spend here, awaiting flights to the Middle East or Russia or China, wherever they're coming from or connecting through. The lounge is on the top floor of the Noovilu Seaplane Terminal, and it's only accessible to travelers transiting to or from Jala.

"Each luxury resort has its own lounge," Maanav, their assigned jadugar, said as he led Sarah and Sam from the international arrivals hall to the seaplane terminal. He explained that, in Hindi, "jadugar" meant magician; at Jala, it also meant "butler." "We make magic happen," Maanav explained with a toothy smile. Unlike at American airports, where non-airport employees are not allowed beyond security, Maanav was stationed at the end of the jetway when Sarah and Sam deplaned, along with a colleague, Sharif, who had been assigned to Krista and Kevin.

Sarah made a feeble attempt at suggesting they only needed one jadugar between the four of them. It seemed gratuitous and a little bit gross, all of this personal attention. Given the state of her and Sam's relationship, did they really want another person all up in their business? But Maanav (and Krista, and Sam) quickly dismissed her suggestion. "This is what we're paying for," Sam said. "Just let them do their thing."

Whether he was referring to the jadugars or Krista and Kevin, Sarah wasn't sure. It was obvious that Sam was less than smitten with their new friends, but he couldn't see Sarah's ulterior motive. Krista could help her. Krista could help *them*.

Of course, it would help if Sarah shared her ulterior motive with Sam. Not that it was so ulterior. It was a grand plan, it was something positive, not underhanded, and she ought to think of it as such. She simply hadn't had a chance to fill him in yet. They were exhausted by the time they got on the flight to Malé, passed out promptly after takeoff, didn't even make it to the bar in the back of the cabin. Krista and Kevin were sequestered in first class, and while Krista said she would ask the flight attendant if Sarah and Sam could come up to visit, "do a caviar bump, have a splash of Dom Pérignon, just for a minute or two," even Sarah felt they could all benefit from a little alone time. For the sake of sleep, if nothing else.

She has to admit that this level of luxury—a resort-branded lounge in which to wait out the two-hour layover before their seaplane flight—is foreign even to her, a seasoned traveler who once went on a press trip that comprised visiting every Four Seasons in Italy. (Taormina was her favorite; this was years before *The White Lotus*.)

But the upper echelon of travel seems to have leveled up since her last jaunt. She surveys the lounge. Krista and Kevin are in sleeping pods in the quiet room, apparently as in need of rest as she and Sam were on the previous flight. Sam, along with the five other men in the lounge, is looking at a screen, headphones on, a dazed look on his face. She glances over his shoulder. He's watching yet more true crime. Can never get enough of those series, pornography for people fascinated by murder but too meek to commit it.

Air. She needs air. She strides toward the far end of the lounge and pulls open the glass door to the deck, which is furnished with rattan chairs and bamboo couches. She pushes herself against the edge and gazes at the seaplanes assembled down below. Several idle next to docks that float on top of the water, waiting for passengers to make their way down and come on board.

She has never been on a seaplane. She is not a nervous flier, but she doesn't relish the prospect of propelling through the air in a vessel that seems as easy to sink as a kite. She is reminded of something Natalie once said about landing in St. Barts: "You're in the tiniest plane in the world, and because of how they built the airport, they basically have to dodge a mountain to land. *Terrifying*. But don't worry, I'll give you half a Xan. That and a glass of rosé, and you'll be fine."

They were drinking orange wine in Natalie's backyard in the Hollywood Hills. Her home was everything Sarah suspected it would be—it featured in many of Natalie's social media posts—but better, lusher and more sumptuous in real life than the version she had seen on-screen. She and Sam had a velvet couch, but it was Ikea's version of velvet, synthetic and bristly. Natalie's was plush and the color of an orchid, like something fit for royalty.

Natalie had uncorked the wine on the couch, in her living room, but as the sun made its descent into the Santa Monica Mountains, she slid open the doors to her backyard and they moved outside to an oblong table of off-white stone and into chairs that looked like those of a Parisian bistro. There was a vase of dahlias on the table and two throws draped over the chairs, like this table had been expecting them. Sarah wondered if Natalie's assistant had set it up specifically for them or if Natalie's house was always like this, camera-ready and ready to receive a three-dimensional audience as well.

The plan was for Sarah to join Natalie and her friends—"the fam," as Natalie referred to them, though none of the members were related and the fam was actually quite incestuous—in St. Barts for New Year's Eve. "Diplo's performing at Nikki Beach, it's going to be beyond," Natalie said. The ten of them would share a villa above Eden Rock, the toniest hotel on the island, and there would be a beach day, a boat day, and a night at the club—"Le Ti, the only one worth going to," per Natalie—in addition to the main evening of revelry.

It would be the first New Year's Eve that Sarah and Sam would spend apart since they started dating. Natalie said Sarah could bring anyone she wanted, but since this was her first opportunity to spend an extended amount of time with Natalie as a friend rather than an interview subject or a source, Sarah thought it best to go it alone. "It's really a work thing," she told Sam, and she tried to convince herself there was truth to what she said. Being welcomed into Natalie's circle could mean big things for Sarah. More followers, more opportunities, maybe a chance to be a guest on Natalie's podcast, which could, if she played her cards right, lead to a podcast of her own.

But Sarah knew in her heart that she wasn't extending the invitation to Sam for other reasons. She feared that Sam would bring her down. He could be standoffish in front of strangers, and she didn't want to worry about whether he was having a good time. What if he put a damper on the celebrations, became the guy the fam talked about behind their backs, in the group chat? What if his inclusion ensured that she would forever be excluded, on the fringes of pop culture's tastemakers rather than at the white-hot center?

She figured it was easier to lie. To Sam, to Natalie, to herself.

It was also a month after she found the text messages. After she discovered what Sam had done. Sam was still sleeping in the guest bedroom. She owed him nothing, and while leaving him alone over New Year's Eve may have been a risk, it was one she was willing to take.

"Such a shame that your huzz can't come," Natalie said once they got outside, topping up their glasses. (Natalie said "huzz" instead of "hubs" because "'Hubs' and 'hubby' sound dopey," she'd said in one of her innumerable social media videos. "It's too cutesy, like something you'd call a stuffed animal.” Her cavalier habit of inventing her own lexicon and the way her followers took it up was one of the many reasons Sarah idolized her.)

“New Year’s Eve is one of Tiffin’s biggest nights, unfortunately,” Sarah replied. A lie. Most of Tiffin’s locations closed early on New Year’s Eve, given the lack of demand.

Natalie gave a what-can-you-do kind of shrug, and they had moved on to talking about other things—the latest billionaire who was courting her, who had sent a helicopter to pick her up to go to dinner in Malibu. “*Such* a loser,” she said. “Talked about himself the whole time. Didn’t ask me a single question.”

“Who is he?” Sarah asked. “What’s his deal?”

Natalie bit the inside of her cheek. “Promise you won’t tell a soul?”

“Of course,” Sarah said, as if programmed. “Promise.”

Natalie revealed that the billionaire was an inventor and electric car mogul, the Thomas Edison of our time. “I know, it’s absolutely insane,” she said, her cheeks flushing with pleasure as Sarah gasped and tried to find new ways to say “No way.” “I’m not into him at all, but I won’t lie, it’s pretty flattering that he’s into me.”

“Are you going to see him again?”

“I mean.” Natalie bobbed her head from side to side. “He wants to take me to his estate in Hawaii, the one on the island he bought. YOLO, right?”

YOLO, indeed. Sarah will never forgive herself for what she decided to do with this information with the additional information that Natalie proffered afterward: what the billionaire asked for in bed, how it reminded her of this other famous guy she had dated, this actor everyone thought was gay. It was a treasure trove, this information. Like stumbling on a locked chest of gold deep beneath the sea.

She had milked that night for all it was worth. Stayed for pizza, stayed for ice cream sundaes and post-dessert espressos. She drove home—windows down, music loud, in awe of what she had learned, of what she had been able to pull out of Natalie with barely a tug. She had to tell someone. She wanted to tell Sam. But Sam was at Tiffin

West Hollywood, as he always was on Thursday nights, so she paced around their living room, wondering if this was it. If this was the scoop of her whole career.

And then she opened her laptop and fired off an email to her editor at *Panache*. This was too good. Potential cover story good. Several thousand dollars in her bank account good. "OFF THE RECORD," Sarah's email began, before dropping names and pertinent details. While it would've been wiser to share these over the phone, or even in a voice note, magazine editors never fielded phone pitches from freelancers, certainly not at this hour of the night. Voice notes? They did not listen to voice notes.

Sarah figured she could couch the story in "allegedlys" and pin the juicy details on fabricated sources, take information given to her off the record and twist it to fit. She could make it part of a bigger story about how influencers were the new ingenues, the ones powerful men and major brands wanted. Natalie would be the star of the piece. It would for sure benefit Natalie, could bump her from being an internet celebrity up to a bona fide. *Panache* would do an Annie Leibovitz–style photo shoot. Hell, maybe even hire Annie herself to shoot it.

Now that Sarah was in with Natalie, it could be the first cover story of many. Sarah would have a font of material that would never run dry. Material to inform multipage spreads, a new novel, who knew, maybe a screenplay, one she and Natalie could write together. Natalie had told Sarah that she had always wanted to write a screenplay, she just couldn't find the time. They could be collaborators for life.

None of this came to pass. The opposite, in fact.

Sarah's editor had not replied to her, had instead forwarded Sarah's email to *Panache*'s digital director—because, as the editor explained later, utterly unapologetic, "given that she's an influencer, Natalie seemed a better fit for the web." The digital director had all but drooled over his keyboard at this gossip, which might as well have been the temperature of a Neapolitan pizza oven, that's how hot it was. He couldn't resist adding it to the forthcoming edition of his newsletter for the magazine, *Scene & Heard*, which would be arriving in inboxes the following morning.

Sarah got the call at 6:00 a.m. Natalie sobbing, "How could you?" "I trusted you." "Never again."

The digital director had performed a sloppy cut and paste, and while he left out Sarah's name, given the timing the morning after her and Natalie's heart-to-heart, and all those names, all those names that had been explicitly stated as off-the-record—but as every journalist knew, once it was in writing, there was a record, and careless people could do with that record what they pleased—it was all too obvious that the information had come from her. Her feeble attempts to explain and apologize fell on deaf ears. No ears, actually, given that Natalie ended the call fifty-eight seconds after she initiated it. Then there was the witch hunt that followed, that took place during the week Sarah was to have gone to St. Barts. The social media accounts and websites that sought to find out who, to quote one, "did Natalie dirty," the Natalie who frolicked with the fam in the bluest water known to man while Sarah cowered under the covers, Sam attempting to soothe her, but there was nothing he could say, nothing he could do, to stop her downward spiral. She had fucked up. She had fucked up worse than she had ever fucked up before.

It didn't take long for fingers to point in Sarah's direction, and the third time someone contacted her asking for comment, she finally said something. The wrong thing: "You don't know how hard it is, being a freelance journalist, living and dying on the strength of your scoops."

You don't know how hard it is, being a freelance journalist?

The number of times she's wanted to kill herself for even thinking that that was the right thing to say. How could she have put it in print? In print via direct message, but still.

It was the whine heard round the world. Memes were made. Takedowns were written. A supposedly feminist website went through her compendium of work and ranked her ten worst stories. Even the *Columbia Journalism Review* did a think piece.

Yes, Sarah lived once. Really, properly lived. Now, she exists as an unwilling participant in the journey of life, feet dragging, weary with regret, wishing for a second chance that will never come.

Behind her, she hears the door of the lounge whoosh open. Maanav appears at her side. "Ma'am, the plane is ready for boarding," he says. "May I escort you and sir?"

"Why not?" says Sarah. What else is there?

~

Sam has imagined holding Sarah's hand as they walk down the floating jetway to board the seaplane to Jala. He would not reach out for her hand if they were walking down a typical jetway, those claustrophobic tubes he always fears will detach from one end. A floating jetway is romantic, a lark, not something you do every day, something they might never do again. The sun is beginning its descent, and the whole boarding area—a marina with planes, essentially—is bathed in a salmon-colored glow, the peaks of the capillary waves glossy and gleaming.

Is this impulse to hold her hand corny? Maybe. But they're celebrating their wedding anniversary. It's okay to be corny, in moderation.

But every time he glances to the side and dangles his hand, testing these particular waters, he sees that Sarah is a few paces out of sync with him. She is quite literally dragging her feet. Maanav has run ahead with their luggage—even their carry-ons have to be stored, given that there won't be an overhead compartment or space beneath their seats—so there's nothing weighing her down, physically.

Psychically, it's anyone's guess.

He knows he should pick his battles; this does not rise to the level. Maybe she's just tired, he tells himself. Maybe things will turn around, once they reach the resort.

He slows his pace until he matches hers. He scoots closer to her.

"How are you feeling?"

"Meh," she says.

"Tired?"

"That, but also"—she exhales dramatically—"I just don't know what I'm going to do with myself. My quote-unquote career. Us." She glances at him, tentatively.

Some men, *most* men, would take up with a mistress if their wife threatened to divorce them as many times as Sarah has Sam. "Take up with a mistress" is putting it nicely—most men would join OnlyFans and take to Backpage or whatever the modern equivalent is, pay for sex, distance themselves from their spouse in the process, develop a deeply seedy habit, like gambling or drinking or—

To be fair, he was gambling and drinking *before* he met Sarah.

His point is he did *not* take up with a mistress, he did not join OnlyFans, he doesn't even know if Backpage still exists or what its modern equivalent would be. Instead, he amassed a small fortune of points and miles and booked them a week in paradise. Her response to this, throughout, has been a resounding "meh."

She has no idea how good she has it. But now is not the time to bring that up. There is never a good time to bring it up, because she is still holding those text messages over his head, those messages she never should have seen, because he could've made things right, he really could've, if he only had one more chance.

Well, it wasn't so much the messages themselves, he knows. There's more to it than that.

"It's been a long journey," he says. "Once we check in and shower up, you'll feel better."

She shrugs. "Maybe."

He finds himself wishing that Kevin and Krista were with them if only because Sarah wouldn't act like this in front of them. But they're either on board already or still in the lounge—or, who knows, if they're as rich as they claim to be, maybe they chartered their own private seaplane. Though, surely, they would've invited Sarah and Sam, given how Krista and Sarah have become, over the past twenty-something hours, bonded so much you would think they shared the same blood.

But maybe he can use their absence to his advantage. Find a common foil.

"Kind of weird that Krista can't remember which of her kids went to Stanford, huh?"

"What do you mean?" Sarah asks.

"I mean, isn't that the type of thing you'd remember as a mom? Especially if you went there yourself and you name-drop the school every five minutes?"

"What do *you* know about being a mother?" Sarah retorts, with a laugh of disbelief. "You can barely remember where you put your phone."

This isn't going the way Sam hoped. "That's different," he says. "That's—I have bad short-term memory, okay? I remember the important things—birthdays, anniversaries."

"I just don't know what your point is," Sarah says.

"My point is that there is something off about them," says Sam. He lowers his voice. "Don't they seem like the key-party types?"

Sarah slaps his arm, but there's some mirth in it.

"I really don't think they want to have sex with us," she says. "Though Krista did stand naked in front of me for entirely too long."

"*What?*" Finally, the tide turns. "When?"

"In the changing room, before our massage. She was talking about . . . I don't even know what she was talking about, she just didn't want to put on the disposable underwear."

"Babe," he says. "That's weird."

Sarah bobs her head in a way that conveys agreement. "I guess it is kind of weird. But maybe I'm reading too much into it. Maybe she grew up in a naked house."

"'A naked house'?"

"Like, with a mom who ran around in her underwear and changed in front of her kids, who didn't act like a body was a thing to be embarrassed of."

"There are moms who run around in their underwear?" He has never even seen his mom in shorts.

"Not ones like ours," Sarah says, "but, yeah. Actually, Natalie said her mom was like that."

Her voice has softened, and now she's looking down at the faux wood planks of the dock. Ah. So that's what this is about. Natalie. Yet again, Natalie.

Sarah fucked up, yes. But everyone fucks up. And she's been too hard on herself for too long. This mess unfurled long enough ago that it shouldn't hang over Sarah's head. She continues to let it. Privately, he thinks this is what is holding her back, her impossibly high standards, which he tries (and mostly fails) to measure up to, that she herself cannot even hope to attain.

They've reached their seaplane. It's pale peach and emblazoned with Jala's name in a large sans serif font.

Sam wraps his arm around Sarah. "You've got to stop thinking about Natalie," he says. "What happened happened. You have to move on."

She looks up at him, tears in her eyes. His heart quietly breaks for her, for this thing that he cannot fix. "How can I?" she says. "No one trusts me. I don't even trust me."

"Ma'am, sir?" Maanav says, regarding them with concern. "Are you ready to board?"

Sarah shakes her head vigorously, wipes away the tears that did not fall. "Yes, sorry," she says to Maanav. "It's fine," she then says to Sam, wriggling out from under his arm. "You're right, I just need to get there, I'll be fine."

He pulls her back to him and plants a kiss on top of her head. She lingers for a beat before wriggling away again. A moment. He had a moment of old Sarah. Enough to ignite the hope that, if he plays his cards right, she might come back and linger longer.

~

Sam doesn't know what it's like, Sarah thinks, gazing out the window of the seaplane. Sam works for a family business, was born with a safety net. He will never know what it's like to turn your life from nothing into something. He will never fully understand what she accomplished and, therefore, what she lost. There was a time when she would've opened up to him about her shame, when she would have unpacked it all. But the degree of her shame and her assumption that he just won't get it has made it her burden and hers alone. What good will talking about it do?

From up above, the islands of the Maldives look like geodes, craggy shapes of emerald and azure surrounded by rings of white and then aquamarine that get progressively darker as the ocean gets deeper. Ombré in real life. It's beautiful. It doesn't entirely take her mind off her existential malaise, but it does make her appreciate her husband, in spite of his ignorance, in spite of his faults.

He booked this trip partially to get her out of her head, she knows that. He thought a change would do her good, would do them good. He might be right.

But what he does not understand is that her problem extends beyond the limits of what even the most luxurious vacation can fix. Wherever you go, there you are, that old cliché about how you can't outrun your problems. Sarah should know, Sarah has tried. Sarah has done this previously, did it with Sam.

They met in college. They were in the same circle of friends. He went to the hospitality management school, world renowned for its culinary classes and internship opportunities; she was in arts and sciences, taking a mishmash of liberal arts classes that mostly taught her how to evade deadlines and how to get the job done when you could no longer lobby for an extension.

They didn't really get close until years later, when they were both working in Manhattan and entertainment industry adjacent, Sam behind the scenes at a restaurant that set the standard for fine dining in the early aughts, Sarah doing tabloid journalism for a major news organization and hating every minute of it, unable to land a position elsewhere or gin up the courage to quit.

He would text her sightings from time to time, tell her which morning show anchor booked the private dining room for a meal with a woman who was definitely not his wife, which Broadway star demanded that her Michelin-starred meal be blended into a soup that she could sip, every single dish mushed into one (disgusting). Sarah had never asked him to do this, and she found it oddly sweet that he wanted to help her in this way. Back in college, he wasn't a man of many words. She wouldn't have pegged him as someone who cared about gossip or followed the news. But he was more than met the eye, and when she insisted on taking him out to dinner on his night off to thank him for all the blind items he'd thrown her way, she realized how vastly she had underestimated him. He was smart and sensitive, witty and wry.

He was also not entirely altruistic, in sending her all those sightings. He liked her. *Liked her* liked her.

She had previously dated men in her field who competed with her, passive aggressively as well as not, and men in finance, consulting, and corporate law who couldn't be bothered with what she did for a living, regarded her career as irrelevant fluff. Sam was different. Sam was not like them.

Sam was also, he informed her, six months after they started dating, moving back to Los Angeles. He wasn't happy about it. A little longer at Per Se and he could seriously think about opening his own restaurant. But his father refused to budge. His father owned the one-bedroom apartment in which Sam lived, an apartment that was much nicer than those of his coworkers, most of whom occupied glorified hovels in the outer boroughs or New Jersey. His father was also underwriting Sam's New York City existence, Sarah learned. He couldn't afford dinner at Momofuku Ko every week on the salary of a line cook, which is what he had ascended to after entering the restaurant as a stage.

"I'm sick about it," he told her. "I don't want to lose you."

They were having drinks at the bar on the third floor of the Time Warner Center, the one that overlooks Columbus Circle. During his tenure at the restaurant next door, Sam had befriended the bartender, who generally rang them up for two happy hour wines no matter what they got. Sarah gazed out at the cabs circling the statue, a snaking ring of brake lights.

"What if I came with you?" she said.

"To LA?" He was incredulous. "But you're New York. You're as New York as they come."

She shrugged. "Maybe I need a change." She had found herself growing ornery, getting irritated about things that didn't warrant her level of response, cursing at cabdrivers when they blew past her raised hand despite their "vacant" lights, slapping a subway scanning machine because it wouldn't read her MetroCard (which she had been inserting backward, incidentally, loath to miss the train on the platform and wait who knew how long for the next one). Her default expression had become a scowl. There was a crease in her forehead that would not go away.

New York would always be, in her mind, the greatest city on earth, but she also felt that there was something provincial about never living anywhere else, besides the suburban New Jersey town where she grew up (and dreamed of one day moving to New York) and the lake-dappled city in Upstate New York where she had gone to college (and dreamed of one day moving to New York).

Surely, there had to be more to the world than New York.

She had never thought of herself as the sort of woman who would move for a man, who would uproot herself to suit him. But Sam wasn't asking her to do that. She was suggesting it on her own. That made it different. And maybe Los Angeles would be good for her in ways she could not yet discern. TMZ was headquartered there, and she already spent the better part of her working hours copy-pasting items from TMZ and lightly amending them so as not to be accused of plagiarism. (Anytime she tried to do something more substantive, she was rebuffed by her traffic-obsessed boss.) If none of the other New York media outlets wanted her, maybe some of LA's would. At least one. All she needed was one.

Beyond that was a thought that she would never elucidate out loud, that she hesitated to even think. By this point, she knew about Sam's dad, the business that he'd built. She knew that Tiffin, while not a Wolfgang Puck–type restaurant, was a juggernaut in the Indian community in Los Angeles, the go-to wedding caterer, the place Salman Khan went for kebabs when he came to town (once, a long time ago, but still, his photo was enshrined above the West Hollywood cash register). While Sam may not have wanted to return to the family business, it was at least a bona fide business, one on which he, and she by association, could rely.

If she had to. If they worked out. While they hadn't been dating for that long, they had known each other for years, had become adults together. She trusted her intuition. She could do this. She *should* do this.

At the very least, she'd get some sun.

Sam tried to talk her out of it, but she stood firm. She would not move with him—she needed a few months to tie up loose ends back east—nor would she move in with him. To do so would be risky, would put too much pressure on their nascent relationship.

She signed a lease on a studio in a low-rise complex on La Brea. She spent a grand total of one night there. It served as a very expensive closet for a year before they dropped the charade and she moved into his place in Hollywood, a condo purchased under the auspices of the family business, Balraj's consolation prize for Sam.

That was nine years ago. It was all coming up roses back then. Before a splashy new Indian restaurant stole the spotlight from Tiffin, almost single-handedly tanking its business. (A bout of E. coli poisoning, brought on by a bad batch of spinach *pakoras*, did the rest.) Before she royally destroyed her connections and career. Before they got married, before they began growing apart, before the notion of divorce was on either of their lips.

Next to her, on the seaplane, Sam places his palm on her knee. She knits her fingers with his, gives him a little squeeze. He cannot know precisely what she's going through, but then, how much can anyone know anyone else, even the person with whom they've entwined their life? He is trying. She will try, too.

Out the window, the arrival jetty of Jala comes into view, and she sees a row of people, maybe a dozen, waving up at them. They're all in uniforms the same peachy hue as the seaplane. They look like members of a cult. Slightly creepy, if you think about it. Must be part of their job description. She wonders what all they have to do to keep their guests happy, to keep their jobs.

"You ready?" Sam asks, turning to her, ducking a little to catch a glance out the window.

"So ready," she says, squeezing his hand again. She tells herself to behave. She can do it. She can be the good wife. Just like Krista.

~

Sam knew what he was signing up for—signed up for it, in fact, because it would be so over-the-top—but he has to admit that he finds the level of service at Jala unnerving. Tough to go from the prevailing American attitude of "fuck you, pay me" to a fleet of staff members falling all over him, offering cold towels and cool drinks and not even letting him carry his own duffel bag, for Christ's sake. It's a bit much. Kind of emasculating, really.

"Sir, really, it's best if you let us handle that," a man in a boxy button-down shirt tells him, prying the webbed nylon handle of the duffel bag from Sam's grip. The feel of a strange man's fingers removing something from his grasp makes him, for a moment, primally possessive, filled with a compulsion to clock this guy. But he's too tired to resist. And you don't clock the help at a seven-star resort, that would be beyond the pale. You give up control, you let them do their job.

He looks at the name tag on the guy's shirt, it's gold; the name tags of the others are silver. Sid. Below it is a title: General Manager. Fine, General Manager Sid, have at it.

Sam has a few inches on the general manager, although the guy is fitter than him, looks like the type to rise at dawn, the better to catch the good waves. His hair is also shinier, blacker, thicker, and he's wearing eyeglasses with chunky black frames. A hipster Indian. A fit, hipster Indian. With a British accent, the worst kind (worst in the sense that they're so much more likable than the kind of Indian he is, at least according to women—"ooh, that accent," as if they've never heard a British accent before).

Or maybe he's Pakistani, or Bangladeshi, or Maldivian, or something else. Sam has no idea. He did a rudimentary amount of research (Wikipedia) after booking the trip, learned that the islands have been inhabited since the fifth century BC by Buddhists from Sri Lanka and India; then the Arabs came in, then the British. Now the Maldives is, like its subcontinental neighbor, an independent nation with a slurry of internal factions and outside influences, but on the surface, especially to a foreigner, it looks homogenous. He felt an instant kinship with the people of this country upon arriving at Velana International, all these brown faces that looked like his, so many under one roof.

But it occurs to him now that beyond the amount of melanin in their skin and the general hue and texture of their hair, he and Sid—he and Maanav, he and anyone living and working in the Maldives—have little in common. They are serving, he is being served. They are of this island nation, whether by birth or occupation, and he is not. He is a tourist, and they probably hate him despite needing his tourist dollars. It's a discomfiting realization, one that applies to all who travel, but somehow it hits different when the place you travel to reminds you of some elemental, ethnic home you never really knew.

Maybe they should've gone to Italy. He would not feel these feelings in Italy. Italians loathe serving anyone, especially people like him.

"How was your journey?" Sid asks, hurling both Sam and Sarah's duffels over his shoulder. Gotta be sixty pounds, both of those bags combined. Who is Sid showing off for? Sam wonders. His bicep looks like a baseball, striations and all. Also, why wasn't their jadugar grabbing the bags? Did this GM not have better things to do?

"Long," Sarah says, though her voice is bright, brighter than it was when they boarded the seaplane. "But it might've been worth the trip for this." She glances around; Sam follows her gaze.

The sun has met the ocean, casting the arrival jetty in a glow of rose gold. Bands of pink streak the sky; the water shines like a sheet of sapphire. Sam takes a moment, takes it in. Yeah, it's pretty dope. And this Sid is just doing his job. The one that Sam's paying him to do. He needs to relax. Let the staff do their thing. Focus on his wife, their life. Big potatoes, not small.

Sam slings his arm around Sarah. Sid is walking on the other side of her, toward a golf cart parked where the jetty and a serpentine boardwalk meet. Sam sees now that Sid is wearing an earpiece connected to a walkie-talkie-type device. He recalls from Sarah's time in television that it's called an IFB. Maanav has materialized behind the wheel of the golf cart, having already loaded the rest of their luggage, and he's got an IFB, too, as do the rest of the employees.

"Honestly," Sam says, "pics don't do this place justice."

"Thrilled to hear that, sir," Sid says, setting down the duffels on the rear-facing seat of the golf cart like they weigh nothing at all. "We strive for seven-star service, but of course we rely on Mother Nature to work her magic as well. Now, you're already acquainted with Maanav, who will be at your disposal for the rest of your stay. Have you made reservations for dinner?"

"They're with us," Krista calls out from behind them. Sam, Sarah, and Sid whip around to see Krista trucking up to the boardwalk, trailed by Kevin and their luggage-saddled jadugar, Sharif. Krista does carry one bag of her own, a Louis Vuitton tote whose thin straps strain against the bulk of its contents, perhaps unwilling to hand it off to the staff lest something get lost or, God forbid, stolen. Krista has Karen energy, and Sam wouldn't put it past her to fill her safe with her gumball-sized diamond ring, collection of Cartier bracelets, and whatever other valuables are in her multitude of suitcases.

It's silly. What Krista probably does not know is that real thieves make off with the safe and bust it open later. The safe will not save her. It's like TSA, a performance of security in lieu of the real thing, which is impossible to guarantee.

"Sorry we passed out earlier," Krista says, closing the gap. "All the cocktails and time zones finally caught up with us. But I hope we're still on for dinner?" She looks between Sam and Sarah, eyes hopeful beneath her tinted designer lenses.

"Um," Sam says. He would like to be alone with his wife.

"Of course," Sarah says at the same time. Sarah looks to Sid. "Do we need reservations?"

"It doesn't hurt, given that we're almost at capacity," says Sid. He proceeds to rattle off several options: There's Veranda, Jala's main restaurant, where the daily breakfast buffet will be served; Riva, which specializes in coastal Italian; Osaka, an outpost of a Michelin-starred Japanese restaurant—Sam is already well acquainted with this one, has made a reservation—and Enchanté, a fine-dining French restaurant that only serves a tasting menu. "Any of which would be a great fit for a group," says Sid, "and please accept my apologies, I didn't realize you all were traveling together." He extends his hand to Krista, introduces himself as the general manager.

"We're not," says Sam. "We just happened to be on the same flight."

"But now we're old pals," says Kevin, draping his arm over Sam's shoulders in a fatherly way (a way that Sam's own father rarely does).

Kevin is a full head taller than Sam, which unnerves him in the same way as Sid's biceps. Veiny motherfuckers, those biceps. Yet another thing to be self-conscious about.

"By the way, I texted my watch guy," Kevin says, looking down at Sam. "I've gotta show you what he sent me, plus there's this whole strategy of working with him that will be way better explained over a meal."

It would be useful to have a watch guy, but Sam really doesn't want to commit to enduring yet another meal with these strangers who still strike him as odd. Something about them is off, he is sure.

"Why don't I text you once we get settled?" says Sam, shrugging off Kevin's substantial forearm. As they exchange numbers, Sam keeps an eye on Sid. Sandwiched between Sarah and Krista, he seems as happy as a clam (if clams are, in fact, happy; who knows what bivalves feel).

Sam wonders if he has to worry about Sid. He's heard stories about hotel employees who get too handsy with guests, who take it upon themselves to sniff out unhappy spouses, who get off on on-property conquests. The last thing he needs is some smarmy GM getting too close to his wife. He feels a surge of possessiveness, or maybe it's just cortisol. He reaches over to Sarah and wraps his hand around her waist. "What do you say, babe, should we head to the room?" She nods; they bid the rest of the group goodbye. Good riddance, Sam thinks. A week from now, they'll hardly remember Krista and Kevin, that funny couple desperate to be vacation friends.

FIVE

In spite of her cargo pants, which, by the time they arrive at Jala, seem permanently stuck to her thighs, in spite of the hour and journey and the humidity thick enough to slice, she must admit, this place is beyond.

She films the winding golf cart ride from the reception area to their overwater bungalow—for whom, she doesn't know, she barely posts on social media these days, simply lurks—and snaps picture after picture of their suite and the expansive, two-story deck. She half pays attention to Maanav's spiel about the bungalow's amenities—remote-controlled shades, heated towel racks, two sets of binoculars, the better for viewing birds and fish. On the upper level is a private pool overlooking the Indian Ocean; below, another sundeck with steps that lead down to the open water. She rolls up her pant legs and sticks her feet in, marvels at the clarity of the sea and the just-right temperature and the way the white sand beneath feels like powder, softer than any she's dug her toes into before.

The only thing between them and the horizon is a trio of overwater bungalows belonging to another resort—a Four Seasons, according to the map on her phone—and those are far enough across the lagoon to not mar the sense of privacy on their deck. She could totally plunge into their pool naked if she wanted to.

But when she scrolls through the footage, sitting on the canopied bed as soft as a cloud, she sees that no camera can capture the most important thing—what it *feels* like to be here.

It feels like heaven. It feels like a slice of paradise that has no business existing in the same universe as the one that contains the 101 and the Van Wyck and death and taxes and all the bad things about being on earth. It feels like she does not deserve to be here.

"Babe?" Sam calls from the shower. One of two—he's in the indoor shower, in the bathroom that is as big as the studio apartment Sarah once occupied in New York. It's inlaid with jade-colored marble or, who knows, maybe jade itself, and the brass rainfall showerhead is the circumference of a hula hoop. There's also an outdoor shower, with a reasonably sized showerhead and its own jade-marble enclosure. It's accessible through the deck and a glass door at the end of the bathroom.

Sarah is supposed to be in the outdoor shower, getting ready for drinks and dinner. But Sarah wants to scroll. In peace. Make herself feel better by comparing her outlandish environs to the humbler abodes of everyone else on social media. Surely, even the Alanas and Natalies of the world cannot compete with this.

But as she ignores Sam and opens the app, she sees a photo of Alana and her daughter. Taken at the new members-only club that courted all the cool kids away from the Soho House. Sarah can feel Alana's radiance from nine thousand miles away, and Alana's caption, "Teatime with the tyrant," conveys Alana's love for her daughter, contentment with her station, and ability to laugh at the inevitabilities of motherhood (dealing with a presumably tyrannical toddler) in a way that makes Sarah's heart ache. Sure, her suite is fabulous, but it is not a child. It is not a purpose, a forever source of joy and pain and all that it means to be human. It's a commodity, and commodities can only carry so much weight.

She darkens the screen of her phone, puts it down, and knocks the back of her head against the woven rattan headboard. This is what it's been like lately—she feels a desire to share something, opens the app, sees something undeniably better than whatever she was going to share, gets discouraged, closes the app, and spirals. A vicious cycle. Sam has suggested that she delete the app from her phone, but she requires the app to stay up on popular culture, and she wants to know what's going on, and she feels like she might actually die if she isolates herself any further than she already has. (When was the last time she went out with a friend? Who does she even consider a friend anymore?)

"Babe?" Sam calls again. He has turned the shower off. He emerges from the stall, a cloud of steam following in his wake. "How an island in the middle of an ocean can have better water pressure than we do, I will never understand, how's the—wait, have you not showered yet?"

He's clad in a towel, regarding Sarah, who is still sitting up in bed.

"I had to send something," she lies.

"What?"

"An email," she lies again. "For work."

"What work?"

"I still work, *Samir*," she shoots back. She almost never uses his full name, generally reserves it for occasions when she wants to drive home the degree to which she is pissed or pleased (a rare occurrence, lately). His question was fair, she knows, and he asked it without malice. But she feels vulnerable, and when she feels vulnerable, she attacks.

And immediately feels bad. He has no idea about the turmoil she's dealing with because she refuses to talk about it. If she talks about it, she believes, she will give the turmoil power, she will let it consume more of her than it already does. If she's not spiraling about the way she sabotaged her own career, then she's spiraling about motherhood. The issue of whether or not to become a mother, whether or not she can, what she's missing out on, whether she is strong enough to handle it—whether their relationship can manage that kind of shift. She is afraid to voice any of this lest she be judged as immature—most women her age have already had a child, if not more than one. She is not sure when she fell so far behind.

"I know," he says, flatly, "but it's like 5:00 a.m. in Los Angeles."

"Which means it's 8:00 a.m. in New York, and you know that's where most of my editors are."

He's looking at her in disbelief.

"I thought maybe I should write about this place," she ventures. "Something about the friends you meet on planes, or traveling to work on your marriage, or something." The latter's not a horrible idea, if only she could find an editor willing to assign her anything. Or perhaps she could make like all the other journalists and start a subscription newsletter, though the critics that would emerge from the dark corners of the internet, the ones who chronicled her downfall with memes and glee, would have a field day with that. Sam exhales, looks up at the vaulted ceiling of the bathroom, which is hung with a fan with blades like butterfly wings. *Try*, you're supposed to *try*, she reminds herself.

"I'm going now," she says, scooting off the side of the bed. She slides her feet into fluffy white slippers embroidered with Jala's logo and plants a kiss on Sam's cheek on the way to the outdoor shower. Maybe the outdoor shower will cure her. Maybe it will rid her of her sins. Maybe it will transform her into an entirely different person.

"I'll be ready in five," she says, yet another lie, but a little white one, or even less severe than that—transparent. It's a lie that her husband can surely see through.

~

Sam is scrolling through sports scores, growing more irritated with every swipe of the thumb. The amount of bets he would like to place. He misses it, yearns for it, the thrill of action playing out on far-flung fields and him potentially getting a piece of it. The gambling app isn't working, as Sam suspected it wouldn't. He has drafted and deleted several texts to his bookie—the new one, the one that Steve introduced him to, the one to whom Sam preemptively announced his travel plans. The guy never responded. Sam's "great to be connected, going to be abroad and unreachable for a bit" hangs beneath Steve's "linking you two here." What a balls-less thing to say, on Sam's part. No wonder the bookie hasn't replied. He can sense Sam's reticence through the screen. He doesn't want to waste his time.

Sam ought not to be fixating on this. He's made a promise to Sarah. But the thing is, he knows how to win the money back, he is sure. And the need to win it back feels all the more imperative given that this trip is, thus far, not having the effect on his marriage he hoped it would. Is it *wise* to cash in all of you and your wife's combined points and miles after losing several thousand dollars on sports bets of various kinds? Define "wise." He needed a grand gesture after Sarah found the texts from his old bookie, Elaine, inquiring in a not-so-gentle manner about Sam's whereabouts. Not so gentle meaning all caps. Many all-caps messages at once. But Sarah didn't have anything to worry about—Sam had been strategically avoiding Elaine and establishing a relationship (read: placing bets) with a new bookie—now also persona non grata, the guy never dealt him a win—so as to pay back the old one.

Okay, maybe Sarah had something to worry about.

Elaine hadn't started out playing hardball. She was always so pleasant over text. She shared his passion for sport and having skin in the game. Novel, to have a female friend like that. That's really how he thought of Elaine, as a friend. A friend he'd met in Las Vegas at the sports book at the Wynn, a friend through whom he could place bets because California hadn't legalized sports betting and wouldn't let him use the meaty part of the sports betting app. He would use the app to assess the lines and then text Elaine, get her thoughts. See what she was up to. It only seemed polite, and she was so kind. So attentive. More so than any of the male bookies he'd ever known.

Nothing untoward had happened. Besides the loss of the money, which Sarah had learned about in the worst possible way, when Elaine's texts materialized on the lock screen of his iPad, just sitting there on their coffee table, the lamest of smoking guns.

He didn't know what Sarah found more reprehensible, the thousands he'd squandered—though he could win it back!—or the volume of messages, or the fact the messages were from a woman. She was vociferously upset about the whole thing. And he understood it, he did. But the thing was, this was his money, his money to do with what he pleased. He hadn't dipped into their joint account, and he had never questioned what she spent her money on, the fitness classes and fancy lunches and Uber Blacks and that trip to St. Barts she never took.

He had played the part of the punching bag. He had let her take her anger about a whole litany of things out on him. They were supposed to let the past be the past this trip. They were supposed to move forward together—or figure out if they were better apart.

His insides make a snarling, gurgling sound. He wouldn't be thinking about his bookies and his bets if they were sitting down for a hot meal. He has already torn through a packet of banana chips in the complimentary snack basket Maanav told them would be replenished every day. He craves something made to order, not microwaved in an airplane or served out of a chafing dish in the back of some hermetic kitchen (although who knows how the meals at Jala are prepared, maybe they have chafing dishes and hermetic kitchens, too). But seeing as how a hot meal will not immediately materialize in front of him, he is seeking ways to distract himself, namely by contemplating all the bets he would place if he only had a way. His other option is to pick a fight with his wife for taking so long to get ready, but no man has ever emerged from one of those spats victorious. So really, scrolling sports scores is *good* for their relationship. It's a way to keep the peace. Because maybe more than anything—than a hot meal, than winning back the money—Sam would like his wife's attention. Does this make him needy? Well, fine, then call him needy, tattoo it on his forehead, sue him if it's illegal to need your wife these days. God forbid you marry someone because you desire them and the way they make you feel.

Sarah's attention is currently occupied by the full-length mirror in the dressing area of their suite. It's oval shaped and ringed by a light with settings such as "Warm," "Cool," and "Evening," and for the past, six, eight, who knows, perhaps as many as *twelve minutes*, Sarah has been futzing with the settings while holding her phone at various angles in front of and above her face, taking selfie after selfie.

He cannot stand it when she does this, when she prioritizes the capturing of the moment over the moment itself.

"Babe," he says, like a sheep bleating, the way he's forever calling out to her. "I'm starving. Can we please go?"

"Our reservation isn't until seven," she says.

"Right, but we were going to get a drink before and check out the gym."

She makes a hmm of vacillation. "We can check out the gym tomorrow morning. I don't know if I need a drink before. Why don't we just wait until we're with Krista and Kevin?"

"About that," Sam says, getting up, going to the mirror. "Can we not do dinner with them? It would be nice to have a night alone."

She puts down her phone. "We have like, seven nights alone. An entire week's worth, all to ourselves."

He rolls his eyes. "I'm sure they're not going to let us get away from them that easily. It's our first night. We should spend it with each other, not with these strangers."

"You keep calling them strangers, but Krista and I have gotten to know each other pretty well."

He feels his ire rising. "How well can you know someone you met literally a day ago?"

"You have no idea how women operate," she says, shaking her head. "It's not my fault that you have trouble opening up to people."

Where the fuck did *that* come from, he wonders.

"Excuse me if I don't want to divulge all my deep, dark secrets to some pedophile I met on a plane."

Her face twists like a lemon. "Pedophile? What are you *talking* about? Kevin could be a great mentor to you, if you could just give the guy a chance."

"What the fuck is he going to mentor me about? Ugly polo shirts?"

"How to, I don't know"—she shrugs dramatically—"run a business? Start a new one? Break away from your dad? You know that he's never going to give you the power to turn Tiffin around, I don't see why you continue wasting your time and potential there."

One day. Not even. They've been at Jala for all of *one hour* and she's already detonated one of the atomic bombs in their relationship, Hiroshima-level shit, the type of topic that makes them want to kill each other and/or themselves when they really start hashing it out.

She has no right. She has no idea. He does not want to start—or end, or spend—their vacation like this.

"You know what? You want to have dinner with them, go ahead. I'm going to the bar."

He turns on his heel and walks out the door.

~

The audacity, she thinks, storming down the boardwalk, the soles of her sandals falling heavily on the worn, wooden planks. She is just trying to help. How Sam doesn't see this, how he fails to register even a hint of her altruism, she doesn't understand. What should a wife do besides help her husband be the best man that he can be? Not that she signed up for this job. She thought that she was marrying a fully formed human, one with ambition and wherewithal and the ability to get shit done. Thus far, Sam has mostly sat on his hands, or no, used his hands to gamble online and open bottles of wine and do pretty much anything but plot a way out from under the family business that's threatening to swallow him—and them, by consequence—whole.

She loves his father, but the guy is a megalomaniac. An aging megalomaniac, the worst kind. All she wants is for Sam to come into his own, to realize the strength of his skills and talents, and she believes the only way for him to do this is to break away from the shadow of his father, to take a hard turn.

Does she understand that Tiffin underwrites the cost of their mortgage, their health and car insurance, their gasoline? Well, sure. But Sam could do better. Sam's future eminently successful restaurant and hospitality business (let's not forget he took a college class in how to run a Marriott-level hotel group) could underwrite an even *better* mortgage, *better* insurance, *better* gasoline, not that there's anything higher than premium unleaded, she's pretty sure.

She can be her husband's greatest champion, which is something he'd realize if he took his head out of his ass.

Perhaps this is harsh.

Perhaps the same could be said about her.

A breeze shifts the palm fronds overhead, which dance in the darkening sky. She crosses her bare arms over her chest. It's not a strong breeze, but she imagines that, given its location in the middle of the ocean and the lack of tall buildings to act as buffers, this place must get hit by winds, gusts, air moving at enough miles per hour that it would be dangerous to be out on the boardwalk unaccompanied.

She could've called for a golf cart, but she thought a walk might help her cool off. She does not want to continue this fight at the bar, or spend the evening bitching to Krista and Kevin about Sam, which is becoming an increasingly real possibility, given that her husband isn't responding to her text messages.

Another breeze sends the hem of her maxi dress momentarily toward the sky and sends a shiver up her spine. Damn. This was not the cooling off she had envisioned. Maybe she shouldn't have embarked on this walk alone—she's still over water, she has not yet reached land. She could've taken one of the bikes—every room at Jala came with complimentary beach cruisers—but it's been a while since she's ridden one, and despite the old saying, she would rather reacquaint herself with the pedals in a place where it would be safe to swerve.

Especially given that there don't appear to be guardrails on this boardwalk. Do her eyes deceive her? She moves closer to the edge to see.

Nope, no guardrail or banister of any kind. Just a steep twenty-foot drop down to the ocean, which she is pretty sure is full of stingrays and sharks. She wonders how Jala gets away with it. The lack of a barrier is aesthetically pleasing, for sure, but it would never fly in America. This place would get sued in a second.

She positions herself firmly in the middle of the boardwalk, stepping more carefully than before. Can't afford to trip in these parts. Who knows what might happen? Since setting off from her room fifteen minutes ago, she's seen two couples whiz by on beach cruisers and one butler in a golf cart. All raised their hands in greeting or smiled and nodded, but if something were to go wrong, it's possible that it would only be her and the birds. And the fishes. And the sharks. And whatever else is down there.

She starts to feel better once the sandbank rises up to meet the boardwalk. Soon, she's firmly on solid ground (well, as solid ground as any existent in the middle of an ocean that's 24,000 feet deep). The palm trees on the main island of Jala are hung with round rattan lanterns that emit a warm, inviting glow, and tiki torches are driven into the sand along the path, their flames illuminating the way to the main restaurant, Veranda. Low, wide marble steps ascend from the sand to Veranda's main entrance, which is framed by a massive rattan arch and more candles than Sarah can count. It's beyond romantic, a realization that makes her wistful. How she longs to be in sync with the man she married.

She steels herself, walking in. Sam had said he was going to the bar. Presumably, he meant the bar of Veranda, although as Maanav told them during the ride from the reception to their room, there were seven bars on the property in total, and Sam could've chosen to post up at any one of them.

She tries to figure out whether she wants to see Sam or not. On the one hand, she did nothing wrong. Sure, she took too long to get ready, and yeah, she could have been more artful in bringing up the family business, but that didn't warrant him abandoning her for a bar.

On the other, the prospect of giving him the cold shoulder for what, a night, seven nights, more than that? It feels untenable. She can be a bitch, but she has a hard time being that principled of a bitch for that long. It's exhausting.

She can already feel the humidity and balmy temperature seeping into her skin, making her looser and more languid than she would be in Los Angeles. It's hard to be a principled bitch when external factors encourage you to be loose and languid. She can always be a principled bitch back home. Lay down the law.

Or, if this week really proves too much to bear, they can part ways at LAX, like in that George Clooney movie about management consultants.

All of which is to say that she's entirely unprepared when she reaches the maître d' stand and finds herself swiftly and firmly scooped beneath Krista's Pilates-toned arm. "We found your huzz," Krista says. Sarah smells rum and cotton candy, either Krista's perfume, some unholy cocktail, or a combination of both. "Trouble in paradise?" Krista asks, turning to Sarah.

Oh no, Sarah thinks, she knows. How embarrassing, to be found fighting on day one. Sarah has read about how many couples fight on vacation, unmoored from the routines that give their days shape and give them space from each other. But usually, those disagreements set in after several days of coffee and Wi-Fi that's not quite as strong as you generally prefer. Who fights on their first day at Jala, the most romantic resort in the world?

"He's just so stubborn," Sarah says. "It's always his way or the highway." This is something Sam has said to her, many times. In truth: They are both stubborn, perhaps equally so, and Sarah knows it. But Krista doesn't. Krista knows what Sarah tells her.

Krista links her arm through Sarah's and starts walking, presumably in the direction of the bar. Krista is wearing a fishnet body-con minidress with holes big enough to fit a quarter and high-heeled platform sandals. Though she has the physique to pull it off—the legs of a dancer, that scar on her knee gleaming like a battle wound—it's the last thing that Sarah would want to wear after coming off more than a day of travel, even in this heat. It's sexy in a lurid way. It's what you'd wear to a club.

A swingers club.

Are Krista and Kevin trying to have sex with them? How embarrassed she would be if Sam has been right all along.

It's also not at all a garment that she expected this Loro Piana mom to own, but maybe Sam was right, she and Krista barely knew each other. Who knew what secrets Krista and her closet held?

Krista stops walking, unlinks her arm from Sarah's, and spins around to face her. "Look," she says. "Men are idiots. They need women like us to teach them how to behave, how to make the most of their potential. And you don't have to do it out of the goodness of your heart." Krista extends a finger and places it on Sarah's heart, or the general vicinity of where Sarah's heart would be beneath the strapless, elasticized bust of her maxi dress.

"Do it because it will help *you*," says Krista. "If you make him better, your life will be better. It's a simple equation."

Sarah sighs. "What's that saying, you can lead a horse to water but you can't make it drink?" The trough in front of Sam might as well be an ocean. "I told him that Kevin could be a great mentor to him, and he didn't want to hear it. That's when he stormed off."

Krista lightly rubs Sarah's shoulder. "You meant well. But I'll be honest"—she leans in—"Kevin doesn't really know what he's doing, either. Who do you think is the brain behind King Holdings?"

Sarah smiles. "Mother knows best."

"She does. And everything will be okay. We bought him a drink—I know that alcohol's an issue, but sometimes you've gotta let them have a treat. Come." She links her arm through Sarah's again. "Let's get you something to take the edge off."

Sarah concedes. What other choice does she have? It's nice to have someone make the decision for her, to be absolved of responsibility if it all goes to hell.

Krista leads the way down the long teakwood bar. Amber uplights illuminate the bottles along the wall, giving them the glow of religious idols. Sarah prays to the god of Campari that she and Sam don't lose control and blow up in front of their new friends, these benevolent souls, or the rest of the people at the resort. Couples are scattered at the high-top tables that surround the bar, fingers entwined above condensation-ringed coasters.

Sam and Kevin are in high-backed chairs toward the end of the bar; he locks eyes with her as she and Krista approach. He's shooting daggers. She decides to turn up the charm, kill him with kindness, or at least give these nice white people the impression that she's the bigger person, thereby making her the winner in their eyes, which might be all that really matters. Impressions.

"Look who I found," Krista trills. "Kev, dearest, can you bring over another chair for Sarah here?"

"Aye, aye, Captain," Kevin says, hopping down from his seat.

"Honey, what would you like to drink?" Krista asks, turning to Sarah. "They make a killer spicy skinny, but there's also a whole encyclopedia of Negronis." She passes Sarah a thick menu. "I know how much you like those."

Sarah cocks her head at Sam. Look how much Krista knows about me. Look how wrong you were.

"*Ooh*, they have one flecked with gold," Sarah says, overly enthusiastic, appraising the Negroni catalog. Honestly, it sounds ridiculous—the drink also costs the equivalent of fifty dollars—but she feels the need to put on a show.

"Well then, that's what you're getting," Krista says, motioning for a bartender.

Sarah panics. It's too much, and she says so. She does not want to make Sam suffer—*them* suffer—by ordering show-off-y drinks that cost as much as a meal. While points covered the cost of their room, they're on the hook for food and beverages outside of breakfast, and she dreads the sinking feeling that, if they order like this, will descend on them at checkout, when they discover that they've spent the GDP of a small island nation on liquor, which is expensive to import into the Maldives and, because it's a Muslim country, also heavily taxed.

Krista grips her shoulder, tighter this time, her French tips digging into Sarah's flesh. "Honey, when are you going to learn?" she says in a low whisper. "There *is* no such thing as too much."

~

Two rounds later and they're punch-drunk, slaphappy, dazed by a combination of overconsumption and jet lag. They've arranged their seats in a semicircle at the bar so that they're able to converse with each other and Hakim, the bartender Krista keeps chatting up.

No, it's more than that. From Sam's perspective, Krista is full-on flirting with Hakim, batting her eyelashes, running her hands through her wavy blond hair, throwing her head back and bestowing throaty laughter on his lame jokes. He's seen this sort of woman before, at the fancy French restaurant where he worked in New York and the not quite as fancy places that preceded it. The well-to-do customer who gets off on being wanted by a member of the staff, who would under normal circumstances never hook up with them—they're the *help*, for God's sake—but who is so hungry for attention that they can't help but prostrate themselves like this.

It's sad, really. Is this who Sarah wants to be friends with? Is this who Sarah wants to be?

"What next?" Hakim asks, coming over to him, rubbing his palms together. Sam's had two espresso martinis. Given the buildup of highly caloric drinks and fatty foods in his system, at this point of the evening, caffeine combined with alcohol is liable to, frankly, kill him, but he needed something powerful to counteract the one-two punch of Sarah insulting him and Krista insisting that he join her and Kevin in what he remains convinced is some kind of convoluted sex game.

Sam offers an apathetic shrug. He's not in a horrible mood anymore, he just can't muster the energy to care. "Dealer's choice."

"Snake venom, then," Hakim says, clapping his hands together and smiling so that his white teeth flash. "My latest concoction, a combination of blue curaçao and tequila reposado."

It sounds about as appealing as being bit by a snake—hence the name?—but sure. Why not. "Hey, man," he says, leaning into Hakim, who's upending a bottle of liqueur the color of Windex into a cocktail shaker. "You get a lot of ladies like that here?" He cocks his head toward Krista.

Hakim gives him a sly look. "Bro, it's my all-time favorite hobby. They come in droves during holidays. Dressed to the nines and ready to"—he puts down his cocktail implements and jerks his elbows back in quick succession. Sam howls. Krista, Kevin, and Sarah, immersed in a conversation about *The Real Housewives of Beverly Hills*—Kevin and Krista live down the street from a recent addition to the cast—turn to see what they're missing.

"Sorry," Sam says, collecting himself. "This guy's hilarious."

"Oh, you mean my new favorite bartender?" Krista says, reaching over the bar to run her fingernails along Hakim's substantial forearm. What do these guys do to work out? Sam wonders. Bunch of statuesque motherfuckers populating this island, an army of Mr. Steal Your Girls.

"I'm bringing you back to LA with me, Hakim," Krista says, batting her eyes at him again. "No one makes a spicy skinny like you do."

"I'll be on the next flight, ma'am," Hakim replies, beaming. "Yours, if I'm lucky."

"Good boy," Krista says.

It's so twisted, Sam can't take his eyes away. Kevin is talking with Sarah about, from the bits and pieces he's overhearing, the long-term viability of pop-up shops in luxury shopping malls, either blithely unaware that his wife is courting a bartender who appears to be half her age—which would be their son's age, now that Sam thinks about it—or unfazed about her extracurricular activity of choice.

Or he knows. Or he knows and they're all going to have a threesome later. Maybe that's the real reason for Krista and Kevin's extravagant trips. Opportunities to engage in orgies with hotel staffers who will never call them out, because who would believe a working-class employee over a monied American couple, even if the employee had the gall to report it? Maybe the employees liked it, too.

And maybe they picked up willing vacationers along the way. What did they call Sam and Sarah in the Emirates Lounge? Incidentals. Giggling as they said it. Sharing one of those looks that communicated that the word meant more than they were letting on. What if "incidentals" were the people they orgied with, if that was even the right way to put it? He and Sarah need to distance themselves from these sickos, stat.

Or.

It occurs to Sam that maybe he's the one with the issue. If Kevin's cool with it and Krista's clearly game and Hakim, well, Hakim said it's his favorite hobby, then who is he to judge? It's not like he and Sarah have some spectacular sex life. He can't remember the last time they were intimate. Two months ago? Five?

He has never engaged in a threesome, let alone an orgy. Perhaps he has been too square. Sarah is generally the one in their relationship who goes on about signs, taking one thing to portend another, and he's usually the realist, dismissing such signs as coincidences or utterly unrelated phenomena.

But maybe he's wrong. Maybe there is a reason Krista and Kevin have landed at the same resort as them. Maybe the universe is trying to tell him something.

It wouldn't be *awful* to have sex with Krista. As for Kevin . . . he is not ready to go down that road. Can't even think about Hakim. But if they want to watch?

He chooses not to think about what role Sarah would play in all of this. Maybe he, Krista, and Sarah can retreat to their own room and the other two can play cards outside or something.

He sees Sarah's eyes start to loll about in their sockets, a sure sign that she's drunk. They need to eat something. Really, they need to sleep, put a cork in this day, send it off to sea.

He reaches out and rubs her shoulder. His snake venom sits on the bar, untouched. "Babe," he says, in a tone that endeavors to convey the gravity of the situation vis-à-vis her empty stomach and rapidly escalating blood alcohol level, grave enough that he's willing to overlook their previous spat in the interest of her not passing out in public. "Why don't we sit down, order a proper dinner?"

"You're sitting with us, silly," Krista says, slapping his arm. "But yes, I'm starved. Kev, want to see if our table's ready?"

"I really don't think—" Sam starts.

"I insist," Krista says, staring him down.

Sam relents, powerless. He does not know what he thinks. He does not know what he wants. A time machine, maybe. Something to take him and his wife way, way back.

~

By the time Sarah sits down for dinner, at a four-top table fashioned out of lacquered bamboo, she is drunk enough to know that she will not remember much of this night. She is laughing too loud, her timing is off, and she flings her hands this way and that as she tries to make a point that gets lost in the increasingly vast expanse between her mind and her mouth.

There are rare occasions in which she enjoys being this drunk. This is not one of them. She wants to excuse herself but does not know how to do that without seeming rude, and by this point, she is convinced that Krista holds the keys to fixing her marriage, fixing her life. Fixing her. Krista is Natalie and Alana and a whole host of other women she follows on social media, rolled into one.

She doesn't want to piss off Krista. She saw the way Krista looked at Sam when he tried to break away.

She orders tom yum soup as an appetizer and spills a good portion of it on herself. By the time her entrée arrives, a Maldivian fish curry that might be the same hue of green as her face, even Krista is suggesting that she drink some water. She takes a sip to appease her and Sam, but water will not save her. She is too far gone.

She needs to sleep this off. She needs to find her way back to righteousness, regain the upper hand. She is not sure when she lost it, in her marriage, in her life, but she wants it back, she wants to be the wife in control who sets the agenda, whose husband is proud to stand by her side. Tomorrow. Tomorrow is a new day. Tomorrow is the day that she'll plot her comeback, with the help of her new best friend, her savior, her guiding light.

SIX

Come on, we're going to be late."

The voice she hears sounds like Sam's, but it's coming from far away, underwater perhaps, or maybe another dimension. Her mouth feels like it's stuffed with cotton.

"What time is it?" she grumbles, groggily.

"Seven thirty. The snorkeling boat leaves at eight. Maanav will be here in ten minutes."

"Snorkeling?" How did she agree to snorkeling? She loathes the prospect of snorkeling, all those unknown predators in the water, slippery, slimy things just waiting to get a bite of grade A leg meat. Probably salivating at the thought of it. If fish salivate. (She figures the less she knows about fish, the less bad she'll feel about eating them. At least, this is what she tells herself.)

"Remember?" Sam says. "We confirmed the boat last night, after dinner."

Of course she doesn't remember. She drank liters more than she was supposed to. One day in and it's all gone to shit, whatever vision she had of herself departing Jala as a new and improved and refreshed human being has disintegrated to dust, dispersed into the ether.

The thought of being on a boat makes her stomach lurch. But Sam is standing over the bed, expectant and irritated, and the more charitable part of her brain, the part that hasn't been soaked in alcohol, sympathizes with him. This is his vacation, too. She is supposed to be trying. Staying in bed and sulking and refreshing all her social media apps is not a good use of her time, not in the Maldives, although—now the hangover chimes in. Isn't self-care what you make of it? Maybe one morning of sulking and scrolling wouldn't be so unforgivable—

Sam sighs. "You-know-who will be there."

She throws off the covers. One thing to disappoint her husband, another to disappoint Krista. She's not sure where it came from, this desire for Krista's validation, for Krista's help with her current situation, but she can't help but think in terms of what Krista would do, say, feel. Would Krista wear this direct-to-consumer two-piece? Probably not, she probably has an Everything But Water's worth of Malia Mills and Vitamin A and Vitamin C and whatever the cool new swimwear labels are, Sarah can't keep track, but direct-to-consumer knockoffs are all Sarah owns. She has direct-to-consumer bikinis for days.

Maybe she should ask Krista about her preferred brands of bathing suits. Maybe she should ask Krista for a hundred-point bulletin about how to be like her.

She eschews a shower, tugs on the high-waist bottom and the square-neck top, and throws a rumpled tunic on top of that. In the mirror, she assesses her hair. A veritable rat's nest. She waves her hand under the faucet and runs it through her shorter layers, which are curling recklessly in the rampant humidity. She shoves a capsule into the Nespresso machine, presses the button, gulps the steaming result, burns her tongue.

"Okay," she rasps, grabbing her sunglasses. Necessary armor. "Let's go."

Maanav is waiting in a buggy on the boardwalk, as promised. By way of greeting, he clasps his palms together as they emerge and briefly bows his head. "Did you have a good night's rest?"

"Slept like the dead," Sarah says.

"Still a bit jet-lagged," says Sam. He's got his phone on his lap. Sarah sees him fiddle with it, toggle between a text chain and sports scores that she tries to read but cannot. It can't be with that bookie. He swore. Always sports scores. Has he deleted that app? She ought to check.

"Snorkeling will set you right," Maanav says. "The salt content of the waters around Jala makes them supremely restorative, they can solve just about anything."

"Even a marriage?" Sam mutters, loud enough for Sarah to hear but out of Maanav's earshot.

She looks at him. He's one to talk.

They rumble along the boardwalk, the early morning sun glinting off the ripples of the water below. They pass a sandbank on which another couple, young parents by the looks of it, are walking with a toddler, the picture of a happy family life.

Then again, maybe they've been up for hours. Maybe the toddler gave them hell overnight. Sarah realizes she can only glean so much from a passing glimpse. That almost makes it worse.

She hates this feeling. Helplessness. She never considered herself the helpless sort until recently, and she'll do anything to feel any other way.

"Maanav," Sarah ventures. "Are any of the bars on the island open now?"

"Indeed, Veranda serves mimosas and Bloody Marys with breakfast," he says. "As well as anything else you might want—you're on vacation, after all."

"Can we swing by there? Do we have time? Or can I pick up a Bloody to go?"

"Certainly, ma'am," Maanav says. "To go is probably best, so as to not miss the boat."

"Excellent," she says. The boat, in Sarah's mind, is the one to oblivion, where regret no longer exists, and she for sure does not want to miss that.

~

While Maanav and Sarah run into Veranda to pick up the Bloody Marys—Maanav offered to go himself, but Sarah insisted on coming along, perhaps to avoid spending time alone with her husband—Sam looks at the text he's drafted to his latest bookie. This morning, he started a new thread reintroducing himself, asking if the bookie can put a hundred dollars on the Falcons on his behalf. It's a relatively measly bet, all things considered. And yet, he can't bring himself to press Send. Pressing Send would definitively break his promise to Sarah, it would break the promise that he made to himself. He could take a roundabout route and ask Steve to cut him in on his bets for the week—Steve gave him the number of this supposed bookie, after all—but that feels like an extension of a bridge that's already too far.

He knows he shouldn't be placing bets at all, but he itches for action. After the dinner with Kevin and Krista last night, after hearing Kevin go on about his watch guy and how much their life costs—"tuition is what'll get you," "fire insurance premiums, forget about it, makes me want to move to Texas"—he yearns to feel flush, craves that charge that comes with a win.

He thinks about it like this: Krista and Kevin picked up dinner the previous night, so why not use that money—parlay that money, if you will—into a venture that could multiply it? Is that not, to some degree, wise?

He stares at the blinking cursor.

Maanav and Sarah return with the drinks in reusable to-go cups, and he pockets his phone, message unsent. Sarah slides in, leans back against the buggy's padded seat, and takes a long sip, as if waiting for the drug to do its work. Sam remembers her saying that she wasn't going to drink a lot this trip. "I need to figure out this novel, my life, what we're really doing here," she said, giving him a knowing look. He wasn't sure what to make of that. "Whatever you want, babe," he said, but maybe he should've been more supportive, because the wife next to him is not the one who used to take pleasure in a glass of Champagne at the start of a flight or a margarita with chips and guac.

The wife beside him doesn't seem like she drinks for enjoyment at all. It seems like she drinks to disappear.

"Are you psyched to see some fish?" he asks, hoping to lift her mood. When she doesn't reply, he tries another tack. "Hey, Maanav, what are the chances of seeing a rose-veiled fairy wrasse, do you think?"

"That's an extremely rare fish to see while snorkeling," Maanav says, over his shoulder. "They usually plumb the twilight level of the sea, where barely any sunlight reaches. But the current is strong today, and you never know what that might dredge up."

"Something to keep an eye out for," Sam says to Sarah, as Maanav brings the buggy to a stop. They've reached the marine and water sports center, a low, open-air structure flanked by rows of Jet Skis and paddleboards lined up neatly in the sand.

"I'm not getting in the water," she says, as Sam comes around to her side of the golf cart.

"What?" he says. "But this is one of the best places in the world to snorkel."

"It's one of the best places in the world to get bitten by a shark and drown, maybe," she says.

"Oh, come on," he says. The boat captain approaches them, smiling, a life jacket in each of his hands. "You can wear a life jacket," says Sam. "Nothing will happen."

"Nothing will happen because I'm not going in the water," Sarah says.

"She'll come around once she's on the boat," he says to the boat captain with an apologetic smile. One of the things they're supposed to be focusing on is shared experiences, according to the couples counselor, and this is exactly that. He thinks back to the lounge at LAX, when she suggested canceling a trip they were technically already on. Why is she doing this yet again?

The captain leads the way to a blue-and-white catamaran called *Search & Find*. "Because of how many fish our guests have spotted during an excursion," the captain says. "Triggerfish, moray eels, barracuda, rays of all types—"

"Barracuda?" Sarah stops in her tracks. "What types of rays? Stingrays?"

"They are native to this region, yes," says the captain, "but they generally keep to themselves."

"Are they poisonous?"

The captain tsks. "It's very rare for them to attack."

"Okay, yeah, no way am I getting in the water," Sarah says. "Actually—I'm feeling kind of nauseous. Maybe I'll just hang back."

At that moment, Krista calls their names. Sam looks up and sees her and Kevin among the six passengers on the boat, sipping to-go cups of coffee (he assumes it's coffee, although who knows, they could also be on the Bloody train) and shielding their foreheads from the sun.

Sam waits for his wife's reaction, almost wants to feel the knife twist, the confirmation that this woman they met no more than a day ago ranks higher on the list of people with whom Sarah would like to spend time than him.

She raises her hand and waves it with faux enthusiasm. "Fine," she says. "I'll get on the boat. But you can't make me do anything beyond that."

Doesn't he know it.

~

Sarah has to admit there was something romantic about the way they pushed out to sea, the engines of the catamaran whirring powerfully beneath the hull of the boat as Maanav and a handful of other Jala staffers waved from the shore. The turquoise shallows expanding into cerulean-blue depths, the churning white froth as the boat carved its course. She and Sam are here to explore, aren't they, to get their feet wet in every sense of the word, and maybe it would be good for her, maybe, to dip a toe in the actual ocean water, to look down, to see what lived beneath.

"You'll be fine," Krista assured her. "I used to hate snorkeling, too, but once you learn how to breathe through this thing"—she tapped the tube affixed to her orange rubber goggles—"it's a breeze."

Sarah nodded as Krista coached her through it, as Krista made her put on the mask and practice. Even Sam supported Krista's intervention, whooping and cheering her on. "You've got this, babe. Come on, it'll be epic!"

But now, anchored near a reef far enough into the ocean that they can no longer see the shore, Sarah's nerves have returned with a vengeance. It's not just nerves. It's also outrage—how could Sam have signed them up for this? He knew how much she hated water sports. Her idea of being sporty in the water is doing a tricep dip to lift herself from the depth of an infinity pool to the edge. A four-foot depth. She doesn't even like to get her hair wet.

Could her anger toward snorkeling be misplaced anger toward Sam for gambling away money that could have been used for other things, for bantering with a bookie instead of connecting with her?

Well, sure.

"Come on," calls Kevin from the water. He's bobbing near the back of the boat, having cannonballed in at the first opportunity. Sam followed suit; Krista dove, yelping girlishly. The other guests on the boat, German brothers vacationing with their German wives, took to snorkeling without drama or fanfare, save for turning on an underwater GoPro that one of the brothers had affixed to a floating pole.

"I don't know," Sarah says. She's not a great swimmer. She feels no urge to see the rose fairy whatever Sam keeps going on about. But she also feels like a fuddy-duddy, given everyone else's enthusiasm. Is there something to snorkeling? Is she missing out?

It dawns on her that this is the sort of thing that would be fun to do with a child. That if she were to have a child, she'd want to dive in with them, maybe even with a GoPro.

Kicking his finned feet, Sam paddles closer to the boat. "Don't worry, I'll be right by your side," he calls out. "Just use the ladder and come down."

"It's quite easy, ma'am," the captain says. He's standing next to her with his hands clasped behind his back, surely assessing her as a freak. "You can just ease yourself into the water from the stern."

When else will she be here? When else will she get to do this?

What does she have to lose? An arm?

Could she sell that story as an essay? Maybe parlay it into a memoir?

"Fine," she says, lifting her oversized tunic over her head so hastily she almost rips the neck. If she doesn't move fast, she'll lose the will to do it at all. She gratefully accepts the life jacket the captain holds out, clipping it around her midsection and tugging the adjustable straps tight. She eschews the fins—so big, so unwieldy, she can't see how they'll help her in the water—but straps on the snorkeling mask and steps toward the back of the boat. The ladder has been lowered, all she has to do is ease herself down the rungs and let go of the steel rails.

She grips on to them for dear life. Why is she like this? She knows how to swim. Well, she learned. Like, twenty years ago. And given her swimming pool proclivities, she has decided to use her skills very little since.

She takes one step down, inhales sharply. The water's cooler here than it was by their villa.

Where she could see and feel the bottom, scrunch it up between her toes.

Which means that this water is deeper. She doesn't even want to think about how far down it goes.

Sam's voice: "Come on, babe! You've got this!"

She takes another step. The water seeps into her swimsuit bottom.

Another step and there are no more steps to go. Unless she wants to go back up. Does she want to go back up?

"Yeah, Sarah!" Krista's voice.

She lets go of the rails. She floats backward. She tells herself not to panic. She's only floating, after all. She flips over and glances down at a school of tiny yellow fish swimming in a serpentine formation. Fascinating! So this is snorkeling. She can see the appeal.

She flips back around and sees Sam. He's farther away than she thought. But she can't have gone that far. There are her friends, the boat captain—oh look, he's smiling and waving. She's fine.

He is smiling, right? The boat captain? She tries to push herself up, slapping at the water, but she can't quite see, and as she flails about, her left hand brushes against something slimy.

Scaly.

Then something hard, like a rock.

"Go left!" the captain is shouting. "You're too close to the reef!"

The reef? Meaning where all the barracuda, titan triggerfish, and moray eels while away their days? How did she get so close to the reef?

She remembers what Maanav said: "The current is strong today, and you never know what that might dredge up."

She doesn't *really* want to lose an arm.

On the boat, there's commotion. The captain and crew are motioning with their hands, like they're doing the wave.

"Swim to me," Sam is saying, waving his hands in a giant X. He seems to be a football field away.

"Over here!" says Krista, who's in a completely different direction.

Her breathing quickens. She can't have a panic attack. Not here, not now, not by a reef filled with venomous sea villains. What if they can sense anxiety the way that dogs sense fear? What if she's already been compromised, nibbled at by anemones too minuscule to see or feel now but whose effects will ruin her once she's on dry land? What if—

An orange life preserver splashes down in front of her.

"Grab on to it," the captain shouts. "I'll pull you in."

She does as she's told. Holds on for dear life, scrambles up the ladder, collapses on the deck. Sam is standing there, as are Krista and Kevin, looking concerned. The Germans are continuing their GoPro reconnaissance on the other side of the boat, blithely unaware.

"Have some water," the captain says, handing her a freshly opened bottle. She accepts it, panting, takes a glug. She kind of hates herself for freaking out. For not being able to hack it. Another loss.

"You're okay, babe, you're okay," Sam says, wrapping a towel around her shoulders. "You caught a strong current, it's just bad luck."

Just bad luck.

Just bad luck?

This strikes her, in her aggravated state, as the understatement of the century.

"This was not," she growls, jerking away from him, "just bad luck. This was a bad decision. Bad luck is something different. Bad luck is, oh, I don't know, losing several thousand dollars on the NBA, NFL, MLB—how many leagues do you bet on, by the way? So many acronyms, it's hard to remember them all."

"Sarah—" Sam starts.

"Or is the real person to blame here *Elaine*, Elaine the bookie who is totally *just a friend*, just a friend you text five hundred times a day, a friend that convinced you to bet on *darts*, on *snooker*. Do you have any idea what snooker even is? Does anyone?" She looks around accusingly; the deckhands shrug and nod. Damn deckhands. Educated in the finer points of British cue sports. They will for sure gossip about this later, this crazy lady who freaked out in the water and threw a fit back on the boat.

"Seriously, Sarah," Sam says.

And yet, even though she knows she's going too far, she can't stop.

"But you know what I'm thinking? None of this is bad luck. This is all a sign. This is a giant, flashing red neon sign that we are not meant to have a child—"

"*Really*, Sarah?" Sam says. "Now? You want to get into that *now*?"

The logical part of her brain—what little remains—can see how this comment comes out of left field. But what if she had been snorkeling with a child—with their child? What if they had run into a reef? What would Sam do then? Their entire marriage suddenly strikes her as reckless and ill considered.

"When else, Sam? When you're at the restaurant? When you're texting with Elaine? When you're losing even more money on even rarer forms of sport? When you piss away dollars that could go toward bigger things for you, for us, for a family?"

Sam's hands, once extended toward her, retract back.

"Not like we're fit to have a child anyway, look at us. At each other's throats in the most beautiful place in the world."

"Guys, surely we can resolve this back on dry land," Kevin chimes in, inserting himself between them.

"Don't bother," Sam says, tugging on his goggles, moving to the edge. "As they say, there are plenty—"

He jumps back in to the fish and the sea.

~

Was Sam's retort harsh? Yes. Way harsh. But to air their dirty laundry in public the way she did—where did Sarah get off? It's like she took pleasure in embarrassing him. In embarrassing them, really. Children? That's on the table again? He had no idea. She hasn't brought it up in months. How was he to know?

He didn't snorkel for much longer, it might've been twenty minutes before the current picked up and the captain blew a whistle, signaling that he and the Germans ought to make their way back. Beneath the surface of the water, he'd blinked at electric-blue parrotfish, going about their business without a seeming care in the world. He wondered if they had marital problems, if they racked up debts, if one of them ever broke off from the school and migrated to some other reef, started anew.

Back on the boat, Sam couldn't look the captain in the eye. Sarah and Krista were engaged in quiet commiseration at one end of the boat; Kevin was sitting on the other and took pity on him, patted the empty spot next to his on the bench. "It's all right, pal," Kevin said. "Things happen on vacation. It'll all be okay. Nothing you can't bounce back from."

Sam wasn't so sure about that. Back at Jala, he mumbled his gratitude to the boat captain and handed him a wad of cash as a tip. No rose-veiled fairy wrasse, no moment with wife (at least no moment he would like to remember). He was 0 for 2.

Or more than that. He's lost track of the losses. They returned to their villa in silence and retreated to separate beds to nap; she, indoors, he on the daybed by their private pool, which offered a panoramic view of the placid lagoon, a vista as beautiful as he was miserable.

In the late afternoon, she reemerged on the pool deck, showered and changed into a breezy white sundress. "I'm going to get a late lunch with Krista," she'd announced. He had been scrolling through the room service menu, debating between ordering a club sandwich and enduring Sarah's silent treatment or nudging her awake and extending some sort of olive branch (maybe in the form of a room service club sandwich).

But seeing as how she appeared uninterested in olive branches or anything else he could offer, he shrugged and turned back to the view. And his phone. Which sometimes blocked the view.

Now, as the sun begins to make its descent, the sound of a jazz band travels over the sandbank and onto the deck. He wonders if Sarah is taking it all in with Krista, umbrella drinks in hand, swaying in the sand. In his predeparture daydreams, that's what he and Sarah were doing at this happy hour, drifting away from the crowd, hand in hand. Stolen kisses and white sand and "Sure, sir, we'll take another round."

Alas, that dream is not to be. There are no happy hours in his Maldives.

SEVEN

Sam is not sure when the first text arrives, but when he turns his phone over at 4:32 in the morning, he has twelve of them. As well as nine missed calls. All from a 310 number he apparently does not have saved in his phone.

He assumes something's gone wrong at one of the restaurants. Was there a break-in at Tiffin West Hollywood? Did the Studio City location get hit by the health department again?

But no, rubbing his eyes, scrolling up, he sees that this 310 number is Kevin's, and he simply never saved it. In the dark, he starts reading from the beginning.

Sam, Kevin King, nice to meet. Small world!
Sam, have you seen Krista? Did she come to your room?
Sam, sorry, just tried calling you, can't find Krista, have you or Sarah heard from her?
Sam, it's an emergency. They can't find her.

And so on. His heart sinks. This is not good. This is very, very bad. Worse than anything he could've anticipated. Krista is lost? What does Kevin mean they can't find her? Where could she have gone?

"Babe," he says, distractedly patting Sarah's back. She's sleeping on her stomach—next to him, he notes, with a hint of reassurance. If she was still cursing his existence, she would've collapsed on the couch.

At his touch, she emits something between a snore and a snort. His phone starts vibrating in his hand. "Babe," he says, louder, shaking his wife's shoulder now. "Get up."

He answers the call, puts it on speaker. "Hello?"

"Sam, sir, so sorry to disturb you." The voice on the other end is lightly accented, and looking at the caller ID, Sam realizes it's a foreign number. "This is Sid, the general manager of Jala. As you may have heard, Krista King, with whom I believe you snorkeled last morning, has inexplicably gone missing. Her husband is quite worried, naturally, as are we all. I'm wondering, is there any chance she might be with you?"

Why does this guy think I would know? Sam wonders, and at the same time he remembers that his cell phone plan does not cover international calling, which means he's getting charged twenty-five cents per minute for this call. Which is already over one minute and liable to go on for who knows how long.

"No, sorry, can you WhatsApp me?" He hangs up. Immediately, he feels guilty. Putting his own wallet over Krista's safety. A stranger, a voice in his head reminds him: You don't know her. You don't know Kevin. You know something is off about them, you feel it in your bones.

His phone vibrates again, this time through WhatsApp. All the commotion has caused Sarah to rejoin the world of the sentient. "What's going on?" she mumbles.

"Your friend is missing," Sam says to her, accepting the call. "Talk to me," he says into the phone, and immediately wants to smack himself for sounding like some wannabe *CSI* character.

At the same time—so many conflicting thoughts at the same time—he cannot deny that this early a.m. crisis is fueling him with some kind of charge, a rush of adrenaline he did not know he needed. There is a problem, and he has been called in to help. He cannot remember the last time his expertise was wanted, courted. When he was last asked, *begged* to be of service in a situation that did not involve an incapacitated chef or a grease fire or a hostess who simply failed to show up for her shift.

"It will be easier to explain in person," Sid says, dispensing with the niceties. "Could you possibly meet us at the service station outside? You can't miss us, we're to the left of your bungalow."

"Give me five," Sam says, and then ends the call. He springs up from bed, flips one of the switches above the nightstand, which turns out to be the master, illuminating all the lights in their suite.

Sarah groans, curses, rubs her eyes, asks again what's going on.

"Your friend," Sam says again, heading toward the bathroom and the dressing area that surrounds it, "is missing. Kevin's called me, like, eight hundred times. I'm going out to help."

"What?" Sarah says, incredulous. She's pushed herself up against the headboard. "Krista? What . . . what are *you* going to do?"

As if he's chopped liver. As if his skills are of no use. As if it's so incomprehensible to his wife that he would be called in to assist in a crisis. *Him*, of all people.

He rifles through his suitcase and pulls on a pair of sweatpants and a matching hoodie. "I told you, I'm going to help. They called me. The general manger called me. Would you like to come?" He comes around the rattan archway separating the dressing area from the bedroom and looks at her expectantly.

"I guess," she says, shaking her head, clearly confused or tired or hungover or all of the above. "I just don't understand why they're asking you," she mumbles.

He can't help himself. "Jesus Christ, Sarah, is it really so hard to believe that someone would come to me in a crisis?"

She looks at him like he has eight heads. "I mean, yeah, since you hate her. Them. Since you hate them."

"I don't *hate them*," he says, "I just didn't want to spend our whole vacation with them, which won't be an issue now, apparently, since one of them is missing."

He sees concern bloom on Sarah's face, as if she's only now understanding the gravity of the situation. Perhaps he can't blame her. After yet another evening with Krista, Sarah's liable to list her as her next of kin.

But there is no point in bickering with her now. He has bigger fish to fry.

"Are you coming?" he asks, shoving his feet into his Nike Air Max sneakers.

"Yes," she says, jumping out of bed. "Give me a minute."

It's not lost on him that the disappearance of her friend lights a fire under her, a fire that failed to ignite when they were getting ready for dinner the other night, a fire that seems only to be associated with events pertaining to Krista. Within moments, Sarah is clad in her own sweatsuit. "Let's go," she says, as if joining the search party was her idea. "Come on."

A spike of panic hits Sam. If Krista is, in fact, missing, is it safe for them to go out there? Is there an attacker or—God forbid—a killer on the loose?

"Stay close to me," he says, reaching the door before his wife. "We don't know what's going on, and I don't want you to get hurt."

She rolls her eyes, reaches over him, and presses down the handle of the door. "What, are you going to be my knight in shining Nikes? Come on, let's go."

~

Sarah worked in news for long enough to know that, in any missing persons case, the first forty-eight hours are crucial, the first twenty-four most important of all—this is also information one could ascertain by watching an episode or two of *Dateline*, but she deems herself extra qualified, having been in the newsroom that broke the JonBenét Ramsey case, albeit years before she got there.

And sure, she mostly covered tabloid darlings who went "missing" due to a drug overdose or ill-advised affair, but given her proximity to the news industry and her relationship with Krista, she feels a sense of propriety over the situation, feels she ought to take charge, given that Kevin is probably a wreck, and Sam—what in the world can Sam bring to the table, really? Curry?

She tells herself to stop. She's not sure why she's being so mean. It's something she and Krista talked about the previous night. "Obviously, the gambling and the stuff with the bookie is not kosher, but he clearly loves you," Krista said. "Have you had an honest conversation about what fueled it all? Because bullying him—that's not going to solve anything."

Sarah was taken aback. Quite a statement, coming from Krista, who seemed to regard men as appliances that needed routine maintenance. Perhaps that's why it has stuck with her. She can't remember the last time she and Sam had an honest conversation. She can't remember the last time she's been honest with herself. Did Krista have a point?

There will be time to mull over all of that later. With Krista. Once they locate her. Because where could she have gone? Sarah charges down the boardwalk toward the roving flashlights at the service station, ignoring Sam's urgings from behind to slow down, be careful, watch where she's going.

"Who's got eyes on her location?" she says, coming to a halt in front of Sid, Kevin, and the jadugar assigned to Krista and Kevin. What was his name? Sharif. They look at her as if she has information they don't. "I mean her phone's location, obviously," Sarah explains. "Easiest way to figure out where she is."

Kevin, poor, puffy-eyed, exhausted-looking Kevin, holds up a phone Sarah recognizes as Krista's, ensconced in its gem-encrusted case. She has been admiring it since she first saw it on the plane. It has a back made up of craggy, emerald-type stones. Maybe they were genuine emeralds, who knew.

"I found it on the edge of the plunge pool," Kevin says, bewildered. "She never goes anywhere without it. I can't imagine . . ." He trails off as his head sinks to his free hand. Sam reaches up to pat him consolingly on the back. "This wasn't supposed to happen," Kevin says, shaking his head. "How could she just vanish, just like that?" Sarah gulps. She realizes that she did not arrive at this service station thinking that Krista was actually missing. She figured that Krista and Kevin had gotten into a fight and Krista had run off, though where she would go given that you needed a boat or a plane to get on or off the island, both of which would have a hard time operating in the inky dark, Sarah did not know.

Well—there are dozens of other rooms that are not her own, and Krista confessed to Sarah some out-of-the box habits of her and Kevin's, things she did to make him jealous, to "light a fire," "keep things interesting." "Do I ever cheat? No," Krista said, "but do I find ways to show him that I'm desired by other people? Absolutely." Sam had been onto something, all his assertions about "swinger vibes." Krista had lingered longer than Sarah for a nightcap at Veranda, and while Sarah didn't see Hakim at the bar, it was plausible that Krista ventured to the back of the house and cozied up to the bartender she'd been flirting with the previous night. The more Sarah thought about it, the more plausible it seemed. If she were going to cheat on Sam—not that she had or had plans to, despite her current enmity toward him—she would think twice about bringing her phone. They shared their locations with each other, and what better way to be caught than to leave your coordinates right there in the open for your spouse to find?

Or.

Sarah's gaze shifts to the boardwalk.

The guardrail-free boardwalk.

The guardrail-free boardwalk twenty feet above dark ocean waters populated with stingrays, sharks, and all manner of aquatic predators she would love never to mix and mingle with again. Sarah recalls the snorkeling boat captain saying that the Indian Ocean is the deepest in the world, with depths that may never be plumbed. The unknown of it all makes her shudder.

"Let's go over this again," Sid says to Kevin. "When did you last see her?" He sounds eerily calm, given the crisis at hand. Sarah wonders if he's been briefed on how to act in this kind of circumstance, or if he's dealt with something like this before.

"Just after midnight," Kevin says. "We were in bed. Well." He pauses, bobs his head, as if debating how much to reveal. "*I* was in bed, she wanted to keep the night going. She had popped a bottle of Champagne and wanted to go skinny-dipping."

"Skinny-dipping," Sam repeats.

Kevin drags his fingers through his ragged hair. "It's her thing," he says with a sigh. "Anytime we're in a place with a private pool, and given that we've got a pool and a bathwater-warm ocean a ladder away, she was not taking no for an answer."

"She wanted to go in the *ocean*?" Sam repeats, as if he doesn't quite believe what Kevin's saying. Sarah certainly doesn't.

"Many of our guests do," Sid says with a sigh, shaking his head. "We warn everyone, of course, about the dangers of going in the open water after dark, unaccompanied—Sharif, you warned Krista, correct?"

Sharif nods rapidly. He looks shell-shocked. It's doubtful Sharif has dealt with a situation like this before.

Sarah tries to remember if Maanav warned them about night swimming, but she doesn't recall any such conversation. It's possible that it happened and she tuned it out. Forget about getting into the open water after dark—after the previous morning, she will stick to land and chlorinated enclosures, thank you very much.

"I told her it was dangerous," Kevin continues. "I said, 'Honey, it'll be light in a few hours, we'll go at sunrise, come to bed, you need some rest.' She got all pouty and stormed out to the deck." Here, he casts a knowing look at Sam. "You know how they get."

You know how "they" get? Who the fuck are "they"?

Sam, to his credit, doesn't meet Kevin's glance, shifts his eyes to the boardwalk.

"I realize this is a delicate matter," Sid says, "and please, don't take my queries the wrong way, but is there any chance that she could have taken up with someone else?"

Kevin arches his caterpillar eyebrows. "What are you trying to say?"

"We have security pulling the surveillance footage from around the property, but of course there are areas where we have no cameras, to protect the privacy of guests," Sid goes on. "I'm merely wondering if there might be a guest she befriended, or even an employee, if there's someone else who may have an idea of her whereabouts."

"There was that bartender from the other night, Harry? Henry? What was his name?" He looks to Sam, seemingly annoyed at either his lack of recall or this line of questioning.

"Hakim," Sam says, eyes still on the wooden planks of the boardwalk.

"That's right, Hakim," repeats Kevin. "She was laying it on thick with him, wasn't she?" He shakes his head. "Krista can be a terrible tease, has been since the day we met."

Sarah blanches at Kevin's reveal, though it confirms what Krista told her the previous night, underlines that the swinger vibes were not all in her and Sam's heads. Then again, given that his wife is unaccounted for and—she doesn't want to suggest it, God forbid—possibly in the open water, Kevin's judgmental statement seems wrong. Terrible tease or not, his wife, the mother of his children, is *missing*. Is the gravity of the situation lost on him?

"You were with her last night," Kevin says, turning to Sarah. "What did she say? Was she with that bartender?"

"Not while we were hanging out," Sarah says. "Where is Hakim? Have we talked to him yet?" As she inserts herself among the investigators, she feels a surge of purpose, a desire to take the reins and right this wrong. Whatever was or was not happening between Hakim and Krista, they had hit it off, and he ought to be interviewed.

Sid says something into his IFB that Sarah cannot hear. "We are summoning him just now, ma'am," Sid says to her.

"Please, call me Sarah," she says. She finds Sid's overly polite manner of speaking grating in these circumstances. Just come out with it, bro.

Sid smiles tightly. "As you wish." He turns to the rest of the group. "While we wait, Kevin, may we come with you to your suite? Again, I do not want to overstep my bounds, but a top-to-bottom search of the suite may help turn up some clues about your wife's whereabouts. Did she take her passport, for example? Any valuables?"

Kevin looks taken aback. "'Passport'? Buddy, what are you not understanding? My wife did not plot some kind of escape—she's *missing*. Time is of the *essence*." He claps his palms together on the syllables, as if this will drive the point into Sid's head. "We need to find *her*, pronto, not her passport or valuables—I'm not even sure why you'd bring those up. You want to case our suite? Scoop up her diamond studs when I'm not looking?"

"Kevin," Sarah says, admonishingly. On the one hand, he's stressed and looking for someone to blame, and who wouldn't? On the other, he's being inordinately rude to Sid and the rest of the staff. Accusing them of theft isn't going to help his case. It seems to Sarah that everyone is striking the wrong tone, but then, are there rules for how to behave in a crisis? She thinks of the adrenaline that would course through the newsroom during a natural disaster or a probable terrorist attack, how her bosses could barely conceal their glee at the prospect of more eyes on their content, of people feverishly refreshing their feeds. Disgusting, yes. But that was the nature of the beast. They profited from pain and chaos and tried to shroud their business plan under the guise of informing the public.

In any case, in the here and now, Sarah feels the responsibility to do right by Krista. Krista's husband is portraying her as a tease. Her own husband, despite his rush to assist, has provided barely any assistance at all. The general manager has good instincts but bad bedside manners. She needs to take this into her own hands.

"Look, what Sid is saying makes sense," Sarah says. "Maybe we'll find some clues in your room. What's the harm? Whatever it takes to find her, right?"

Maybe it's the light or lack thereof, but Sarah detects a flicker of irritation in Kevin's eyes. "Yeah, sure," he says. "Whatever it takes."

~

Sam may not be the brightest bulb in the box, but he considers himself a pretty good judge of character. Back in college, he saw through Sarah's faux-intellectual veneer from the start, the fact that, though she styled herself as the type to lie about the quad, discussing Foucault or Proust or some poet whose name he couldn't pronounce, she did, in fact, care about material goods, she was a classic American capitalist, and even though they were not close during those four years, he knew that she did not really want to stay in the dorms discussing second-wave feminism after 10:00 p.m. on a Friday night. He was never surprised when he saw her out at the bars. She contained multitudes, which was one of the many things about her he loved. A million people in one package, his wife.

He has always known that Ronny Lee, the chef of Hawker Stand, is a slimy motherfucker, even if he hasn't always had the proof. He knew that Thomas Keller—the mastermind behind Per Se, the French Laundry, and an army of Bouchons—was the chef to work for, which, sure, mostly had to do with the man's résumé rather than his personal character.

But even Sarah, in good times, has praised his ability to know a bad egg when he sees one. "You knew before I did," she told him, when her gambit with Natalie and *Panache* came crashing down. "You always said there was something off about my editor," the one who threw her under the bus by forwarding her pitch to *Panache*'s digital director, who outed Sarah with all the subtlety of a fire alarm. They'd gotten drinks with her editor at a dive bar in the East Village the last time they were in New York. The thing that was off? The editor excused himself to the restroom when the bill dropped, forcing Sam and Sarah to pick up the tab. He knew things were bad in media, but if you're on staff at a major publication and you let a freelancer or, worse, a freelancer's significant other pay the bill, there might just be a special place in hell for you. (Right next to Ronny Lee's.)

All of which is to say that he is still convinced there is something off about Kevin and Krista. It's not that they're swingers—well, maybe they are, he still can't be sure. But Krista's disappearance doesn't feel—how should he put it?—accidental. It's like Kevin's been down this road before.

Sam tries to think if Kevin ever mentioned anything like this happening before. He and Kevin shared intel from their recent trips, as people do on vacation—what hotels lived up to the hype, which supposedly must-see beaches were secretly thronged with mosquitos. Nothing in their previous conversations hinted at a streak of behavior like this, periodic lapses in judgment that resulted in one party going AWOL at a luxury resort. Kevin mentioned to Sam at the bar on board their flight from Los Angeles to Dubai that he and Krista had been in Puglia the previous summer. "Stayed at this incredible compound, Borgo Fasano," he said. "They hosted the G7 and some big fashion show—what was it, honey? Dolce Vita?"

"Dolce & *Gabbana*," Krista corrected him, sounding out the second half of the name like that character in *The Devil Wears Prada*. "Beyond fabulous," she said. "Except for this."

Sarah was in the restroom, so there was enough room for Krista to extend her leg on the bench seat, lift up the leg of her Emirates-brand pajamas, and display to Sam, below her left knee, a scar the size of Madagascar. It was shiny and new, with ridges that looked like topography.

"Yikes," Sam said. "What happened?"

"Tripped while running," Krista said. "Can you believe it? Four marathons and this is how my storied career ends."

"Oh, hon, you can run," Kevin said. "The PT cleared you."

"Well, these old bones ain't as limber as they used to be," Krista said, letting the leg of her pajamas down again.

"Your performance last Friday begs to differ," Kevin replied, elbowing Sam in the side and yukking it up. Sam laughed uncomfortably, briefly imagined what Kevin might reveal if Krista wasn't sitting right there, what overshares lurked on the tip of his tongue.

Now, as the search party advances down the boardwalk to bungalow no. 17—farther along the double helix above the water than Sam and

Sarah, who were assigned to bungalow no. 7—Sam wonders what it is about Kevin and Krista that rubs him the wrong way, beyond all the public displays of affection and sexual innuendo. Beyond the big watches and talk of money and mortgages.

Is it their audacity? The way they move through the world like they own it? But he's met plenty of people like that—Ronny Lee, for one. What is it about *them*?

At the same time, part of him wants to turn around, turn back to their bungalow, deadbolt the door, turn off his phone, and pretend this night never happened. Pretend this association never occurred. What foul luck that he and Sarah happened to be on the same plane as these head cases. He had been raised to not concern himself with the problems of strangers. "Don't get involved," his father would say. "No good deed goes unpunished."

Typical Indian mentality, and you couldn't blame the old man, that was how he was raised, to keep his eye on the prize lest he lose it to one of a billion other aspirants. But you can't have children in America and expect the whole "love thy neighbor" thing not to infect them in some way. Sam always had a hard time looking past panhandlers. It just felt wrong, to witness another human being suffering and do nothing, even if their cardboard signs and pitiful pleas were all part of a scam. What was life, after all, if not the biggest scam of all?

They reach the door of bungalow no. 17, which is identical to the doors that line either side of the boardwalk: hulking, arched, made to look as if it were rendered out of lacquered palm fronds but surely—hopefully—constructed from something sturdier, given that they were in the middle of the Indian Ocean, closer to the open, unobstructed water here than the single-digit bungalows, which at least had each other as buffers. Bungalow no. 17 was at the end of one strand of the double helix, with uninterrupted 270-degree views of the sea and sky.

Sam notices something. There's only one vanilla-hued beach cruiser in the bike rack next to the door. Shouldn't they have two?

There's also a flag strung up on a pole by the front door. An American flag.

"What's up with that?" Sam asks, almost to himself.

"Perk of staying at bungalow no. 17," Sid says. "Whoever books it gets to decide what flag flies there."

Sam shrugs. Fair enough. Though he wonders why bungalow no. 17 gets that right as opposed to any of the others.

Before he can inquire about that, Sid brandishes a master key and swiftly pushes open the bungalow's door. "Hey," Kevin says, "let me," but Sid is already charging inside, flipping on the master switch. Is it strange that all the lights aren't already on? Sam wonders. This wasn't one of those resorts that made you insert a room key into a slot in the wall or on the door to activate the electricity. You could keep the lights on all the livelong day if you liked, presumably a luxury demanded by the .01 percenters who frequented Jala. Kevin and Krista didn't strike him as the types to compost, to care about the world beyond what they inhabited currently and planned to in the future.

It quickly becomes apparent why the occupants of bungalow no. 17 get special privileges. While the bungalow looks similar to Sam and Sarah's on the outside, once inside, it's easy to tell that it's bigger. Exponentially so. "Our ocean grand villa has many nooks and crannies, so many spots where one could get lost, if you will," Sid is saying, proceeding purposefully through the foyer. Sam and Sarah's bungalow does not have a foyer, but then, Sam now realizes, Kevin and Krista are in a villa, a completely different category of "room," one that has more in common with a house, given its multiple wings and cost. He recalls seeing online that Jala's villas started at $10,000 per night, and the ocean grand might be the grandest of them all.

There's a kitchen with a wall of cabinets the same dusty rose hue as Jala's logo. On the island is an unopened bottle of Veuve Clicquot and a small purse with interlocking *C*s on its clasp and a gold chain strap—Sam vaguely remembers Krista futzing with the strap while they were at the bar of Veranda on their first night; it kept slipping down her shoulder.

Sam follows Sid, figuring it's the path of least resistance and also the best way to get a tour of the villa without seeming like a gawker; Sarah trails behind, talking in hushed tones with Sharif.

From the kitchen, they venture into a secondary bedroom. Sid opens the closets and peers inside, as if Krista might simply be playing an elaborate game of hide-and-seek. "Dude, this isn't right," Kevin says, chasing after him. "This is a violation of privacy. You don't think I've already checked everywhere? She's not here."

"We must do our due diligence, Mr. King," Sid says, lowering himself to look under the bed of another secondary bedroom. "I do hope you understand."

There is a gym with a treadmill, a Pilates reformer, and floor-to-ceiling windows. Krista is not there. There is a spa with an infrared cedar sauna for one and massage beds for two. Krista is also not there.

Finally, Sid pushes open the door to the primary suite. Kevin is still grousing about the invasion of privacy, which again strikes Sam as weird. If Sarah disappeared on an island in the middle of nowhere, he would happily let the powers that be turn the place inside out, would beg them to find her by any means necessary.

Assuming, of course, that he was innocent. Which begs a bigger question.

Sam has watched enough true crime shows to know that it is almost always the husband. The thought had first occurred to him when Kevin mentioned what a "terrible tease" his wife was. Not the most charitable of descriptions. And to say such a thing when she wasn't there to defend herself—bad form for a spouse, even under the best of circumstances.

People who come out swinging usually have something to hide.

"Again, this is extremely unnecessary," Kevin is saying, growing gruffer by the minute. Sid chooses to ignore him, poking his head into the walk-in closet and egg-shaped bathtub. Finally, Sid slides open the ten-foot-tall doors between the dressing area and the primary bedroom. The group, aside from Kevin, lets out a collective gasp.

On the bed is an array of sex toys—furry handcuffs, a hot-pink dildo, ties that might hold back curtains but, given the context, are probably meant for something else. Kevin presses his thumb and forefinger to his temples. "This is *why* I didn't want you to *paw through* our room," he grouses.

"Sorry, sir," Sid stammers, retreating quickly through the doors. "So very, very sorry." Sam sees that Sid's turned the color of a tomato. "Why don't we take a seat in the living room, take a pause?"

"Brilliant," Kevin deadpans, following him out.

But instead of the living room, Sid, visibly flustered, veers into the kitchen, opens the refrigerator—a massive, hulking thing more appropriate for a fine-dining restaurant than for an overwater vacation home where no one would ostensibly lift a knife—and helps himself to a mini bottle of Pellegrino. He takes a swig and leans back against the refrigerator's brushed stainless steel door.

"I hope you don't mind," he says, meeting Kevin's eyes.

"You're not charging me for that," Kevin says.

"Of course not," says Sid. He moves toward the kitchen island, Carrara marble by the looks of it, places the little glass bottle and the heels of his hands on its surface, and stands back. "Well, what do we know? Krista and Hakim hit it off—"

"Where is that guy, by the way?" asks Kevin.

Sid looks to Sharif, who gives him a curt nod, an indication to go ahead.

"Hakim is indisposed," says Sid. He clears his throat. "The staff supervisor alerted me that he is suffering from some kind of stomach bug."

"What?" Kevin says, screwing up his face. "Get him here now, I don't care if he's exploding out of both ends." Gross, Sam thinks.

"I'm afraid we won't be able to do that for at least a few hours, sir," Sid says. "In any case, there has been no sign of Krista at the staff quarters or elsewhere on property. Security is still pulling the surveillance footage—we have more than two hundred cameras on the island, so it might take some time—but the fact remains that we must figure out next steps with the information we have so far."

Does Sid always talk so formally, or is the situation bringing out this side of him? Sam wonders. Suppose you couldn't blame the guy. If he were Sid, he'd also be wary of Kevin and his all-American attitude, the pay-attention-to-me braggadocio and probable penchant for lawsuits, the watch that signals that money is no object and funds to fuel a drawn-out legal battle could surely be wired from points far and wide.

"I'd like you to call the cops," Kevin says. "And bring this Hakim in for questioning."

"If I may, sir, if at all possible, we would like to resolve this matter in-house with our array of resources, including a scuba-certified search and rescue team, should it come to that."

"There's a search and rescue team?" Kevin says, turning up his palms as well as his volume. "Where the fuck are they?"

"They're called in to assist with water-related accidents," Sid says, "and so far, we've been combing the property. It's also nearly impossible for them to do their work in the dark."

"Uh, didn't Krista want to go skinny-dipping?" Sarah chimes in. "Shouldn't they be searching the water? Can we get them headlamps or something?"

Sid flattens his mouth into a line as he turns to her. "I suppose it's not the worst idea to call them in, now that dawn is nigh."

Nigh? The whole eighteenth-century-lord shtick is beginning to make Sid seem suspicious. Really, who talks like that? And why does he seem so reticent to call the cops, hand this off to the appropriate authorities?

"I'll page the team presently," Sid says, taking out his phone, "but in the meantime, is there any stone on dry land that we've left unturned? Does anyone have anything to add? No detail is too insignificant, anything you may have seen or not."

A thought occurs to Sam: the bike. Or rather, the absence of the bike.

"One thing," Sam says. "Shouldn't there be two bikes outside? When we came in, there was only one."

Sid locks eyes with him in an accusing, how-could-you-not-have-told-me-this-earlier kind of way. Sarah and Kevin are giving him similar looks.

Sam shrugs. It's his first missing persons case. Cut him some slack?

~

Outside, the sky has turned from ink to sapphire blue. On the eastern horizon, violet bands streak the sky. Sarah feels a perverse urge to take out her phone and take a picture. It's undeniably beautiful, but now is not the time.

The four of them are peering at the bike rack, which ought to have two cream-colored beach cruisers and only has one.

"So she took the bike," Sarah says, to fill the silence.

"She took the bike," Kevin repeats, flatly.

"And she had been drinking," Sid says.

"And there are no guardrails on this boardwalk," Sarah says. "How can you have no guardrails, by the way? Isn't that dangerous?"

"The decision was made by our owners," says Sid, "for aesthetics' sake."

"Well, for *fuck's sake*," says Kevin, "now my wife is missing, and God help us, if she's in the water, and if she got there because of your idiotic owners and their decision to prioritize aesthetics over common sense and *safety*, mark my words, I will burn this motherfucking place to the ground."

Odd, Sarah thinks. Odd for a husband to prioritize vengeance over locating his wife, who has not, to their knowledge, fallen overboard (or over boardwalk). Sarah still feels like Krista is holed up with Hakim. She has no proof, and she can't explain why, it's just instinct, or maybe it's a female thing. She just doesn't see Krista as the type of woman to go cruising around on a perilous boardwalk after dark. Krista, from everything Sarah knows, gets off on a different sort of danger, seeks other types of thrills.

She turns toward the east, where the violet has bloomed into fuchsia, on its way to pink. Not far from the pillars elevating the boardwalk, something catches the light.

Something gold.

Something heart shaped.

Something engraved with *K&K.*

A pang strikes Sarah's heart.

"Guys," she says, casting about for a hand, a limb, anything to steady herself. She wraps her hand around an arm she thinks is Sam's, but it turns out to be Sid's. "Come quick."

EIGHT

Midmorning at Veranda. The clatter of forks against plates, the smell of croissants and coffee. Sarah blinks at the menu a server placed before her who knows how long ago, a leather-bound book the size of an atlas, advertising (among other things) eggs in purgatory simmered with San Marzano tomatoes and topped with twenty-four-month aged Parmigiano Reggiano. "A divine dish from the south of Italy reinterpreted in the southern Indian Ocean, served with a side of house-made Calabrian chili sauce."

She has read this line more times than she can count. Fitting, given that she herself is in purgatory. She keeps trying to regard the rest of the menu but keeps flashing back to four hours ago, when the authorities pulled the body from the water.

The body. She can't bring herself to say it was Krista's, she can only refer to it as "the body." Owing to the presence of the search and rescue team and the authorities Sid was forced to call once the gravity of the situation became clear, Sarah couldn't see the body closely, even if she wanted to.

She let out a sob when she saw the tangle of hair emerge from the water, dripping. Poor Krista. Poor, dear Krista. How could this happen? How could it have happened to her?

Rich white women did not meet this fate, not often, and certainly not at a luxury resort. The inhumanity of it makes her heart ache. It feels so unfair.

Would she feel this way if Krista were not a rich white woman? Would she feel this way if Krista were not a rich white woman on whom she had projected her hopes and dreams for her own marriage, her own life?

Who's to say?

Granted, she only met Krista, what, three days or so ago. But Krista was supposed to be her savior. She is allowed to mourn the death of her savior in her own, private way. She is allowed to feel bad. Krista had a plan, which meant that Sarah had a plan, one that they could execute together to get Sarah's life back on track. What is she going to do now?

"Ma'am? Do you have any questions about the menu?"

A server is standing above her, looking concerned.

"Oh, no," she says, distractedly. "Can you give us a few minutes? My husband's in the restroom, he should be back by then."

"Certainly," the server says, retreating.

Sarah leans back against the upholstered banquette, sets down the menu, and lets her eyes close. Veranda, where she and Krista lingered over vessels of sauvignon blanc and plates of tuna carpaccio last night, is also where the daily breakfast buffet is arrayed, and she cannot get over the fact that just a handful of hours ago, she was having a heart-to-heart with a woman now dead.

How can life change so quickly? The sheer randomness of what could happen at any given moment was enough to make your head spin, debilitate you if you thought too much about it.

She would like to not think.

She would like, she realizes, another drink. She doesn't want to want alcohol, but the drug has her in its clutches, and the only thing that will quell the anxiety creeping up on her like a spider up her spine is a glass of Champagne, or a shot of mezcal, maybe a Bloody Maria—something to take the edge off.

This will, by consequence, remove her once again from the high horse that she's been on regarding Sam and his drinking, but given her behavior over the past few days, that horse has ridden off into the sunset, to greener pastures, or perhaps it's fallen into a ravine and been turned to glue. The horse no longer exists, is the point.

"Sorry," she hears Sam saying. She opens her eyes and he's back, scooting out the dining chair in front of her, a cushioned thing with a low, curved back of bamboo.

"My stomach's not feeling so great," he says.

What a shock. Sam's stomach never feels great. She is convinced that his drinking has a lot to do with it, but she's certainly not in a position to bring this up. She's also convinced that he's gluten intolerant, doesn't eat enough fiber, and needs to focus more on fruits and vegetables, but every time she brings this up, he shoots her down, says he needs more protein. Protein, protein, protein. You'd think he was in the business of lifting monster trucks over his head, the way he's consumed with consuming protein.

"Maybe have some yogurt," she suggests, half-heartedly, because she would bet money on his response.

Sam makes a face. Of course he makes a face. He also dismisses evidence about the brain-gut connection, does not believe in probiotics. You can lead a horse to water, but you can't make it drink. (Why is she so fixated on horses? She's afraid of them in real life. Has never been on one, what with Christopher Reeves and her general discomfort around animals large and non-cuddly, her fear of what they might do.)

Her husband scans the menu. "Ooh, lobster Benedict," he says. "Did you see that there's a live dosa station?"

She looks at him, aghast. She has not seen the buffet or any of the live stations. She is barely aware that the buffet and live stations exist.

"How can you be thinking about dosas? Krista is *dead*."

"Babe," he says, putting down the menu, leaning in. "We barely knew her. Come on. We can't let this ruin our vacation."

"'*This*'? That's how you refer to the death of our friend, like she's some smudge on your sneaker?" She wonders aloud if Sam has no heart.

He narrows his eyes at her. "I have a heart, Sarah, I'm just more discerning about how I use it. I really don't see how this chick getting drunk and biking off a boardwalk is our concern."

"Oh, so now she's 'this chick.' How evolved of you. How *discerning*."

He rolls his eyes. "You know what I mean. She was practically a stranger. What do you want me to do, cry? Organize her funeral? We didn't *know* her."

Her nose prickles. She feels her cheeks getting hot. She tells herself she will not cry. She is wearing a triangle bikini top and a caftan robe, and she would look, frankly, tragic crying in a triangle bikini top and caftan robe. Like some *Real Housewives* wannabe. She will not allow it.

Perhaps sensing her distress, Sam reaches his hand across the table, palm up, relenting. Her hands are in her lap, fingers twisting.

"Come on, we did all we could," Sam says, gentler now. "There was nothing we could do, honestly. It was a horrible accident, yes, and I know you two hit it off. It's sad. It's awful. You have every right to be upset. But . . . this woman was not in our lives seventy-two hours ago. Do we really want to have a cloud hanging over our whole trip? It's up to the authorities to handle now. It's not our job to get involved."

She is not stubborn enough to not see his point. But his ability to so quickly move on from what happened, to just swipe it away—it hurts her. She wants him to feel what she feels. Lost. Bereft. Irate and confused about how such a terrible thing could happen to such a generous person.

Scenes from the early morning flash through her mind on a loop every time she closes her eyes. The glint of Krista's locket in the crystalline waves, the frame of the missing beach cruiser floating off to the side. Maanav arriving on the scene, beside himself; the somber quiet that descended over the end of the boardwalk as the authorities lifted the body from the water. It was early enough that no other guests saw the spectacle, and Sid's urging that Sarah and Sam not talk about what happened seemed superfluous. This isn't the type of topic you broach over piña coladas at the pool bar. Maybe if Sarah didn't know Krista, maybe if this were all just a piece of gossip. But Sarah cannot see it as anything but a tragedy.

She's not sure why Sam's not in mourning, too. If she's upset, can't he be upset by default? Why does he have to question everything?

Did his insistence on formulating his own opinions once endear her to him? Well, yes. But that was then, this was now, and Sarah wants a partner in outrage.

"I don't know," she says. She reaches out her hand and places it on top of his, curls her fingers in to meet her palm. "I can't dismiss what happened that easily. It just doesn't make sense. Krista does not strike me as someone who would be reckless enough to go biking above the water after dark, especially after drinking as much as she had." The previous night, Krista graduated from wine to tequila and bid Sarah farewell with a wave of a chewed-up pineapple wedge from an empty spicy skinny.

"How late were you out?" Sam asks. "I didn't hear you come in."

Sarah shrugs. "Maanav gave me a ride back."

"What were you two talking about?"

Sarah sighs. "Oh, it doesn't matter now." What was the point of sharing how Sarah, once again, bit her tongue when the big topic came up?

"You know," Krista said, "a kid isn't a status symbol, and lest I emphasize the obvious, it's work, being a parent, it's work you can never fully escape." Krista had asked why Sarah wanted to be a mother, deep down.

What was the correct answer to this question? Sure, she fantasized about the covert clubs she'd be let into if she became a mom, but she knew that a child was neither an accessory nor a Band-Aid to be applied over a preexisting problem. A child could not "fix" her, nor could it fix her and Sam. She could make conjectures, based on what she knew and saw, but she had no idea, fundamentally, what becoming a mother would do to her. How could you explain opting into the unknown?

What she does know is that she wants more out of life. She wants the most. She wants to fire the menu, order the entire bounty that life has to offer. Creating life—that sounds like firing the menu. She hasn't always seen it that way, but she does now.

The thing is, she was afraid to say this to Krista. She is afraid to say it to anyone. She is afraid to want a child too much, because what if it doesn't happen? Given how long she's waited, given all the ways in which she's abused her body, what if she can't get pregnant? What then?

She doesn't know if she could handle the heartbreak. So, perversely, she's abused her body even more, as though, if she drank enough, she would stop wanting children, she would make it so that she *could not* have children, she would eliminate the possibility and thereby save herself.

Because here's what terrifies her even more than the prospect of not being able to have children: All the things that could happen once they came into the world. All the things that could go wrong.

What she told Krista, in the moment: "I don't know." She didn't want to get into it. Call it her fatal flaw—it's why she and Sam have mostly danced around the conversation, even when her maternal ambivalence crystallized into the affirmative. It felt wrong to have once not wanted children—to have prioritized a life of indulgence and pleasure, to have thought hedonism would make her happy—and then changed her mind. It felt like something she couldn't talk about. Like she would be forsaking her past self in favor of an uncertain future.

"Well, look," Sam says now. "What are we going to do? Maybe she got on the bike. Maybe she didn't. Maybe she was pushed. We could spend the rest of our lives wondering about all the things we'll never know. I need a mimosa."

He lifts his hand and motions for the server, which she hates. The brashness of the gesture. Willfully disregarding what happened to one human being while summoning another. Sam normally hates it, too, working in the industry, says people who snap their fingers and say "Check, please" have small-dick energy. She supposes that his own alcohol anxiety, surely coursing, has something to do with it, along with the compounding effects of jet lag and having participated in a police investigation in the wee hours of the morning.

But her mind goes back to something he said: "Maybe she was pushed." It's a thought she has been thinking but has not yet voiced.

She has not watched a lot of true crime, but you don't need to be as addicted as Sam to know that, generally, it's the husband's fault. Kevin's initial response to his wife's disappearance struck her as weird. The way he said he'd burn Jala to the ground. Shouldn't he have been more grief-stricken, more laser-focused on finding his wife, than threatening to sue or literally set a resort on fire? (Could you set a resort in the middle of the ocean on fire? It sounded counterintuitive.)

Maybe this is how rich people act in a crisis. She remembers the harsh words Natalie lobbed at her in that tearful 6:00 a.m. call. "There is a special place in hell for you, and it's called never being invited to an event worth attending again." Natalie must have had special powers, because that's exactly what has come to pass. Natalie knew people who knew people who could revoke someone's access, which was, for someone like Sarah, an outsider forever hoping to be let in, the harshest punishment of all.

"Well, look what the cat dragged in." A booming baritone coming from behind Sarah brings her back to the present. She registers the shock on Sam's face, whips around, and finds herself looking up at Kevin. His hair is slicked back and he smells of aftershave. His cheeks radiate a just-exfoliated sort of glow. He is dressed in a seafoam Palm Angels bowling shirt printed with canary yellow pineapples and matching swim trunks. For a guy whose wife has just died, he is trying way, way too hard.

"Got room for another?" he asks, coming between them and clapping his palms together. "As you might've heard, my plus-one is now a plus-none."

~

Sam doesn't know how to react. He releases a sound of disbelief, a mirthless sort of laugh. Is Kevin in denial? Is he having some sort of meltdown?

"Uh," he says. "Sure?" He wants to spend no more time with this couple, or the memory of this couple, if that's the correct way to think about it, and certainly no more time with Kevin. But to deny a seat to a man who's freshly widowed seems beyond wrong. Sam is fronting like he's over it all—largely to keep Sarah from sinking into the depths of despair—but internally, he quakes at the thought of the calls Kevin must have made this morning, to their kids, to their extended family.

They can handle another half an hour of being polite. What's the worst that could happen?

Kevin motions for a server to pull up another two-top, bring over another seat, and set another place. The server regards him warily. Surely, all the employees know by now what happened, although no one seems eager to bring it up.

"We ask, for the comfort of the rest of the guests, to please refrain from talking about this incident in public areas," Sid told Sam and Sarah. They were at the arrival and departure jetty. The sun had emerged in full; the authorities had just left with the body bag, the thought of which, even now, at breakfast, makes Sam shudder, despite his want to forget Krista, to forget what happened.

"This was a tragic, horrific accident, and we don't want to stoke any fear on the property," Sid continued.

"Of course," Sam replied, "but don't you think you should warn the other guests about the dangers of biking after dark? Or put up a barricade, or something?"

"We cannot do the latter without alerting our owners, who are currently offline in Mallorca, and I'd prefer to handle that matter with them one-on-one when they are next here," Sid said. "As for the barricades—it's common sense, no?" Sid looked at them both for confirmation in the way brown folks do, in a way that says "Stupid, reckless white people" without actually saying it.

"I guess," Sarah ventured, "but still, it's not that big of a boardwalk, it's what—ten feet wide? Anyone could easily swerve."

Sid smiled tightly. "I'll take it into consideration." Sarah and Sam turned and walked back to their overwater bungalow slowly, eschewing Maanav's offers of a buggy ride, each lost in their own world. And that had been the end of that.

Or so Sam thought. Because now, all Kevin wants to do, understandably, is talk about what happened, in the very public area that is Veranda. Other guests are having breakfast, sipping coffee, and tearing into croissants that crumble all over their cream-colored cloth napkins and rumpled linen shirts. Overhead, fans swirl lazily. The air feels thick, redolent with the smell of freshly roasted espresso, fried dough, and something ineffably South Asian, the vague aroma of ginger, garlic, chilis, and cilantro frying somewhere in the background.

"Here's the thing that I don't get," says Kevin, leaning one elbow on the table. He's sitting next to Sam, who can practically feel the righteousness radiating from him, the sense that he will not stop until his point of view is accepted as the only one that matters, the only one that could be correct. "How can they not have barriers along this boardwalk? How in God's name is that allowed? Have you ever been to the Rosewood Miramar?"

Sarah nods, tentatively. She took Sam there a couple of years ago, on assignment for a travel magazine that had tasked her with writing about places to go in the tony Southern California hamlet of Montecito, home to Oprah Winfrey, Meghan Markle, and Lucky's, a steak house that served (in his opinion) the best onion rings on earth.

"So you've seen those train tracks that run through the property?"

Sarah nods again. A server places Sam's mimosa on the table, and before he can reach for it, Kevin wraps his hand around the stem and takes a glug.

"Sorry, pal," he says, clapping Sam on the back. "This round's on me. Or, shall I say, on Jala—I'll be damned if I'm paying a goddamn cent to this place—but what was I saying?"

"The train tracks," Sarah says.

"Right." Kevin takes a second gulp. Sam desperately tries to catch the server's eye so he can order another mimosa, to no avail. "They've got a staffer posted at those train tracks twenty-four seven," says Kevin. "Sundays, holidays, 3:00 a.m. on New Year's Day—it doesn't matter, someone is always standing guard, plus there's an iron gate on either side that has to be physically opened. You can't just wander onto the tracks, drunk or suicidal or whatever.

"Rick Caruso knows what's up," Kevin goes on. From this, Sam recalls that Rick Caruso, the only real estate developer in LA with a portfolio to rival Kevin's, owns Rosewood Miramar. "You leave those gates unlocked, those tracks unguarded, snakes, scum-of-the-earth types, will slip and fall, lose a finger, lose a leg, and sue you into oblivion." Kevin takes another gulp and the mimosa's gone.

"Wouldn't snakes slither?" Sarah says, almost to herself. Sam cracks a smile.

"You know what I mean," Kevin says, elongating his vowels.

Is Kevin drunk? Did he drink before this? Sam can't blame him, but again, the reason for Kevin's vitriol seems misplaced. What are the stages of grief? He remembers denial, anger, and acceptance. To Sam's knowledge, Kevin has been rooted in anger since the moment Krista disappeared. Maybe he's remixing the stages. Aren't there no rules when it comes to grief? He heard that once, somewhere. Maybe denial will come next.

"The point is that normal luxury resorts, *American* luxury resorts, protect against shit like this," Kevin says. "They see the lawsuits coming a mile away. This place, on the other hand." He takes a withering look around Veranda. Sam tries to see through Kevin's eyes: a sea of brown faces serving clients that are, by and large, white. The have-nots versus the haves.

"They're practically asking for it," Kevin says with a shrug. He picks up the empty mimosa glass and tilts it, spins it on its base. "And you know they're in the middle of an acquisition."

"By whom?" asks Sarah.

Kevin looks from side to side, as if to check if anyone's listening. He stops toying with the glass and leans in.

"Hyland," he says, conspiratorially. "It's not public yet, but I know someone on the inside."

Hyland is a multinational hotel conglomerate based in Dallas, Texas. Founded by Nelson Hyland in 1925, it's got scores of properties around the world, everything from airport hotels with coagulated, clumpy eggs at the breakfast buffet to Ritz Carlton–level emporiums of luxury. Sam has stayed in many a Hyland. They tend to be fine. The type of places you can rely on, with an Honors club and a proprietary points system and the same Wi-Fi code throughout the portfolio, so management consultants don't have to key in a new one when they arrive at the Raleigh-Durham Hyland at eleven o'clock at night.

"Interesting," Sarah says. "Didn't the company just change hands?" She mentions Nelson's recent passing and April, his eldest daughter, taking the reins of Hyland.

Sam saw that headline, too. Meant to read the article. Internalized the news, wondered if it would take his father dying for him to finally grasp control of the family business.

"You know your stuff," Kevin says, appreciatively. "She inherited the whole kit and caboodle last month. Daddy finally croaked. What a tool, that guy. Knew how to run an empire, though. God knows what'll happen to the company now, given that April knows diddly-squat about business."

"She has a few companies, doesn't she?" Sarah says. "Pretty successful in their own right."

Kevin scoffs. "If you call a cleaning spray a company. Baby girl knows how to deejay and pose for pictures, that's about it."

"Hey, buddy, I'm going to check out the breakfast buffet. Want to come with?" Sam says, abruptly standing up and pushing in his chair. He can see Sarah bristling at Kevin's barely concealed misogyny. It's kind of out of character. He was as inoffensive as vanilla around Krista, but again, Kevin's been through the unimaginable. Sam cuts him some slack. "Might be good to get a bite. I know I'm starving."

"Not I, my friend," Kevin says, sitting back. "Not I."

"Come on," Sam says, nudging Kevin on the shoulder. "Have you seen the dosa station? Have you ever even had a proper paper dosa? I bet you haven't. Bet you don't even know what a dosa is."

One side of Kevin's mouth turns up. "You got me," he says. He pushes away from the table. "Fine," he says, standing up. "Suppose a bite wouldn't hurt. Gonna need energy for what comes next."

"Next?" Sarah asks, looking up at them.

"Wait'll you see what's in store," Kevin says. "I'm bringing in the big guns."

~

Sam would like to focus on the machinations of the chef behind the live dosa station, the delicate and precise twist of his wrist that, in one fell swoop, transports a ladle full of fermented rice batter from a stainless steel vat onto a *tawa* bigger than a tire. The way that, each time the chef does this, the batter forms a perfect circle, like magic. The way the edges of the dosa cook and crisp in mere seconds, the way the chef knows exactly when to slide a spatula under the golden-brown disc and fold it, stuff it, serve it.

The guy could teach his guys a thing or two. But Sam can't concentrate on any of this because next to him Kevin is going on about his grand plan to "burn Jala to the ground"—he keeps saying this—carrying on in a maniacal way that makes Sam wonder if Kevin's on uppers or coming apart at the seams or both.

"You see these sorts of cases all the time," Kevin is saying. "Gross negligence. Major cash payouts. You have no idea how often it happens, how many companies settle instead of going to court, all the bad press. You think this place wants to be known as lose-your-wife central? What with Hyland coming in and taking the reins? Not a chance."

Sam side-eyes Kevin as Kevin keeps ranting.

"You're nothing without your reputation, and this place can't afford to go up against me and my legal team, not a chance in hell. You know how much business they have to do here just to break even? You know how the reviews would tank? You would think they're rolling in it, what with the rates they charge, but I've crunched the numbers and—"

Meth. Kevin sounds like he's on meth.

"It sounds like you've given this a lot of thought," Sam says. He crosses his arms over his chest, keeps his eyes on the dosa chef.

"What do you mean?"

"I mean, you've got this whole plan figured out." What Sam means is that it seems pretty well plotted for a man who lost his wife mere hours ago, but he does not know how to say this in a delicate way.

Kevin moves his body—his substantial body, he's wider than Sam and taller, too—so that he's now blocking Sam's view of the dosa station. He lowers his voice. "Are you saying that I planned this?"

Sam waves his hand to deflect this suggestion. "I'm just saying that you seem to have a lot of experience with lawsuits." Sam is, in a roundabout way, asking whether Kevin planned this. But he's not ready to say that directly in front of the dosa station, or anywhere else, for that matter.

Kevin's face softens. "Well, sure. Happens all the time in my world. I've paid out more scam artists than I can count, idiots who fell down a stairwell when they should've taken the escalators to the parking garage like everyone else."

"I guess," Sam starts, choosing his words carefully. "What do you hope to have happen? If you can't bring her back . . ." He trails off. Maybe he shouldn't have gone down this route. He thinks of the son in college, the daughter sashaying between bistro two-tops in Europe. He can't imagine what they make of what's happened, if they, in fact, have any clue.

Kevin's face hardens once more. "Do you have any idea the phone calls that I've had to make today? I wouldn't wish this on my worst enemy. No way can I slink away from here with my tail between my legs, accept this. It's unacceptable. One thousand percent."

"But money—"

"But nothing," he hisses. "Money is all there is. Money is proof that they fucked up. And if they don't want to go that route, I'll take them to court. My lawyers will be here by the morning. Preston and Wycoff, white-shoe New York law firm, got an office on Park Ave and everything. These Jala motherfuckers are going to feel the full force of Kevin King."

Sam wonders again about the kids. Kevin's made no mention of them. Shouldn't they be on the next flight out? Or did Kevin decide to spare them from the lawyers, from the nastiness of it all?

The whole performance—is that what this is?—strikes Sam as over-the-top. Vaguely comical. But what does he know?

Blame it on the Palm Angels set. You really wouldn't think a guy in Kevin's position would have the wherewithal to put on a Palm Angels set. One printed with pineapples, no less.

"Masala?" the dosa chef asks Sam tentatively, lifting his eyes from the tawa.

Sam nods. "Extra mirch, my man." He can't tell whether Kevin is right side up or upside down, he cannot understand how he's gotten involved in an accidental death that he wants no part of, but he can control the level of spice in the masala being ladled onto his dosa, and given that it's the only thing he seems to be able to control in his life at the moment, he wants more.

~

Sarah did not want to go up to the buffet with Kevin and Sam, not with Kevin frothing at the mouth, fiending for revenge, but after they saunter over to the live dosa station, after she tires of trying to read the à la carte menu for what feels like the thirty-fourth time, she slips out of the banquette and goes into an air-conditioned room arrayed with salads of various sorts: fruit, green, a mélange of the Mediterranean's greatest hits—Greek salad layered with thick blocks of feta, tabouli with leaves of parsley splayed open wide like a fan, *muhammara* with red peppers roasted into submission and studded with nubs of walnut, more of a spread than a salad, but vegetal in essence. It belongs to this spread in the way Sarah wishes she belonged to anything.

She cannot tell whether or not she's hungry. She feels something in the pit of her stomach, the kind of yearning that she intrinsically knows food cannot quell. But filling a plate with spoonfuls of the salads and stacking a little tower of cucumber and carrot sticks makes her feel, for a moment, virtuous, like the person she had planned to be in the Emirates Lounge at LAX, like someone in control of themselves, who tracks their vitamins, maybe the sort of individual who wears a glucose monitor and an Oura ring, who sees a trainer and a nutritionist and definitely, *definitely* does not stake their future on the advice of someone they just met who is now dead.

She catches sight of a chafing dish full of bacon. Oh no. Does she want this spread of exotic salads, or does she want bacon?

She sets down her artfully arranged plate and picks up another.

"Can I tell you a secret?"

She pauses her tong-enabled search for the crispiest piece of bacon in the chafing dish and finds herself face-to-face with Sid. He appears to have showered and changed since they last saw each other on the jetty. He's wearing another boldly patterned shirt, this one sprayed with curving lines that occasionally come together to form the outline of a wineglass. He's holding the salad plate she set down by the beginning of the "Western" wing of the breakfast buffet.

"Sorry about that," she says, glancing down at the plate. "I was going to go back for it."

He smirks. "Sure. In any case, with regard to your reconnaissance for the finest specimens of pork belly, you should know that Chef Dave keeps the crispiest pieces in the back."

"What, really? Why?"

Sid shrugs. "He claims that no one in this Muslim country appreciates Canadian-born-and-bred bacon, and he likes to snack on it while he's on his shift."

"And you let him get away with this?"

"He makes the best breakfast sausage I've ever had. Call it a concession. How many pieces would you like?"

"Three?"

"I'll bring them to your table," he says. He's holding her plate of salad like she can take it or leave it, he's not going to judge either way. She takes it, thanks him, and, seeing that Sam and Kevin are still at the dosa station—and still wanting nothing to do with that conversation—heads back to their table.

She wonders if Sid is this solicitous with everyone or if she's getting special treatment because of what happened with Krista, whether Sid will go above and beyond to help her and Sam have a semblance of a normal vacation. Not that they can now. Nice of Sid to make the effort, though.

She's stabbing a cucumber stick with a fork when he reappears with a plate bearing four pieces of picture-perfect bacon. Like something out of an Arby's ad. "One for good luck," he says.

"Why don't you wear a uniform like everyone else?" she asks, eyeing his shirt again, the way it hangs on a frame that she'd describe as "protein shakes for lunch." Chiseled, but not overly so.

"Because I'm not like everyone else," he says. He glances down at the bacon and the salads. "You must be hungry after that horrendous morning."

She puts down her fork, picks up a piece of bacon, and bites off a hunk, letting the blackened edge melt on her tongue.

"I don't know what I am," she says with a sigh. The sight of all this food sourced from various corners of the globe—what is muhammara doing, mingling with Canadian bacon on an island in the Indian Ocean?—suddenly strikes her as vaguely disgusting. Unholy. She should've just gotten a yogurt. She shouldn't even be here. She should be doing something purposeful, like figuring out what really happened to Krista, given that Kevin seems more intent on suing everyone under the sun than finding out why Krista would've taken a midnight bike ride, a story that Sarah still does not buy.

Though her brain could use a break.

She thinks again about the drink that will calm her mind and soothe her nerves, even while restarting the retox-detox spiral. Might as well. Isn't she destined to go down that route anyway?

She catches the eye of a waiter, asks if she can see a beverage menu.

"Never mind all that," says Sid, cocking his head toward the outside. "I've got a better idea." He stands up with authority, a man with a plan who seems to have sensed her unease, which, though she doesn't quite want to admit it, she finds awfully attractive.

In the abstract, at least.

She follows him across the expanse of Veranda's dining room, down to the sand and around to a shack that looks like it's made of driftwood, but in a considered, thoughtful way. As if it's always stood there, as if the island came with it, even though it was most likely conceived by a marketing department to add "authenticity" to the resort.

Sid slides a key card out of his pocket and hovers it over the sensor on the handle of the door. "Welcome to our rum hut," he says, as a wall of air-conditioning envelops her, sending goose bumps up her forearms, exposed as they are by the billowing sleeves of her caftan.

"I'm generally not one for rum," she says, but she can't help but find the whole thing charming. The windows of the rum hut are beaded with condensation, all four walls are arrayed with bottles, and the sun is hitting the mirrors behind the bottles in a way that lights the place up like a jewel.

Also charming: that Sid seems to know intrinsically what she wants. Charming and unnerving. Like he has a sixth sense.

"We call it the rum hut, but in fact, we've got all kinds of liquor here," he says, moving toward a row of long, elegantly curved, decanter-shaped bottles on the farthest wall. "Top-shelf, limited-production spirits, gifts from repeat guests and suppliers who've graced us with their presence."

"Huh," she says. "You don't want to use it in the regular bars?"

He shrugs. "Figured it's better to keep them in their own place, since they're such special bottles. Like this one." He reaches for a matte-black decanter-bottle with a bell-shaped top covered in multicolored beads. "Are you familiar with Clase Azul?"

"I sure am," she says. It's her favorite tequila producer; she once went to Mexico to write about their production process and cult following. She had gushed all about it to Sam upon her return, but Sam seemed unmoved by her enthusiasm and unwilling to sample any of the bottles she brought back, claiming to be averse to agave spirits, even though she'd seen him take down shots of tequila without an apparent second thought. She'd scored the cover of the *Wall Street Journal*'s Marketplace section with that story; for all she knew, Sam hadn't read it.

"Have you tried their mezcals?" he asks, uncorking the bottle. From an island at the center of the rum hut, he grabs hold of two crystal glasses.

"I have," she says. She recognizes the bottle in his hand as the Durango, her favorite of Clase Azul's mezcals, perhaps her favorite mezcal of all. Under another circumstance, with another person, she might've revealed all of this, might've gushed about how much they have in common, all "what are the odds," but seeing as how Sid read her mind regarding her desire for crispy bacon and a drink, she's curious to see how far he can take this on his own.

Is this wrong? She hasn't done anything wrong. She feels nothing for him physically.

Though, the fact that she wonders whether it's wrong might signal that it could be.

She is also the type to be won over by personality before physical appearance. Sam got her with his humor, hook, line, and sinker.

"Then you must know about the healing properties of Durango," Sid is saying, pouring two fingers' worth of the clear liquid into each glass. "It's what I reach for after a tough day, and after the morning that you had, I think you're entitled to the entire bottle, should you care to go down that route."

She laughs. "You had the same morning."

"No," he says, holding out a glass for her. "My morning was worse. But you're a guest, and a guest should never be embroiled in such a disaster. It's an embarrassment."

As she accepts the glass, their fingertips lightly touch. "You couldn't have known what would happen," she says.

He shrugs again. "You have a point about the barricades. It's just such an eyesore. And in all my time here, ten years, we've never had a tragedy like this."

"Does anything else even compare?"

Sid looks up at the rum hut's vaulted ceiling. Sarah notices his neck, the muscles beneath the skin. Virile. That's the first word that comes to mind.

"There once was a woman with a Birkin bag," he says. He chuckles. "Sounds like the beginning of a bad joke, which it was. She took it out in a storm with gale-force winds and accused us of negligence when the leather got damaged, wanted us to buy her another."

"Wild," Sarah says, shaking her head.

"Some guests don't know their limits. Or ours. They think we can give them the sun, moon, and stars."

"You don't control the weather," she says.

"No, but I do try to ensure that guests have as good a time as possible on the island, and I don't think I'll ever be able to forgive myself for how your trip started."

Sid had said he didn't want them to talk about "the incident" on property, but since he brought it up, she wonders if she should test the waters that Sam seems so bent on avoiding.

"What's your thought on what happened, honestly? Do you really think she biked off the boardwalk?"

"Honestly?" he says, raising his glass. "I think we should take a sip of this first."

She raises her glass to meet his. It occurs to her that it's somewhat odd Sid didn't wait until Sam returned from the buffet to invite him to the rum hut as well, but perhaps that's because he was with Kevin, and she is pretty sure Sid would put an ocean between himself and Kevin if he could.

Their glasses clink. He locks eyes with her. She looks away first. It's almost uncomfortable, the intensity of his gaze. "Cheers," she says.

They draw back and each take a sip. It burns, going down her throat, but in a pleasant way. Like swallowing incense. There's something medicinal and magical about mezcal. Sam took a whiff of the bottle she had brought home and denounced it as lighter fluid, sneered when she mentioned its spiritual connotations. "Do you really believe that?" he said. "You've got to know that it's all a marketing ploy."

She's never shared a glass of it with someone until now.

"Needed that," Sid says, setting his glass on the driftwood island. "Now, do I really think she biked off the boardwalk? Not in the slightest. Even drunk, one would have to have a death wish. She did not strike me as that kind of woman."

"That's *exactly* what I've been thinking," Sarah says. Ah, the sweet taste of vindication. She takes another sip. "It's not adding up."

Sid shakes his head. "I have a few theories." He takes another sip. "Perhaps we should compare notes?"

"Not that I have any formal ones," she says, "but yes."

"Here," he says, whipping out his phone, "program your number. This is my personal phone, not Jala sanctioned. I unfortunately have to rush off to another staff meeting—business as usual—but perhaps we can link up later?"

"Sure." As she accepts his phone, their fingers graze again.

She tells herself it's not a spark that she feels. She's just out of sorts. It's just the morning. This particular morning. It's just the alcohol. This particular alcohol.

It's certainly not the fact that there's a virile man who can read her mind and happens to share her taste in alcohol as well as the hunch that Krista's death is not the accident that Kevin is making it out to be.

It's certainly not that at all.

NINE

Full sun. Popcorn clouds out yonder. A huff of frustration to his left.

"It's just not making sense," Sarah says. "Him in that Palm Angels set, going on about lawsuits."

Sam looks up from the sports scores he's scrolling in an attempt to feel some sense of normalcy. A Sunday afternoon just like any other. NFL and the sound of the RedZone app, some player scoring on some far-away field.

Except, of course, this Sunday is different. And while he doesn't mind his wife interrupting this purely voyeuristic tour of games whose outcomes mean nothing, materially, to him—he's given up on texting the new bookie, doesn't know what to say, doesn't know what he wants to hear—he does mind talking about Kevin and Krista yet again. These people have disrupted his peace for long enough. He would like to do away with them, has actually considered checking out of Jala and into another Maldivian resort just to distance them both from the whole sorry debacle, but he abandoned that plan before saying anything to Sarah because he does not have the patience to get on the phone with American Express and attempt to recoup the hundreds of thousands of credit card points that he's already cashed in.

He thought about whether the American Express Fine Hotels & Resorts representative would take pity on him, given what's taken place at Jala, but he and Sarah had signed some forms that Sid gave them in the early hours of the morning, as the authorities were leaving, and he doesn't know if he's allowed to say anything, or what the forms were. He never reads forms, and while, sure, it may have been prudent to see if it was an NDA or an agreement to enter into arbitration, should they decide to sue, or, hell, his own last will and testament, by the time Sid handed them the forms, he had been up for too many hours and endured too few nights of rest. He would've signed his life away for a chance to lie down in bungalow no. 7's king-size bed.

Did he sign his life away? Maybe Sarah knows.

He generally trusts her to read the fine print. He's not sure if he's ever told her that.

He turns to her, on the chaise lounge beside his. It's thick and covered in high-quality beige-tone canvas, with a plush white beach towel tucked on top. They're at Jala's main pool, next to the open-air restaurant, Riva, which serves an improbable menu that includes wood-fired pizza, Maldivian fish curry, and hookah. As they walked in, he saw a couple not unlike them—youngish, without kids in tow—smoking a hookah fitted with a pineapple bowl, smiling, laughing, chatting in an animated way as they passed the pipe back and forth.

"Well," he says to his wife now, his not smiling, certainly not laughing wife. "Of course it's not making sense. Nothing about Kevin makes sense. But can we please talk about literally anything else? Our entire morning—our entire trip, pretty much—has been the Krista and Kevin show, which I couldn't even escape at breakfast. Where did you go, by the way?"

He had been ready to stab himself with a butter knife by the time Sarah came back to their table, very clearly under the influence of some alcohol or another. Her eyelids looked heavy, her gaze kept shifting.

While she was gone, he had consumed two dosas, two mimosas—"just a splash of OJ"—and excused himself from Kevin's tirade two other times, inventing urges to use the restroom and cruise the table piled with baked goods, croissants filled with deliriously sweet pandan custard and raspberry tartlets with crusts that crumbled like castles of sand. He had one of each while waiting for Sarah, while the hunk of dosa he had saved for her grew cold. Sarah didn't even explain where she'd gone, just slid back into her seat with a mumbled apology of having to take care of something, whatever that meant.

They'd only lost Kevin when Sam announced, loudly, that he really didn't feel well and needed Sarah to accompany him back to the bungalow so they could find the Imodium A-D. Sarah had given him a withering look, but he was pretty sure she knew that he was telling a white lie, and in any case, he didn't really care. He just needed to get away from Kevin. He hailed a golf cart and told the driver to take them to the biggest pool on the property, a place where he imagined they could relax and perhaps even rejoice, away from all the drama, and here they were, rehashing the nightmare all over again.

"I went to get a drink," his wife says now.

"Where? I looked for you at the bar of Veranda."

"The rum hut," she says. She explains that it's a standalone bar where all the special bottles are kept. "Sid wanted to show it to me."

"The general manager?" he clarifies, though he knows exactly who she's talking about. What he did not know was that they were on a first-name basis.

She murmurs in a way that indicates that he's correct.

"Huh," he says. "Okay." Is Sid trying to flex on his wife? What kind of resort manager would do that? Especially when the resort in question has been named the number one most romantic by *Travel & Leisure* four years in a row? "How was it?"

"Fine," she says, although he can tell by the tone of her voice that there's more to the rendezvous than that. "Apparently he deals with guest-related disasters all the time, though nothing as awful as this."

"One would hope," Sam says, turning back to his phone.

"But he doesn't think we know the whole story," she says.

"What do you mean?"

"He also does not believe that Krista would've ridden her bike off the boardwalk," she says, "that she would've been that careless. He thinks Kevin did something."

Sam sighs and plops his phone face down on the chaise, which, as it's covered in layers of plush fabric, does not elicit the satisfying sound he was hoping for. It does not elicit any sound at all. He sits up and turns his torso toward his wife.

"You know what, maybe he did. Maybe he poisoned her. Maybe he hit her in the back of the head. Maybe he stabbed her with a corkscrew and threw her in the ocean and threw the bike in after her to make it look like an accident. Honestly, though? I don't care. I could not care less. These people were strangers to us a few days ago, and they will continue to be strangers to me going forward. If you want to get wrapped up in all the little details, the what-ifs and if-then, now-whats, go right ahead, but please leave me out of it."

He does not really want her to get wrapped up in all the little details, but he is frustrated, and he doesn't know how else to put it. All the advice of their couples counselor feels as hard to reach as the edge of the cumulus cloud hovering over the horizon. What is he supposed to do in situations like these? Pause, reflect? He is too heated to pause or reflect.

"Quite a vivid picture you painted just now, Bob Ross," she says.

"You watch enough true crime, you begin to freestyle," he says.

"Comforting," she says. "But you're really not curious? You genuinely don't want to know what actually happened?"

He looks at her. She has also sat up and twisted her torso to face his. She's wearing that bikini he likes, the dark-pink one with the fabric that looks like the frosting you pipe onto the edge of cakes.

"I'm going to take a dip," she says, pushing up from her chaise lounge, sauntering away.

There's no malice in her voice. He understands what he's up against—an eternally curious questioner, the forever contrarian, the person he fell in love with, all those years ago.

She is still the same, underneath the jadedness that's built up over time, underneath the layers of resentment. She enjoys asking the questions others don't think to ask. When he would send her those bits of gossip from the restaurant, like Lady Gaga waltzing into the private room in a dress made of meat and ordering off the raw vegan menu, she would ask follow-up questions that never would have come to him.

"How aged was the jamón part of her skirt? Two years? Three? If you had to guess." He had screenshotted that message, saved it as one of his favorites, still looked at it from time to time, when he needed to remember who he had married.

The audacity Sarah had, to give up everything and everyone she knew in New York and move across the country, not just to be with him, she made that clear, but the fact that they were in love had everything to do with it.

When they were both living in New York and she had to fly to LA to cover the Oscars or the Emmys or some other awards show, she would return with nothing but hate for the 101, the way you had to drive everywhere, the lack of bodegas. She would rib him about it, affectionately. "How could you have come from there?" As if he had risen from a wasteland.

And now she calls it her home. Because of him. They've made a life there, together, one that she's been happy with until not that long ago.

Until that backstabbing editor ruined her career, specifically. Until she got consumed by what everyone else was doing—Natalie, Alana, whoever she followed on social media who, she assumed, had a more fulfilling life than her, who filled her with self-doubt, who made her question what she did for a living, her purpose.

He wishes she didn't have to work. He's never said that, because he's afraid of the response that she would hurl at him—what, does he think she's just some layabout, some housewife, some ambitionless Stepford type? Is that how he *wanted* things to be? Does he secretly want her to be like his mother, who never held a salaried job a day in her life, who never, to his knowledge, envisioned a life beyond having a family and taking care of that family?

It occurs to him that he ought to ask his mother about that.

But the thing is, that's how it's supposed to be, in his mind. Call him old-fashioned. He feels that a man should take care of his wife. If she wants to work, wonderful. She ought to. If Sarah wants to move mountains, he'll be the first person at her side, ready, willing, and able to help. But as far as he can tell, lately, the notion of work, of writing, of interviewing anyone who deserves her attention, fills her with angst, makes her miserable.

She still takes the odd assignment here and there, top ten lists, her running gig with the members-only restaurant reservations app, stuff that pays pennies when her words are worth gold. She did it so she could contribute to their mortgage and pay her credit card bills, which don't amount to much, given that she's stopped going out and shopping. She has never asked him for money, which is a good thing, because he doesn't have much to give. If he had the power that he so craves at Tiffin, it would be another story. They'd be flush. Rolling in the Gs. She wouldn't have to take on any work that didn't move her. She could spend a decade on her novel, or start a new novel, or start a quirky business, like whatever Krista had, needlepointing cheeky pillow covers. Whatever she liked.

If only.

He longs for the halcyon days when they felt on the precipice of making it. When there was only possibility ahead. When his father seemed sure to hand him the reins to the restaurant empire any day now, when his father *promised* he'd hand over the reins "in January, in July, I'm getting old, too old for this, it's time for you to step up, I built this all for you."

And then night would fall, and his father's feelings would change, and, often with no explanation, they'd be right back at square one. Balraj as the big boss, his son as the bitch boy.

It could make you crazy, a family business. It's a specific type of torture. An exercise in filial manipulation.

It's poisoned his marriage, made him doubt his self-worth to the degree that, in his lesser moments, he's wondered what Sarah sees in him. He saw through her lie, that time she was supposed to go to St. Barts with Natalie. Work trip, his ass. She was embarrassed to be seen with him, and the worst part was that he couldn't blame her for feeling that way.

No, the worst part was that the implosion of her career, after that *Panache* story came out and Natalie put a hex on her, made him, if only for a moment, kind of, sort of perversely happy. Happy because now she wouldn't be going to St. Barts to party with the beautiful people and quite possibly fall in love with the deejay at Nikki Beach or one of the scores of French men who poured rosé across the island and for sure cleaned up in the bedding department, what with their accents and their scruff and their laissez-faire attitude toward adultery.

That was his insecurity talking. Because now that he's had a taste of Sad-rah, he wants her to go back to the person she once was. Misery may love company, but he loved bubbly, effervescent, ambitious Sarah more, the girl he fell in love with, the woman he married, the woman for whom he'd move mountains.

Which brings him back to the present, staring at his wife, emerging from the infinity-edge pool, his very own Bond girl. He wants so desperately to be on the same page as her again. He remembers a bit of relationship wisdom imparted to him by one of the wine suppliers he'd gotten chummy with while working at the fancy restaurant in New York: "You and your girl won't always be on the same page, so enjoy it when you are." Back then, before rings and vows and cross-country moves, Sam had amiably accepted this advice but secretly scoffed. He and Sarah saw eye to eye about all the important things. He couldn't fathom that changing.

What an idiot he was. Now, he sees an opportunity to get on her level. Does he want to care about Krista's death and Kevin's vendetta? No. But will caring, or feigning to care, endear his wife to him? Quite possibly, yes.

Krista's body had been fished out of the water; the authorities left hours ago. The way he saw it, if he played along now, Sarah would be ready to close the book on the whole sorry saga by sunset. Perhaps he could find it within himself to care—or pretend to!—for a few more hours. Let it be her idea, to let go of these people. Let her see the light.

He slides off his sunglasses and assembles his face in an expression of conciliation.

"All right, fine," he says, as she approaches. "You're right." He knows that women love nothing more than hearing that they're right. "It's not adding up. But what are you saying? Do you want to, like, investigate this?"

He clocks her little smile of satisfaction, the sun emerging from the clouds.

~

Sarah initially packed a notebook thinking that the Maldives would compel her to work on her novel. Or come up with a new idea. Or write for herself about anything at all. She's gotten so accustomed to computers and keyboards, she's practically forgotten how to write freehand. She had kept a diary since childhood, but sometime in her twenties she stopped. She kept meaning to pick up the habit again. Maybe Jala would inspire her.

She certainly never envisioned using the journal, a gift from the high-end sweatshirt maker Madhappy, with rainbow swirls on the cover, to record what they knew about Krista and Kevin and the questions surrounding Krista's death. It's the antithesis of the typical reporter's notebook. The word "Gratitude" is printed across the front in a bouncy, bubbly font. Most reporters lack gratitude, have, if anything, a glaring lack of gratitude, a great, big grudge against the world.

But using the heavy rose gold Jala pen to write about, actually write about, what's transpired over the length of their trip makes her surge with a sense of purpose she didn't realize she could still access, even as it makes the events of the morning feel freshly horrific.

Poor Krista. Poor, dear Krista. She can't get over it. How something so awful could happen to someone so nice.

"What were their kids' names again?" Sam asks.

Sarah has the back end of the pen between her lips. "One is Connor," she says. "I think he's the one who went to Dartmouth."

"The one she couldn't remember," Sam says. "She said he went to Stanford, but apparently it's the daughter who really went to Stanford."

"Alexa," Sarah says. "Right." She leans back against the lounger, the weight of these motherless children suddenly hitting her. The knot in her stomach moves to her throat.

"I can't even imagine," she says, shaking her head.

"It's tragic," Sam says, but he's leaning forward, legs crisscrossed on the lounger, torso bent over the phone in his right hand. "There are a bunch of Connor Kings on LinkedIn, but none of them seem to be the right age."

Sarah pulls herself together and opens the laptop she retrieved from their overwater bungalow along with the notebook after Sam finally agreed to participate. Actually—Maanav retrieved them for her, said when she WhatsApped for a buggy that it would be his pleasure: "If you can tell me where to find them, I'll bring them straight to you."

A previous version of her might have balked at the idea of a resort employee rifling through her luggage. What if he steals her passport, her money, her fine jewels? But she knows from her past writings about luxury travel that passports are the last thing that get stolen at places like these, at least by the staff. They'd be fired and blacklisted if they were caught, it's not worth the risk. And she has neither money nor fine jewels, unless you count the necklace of golf-ball-sized beads she got from Baublebar a decade ago. (Why did she bring it?) Beyond the laptop, the most valuable thing in her possession is a hair straightener she knows she will not use, given the humidity and her general unwillingness to spend more than fifteen minutes getting ready. If Maanav really wants the hair straightener, he can have it.

It feels nice, being waited on. And it's nice working on a project with Sam. A project unrelated to them and their issues.

When they were arguing about having children—when the prospect of having children was even an issue that could be on the table, before his gambling got out of control, before she found out about Elaine and how much he'd lost with her, before her career imploded, before the strength of their union came under question—the couples therapist had told them to make a pro-con list. "Without drinking," she specified. "Have fun with it, and talk while you do it." They'd lasted all of eight minutes before Sam shut down and said he'd had a terrible day at work, he wasn't in the mood.

But now, he's fully present. At least, he's more present than he has been in a while, which is maybe a function of the fact that she's also actively thinking and participating in the here and now.

Sarah used to think that the business of energy and people's vibes was hogwash, a bunch of woo-woo mumbo jumbo borne out of, surely, some yoga studio in Venice Beach. Lately, though, she's realized that she and Sam feed off of each other's energy. If he's in a bad mood, before long, she will be as well. Maybe this is what happens when you spend enough time, enough years, by someone's side. It's not something she thought about before committing to a life together, but now it seems just as important as anything else.

"Bringing out the big guns, huh?" Sam says, gesturing at her laptop.

Sarah nods. "Trying to find the son's social media." She googles "Connor King Dartmouth Los Angeles," figures that will turn up something, if, in fact, he's online. These Gen Zs—or would Connor be a member of Gen Alpha?—don't always have an internet presence, having seen how many millennials have lost jobs and been summarily canceled courtesy of old Facebook photos of them wearing an Afro wig or Native American headpiece on some long-forgotten Halloween.

There's nothing. She tries a few different spellings. There are some Connor Kings who live in Los Angeles, but none of them appear to be him, and there is no record of a Connor King who graduated from or is currently attending Dartmouth University. But again, this isn't surprising. The kid could be on TikTok as buttlover2002 for all they know.

On to Alexa. "Krista said the daughter majored in psychology, right?" Sarah says. She knows she's right, but she likes involving Sam in the process.

"Yeah," he says, "but now she's *Eat, Pray, Love*-ing her way through Europe. Must have vlogs for days."

"You'd think," Sarah murmurs, squinting at her screen. Even with the brightness turned all the way up, even though they're under the shade of an umbrella with a span of a basketball court, it's hard to read the results under the midday Maldivian sun. Not that there are any that seem to be relevant.

She glances up from her screen and sees a server handing a coconut to a woman reclined on a lounger across the pool. Could a coconut—or better yet, a piña colada—help her reconnaissance? It couldn't hurt, could it?

She asks Sam if he wants one, too. He nods and casts about for a server.

It's strange that Alexa would have no social media presence, what with her Euro trip and status as the recently graduated president of Stanford's chapter of Kappa Alpha Theta. Wouldn't you have to be on social media to get elected as the head of your sorority? You'd probably have to be on LinkedIn as well. Maintain some sort of honorable public profile.

"Maybe they're private," she says, though she herself has a hard time believing this. "Like, no-online-record kind of private."

"Didn't Kevin say something about how rich people get eviscerated?" Sam says. "How that's why he doesn't have social media at all?"

She turns to Sam, pleasantly surprised he remembers something she did not. Something useful. Something worth noting.

"Great point, babe," she says. They make a good team, when they're not at each other's throats. Funny how easy it can be to forget that, when you're in the muck of marriage, cursing the other person for stacking the dishwasher wrong or "forgetting" to take out the trash.

"Spectacular day for one of these, isn't it?" Sarah hears Sid's voice over her shoulder and is immediately pierced by guilt. But why? She hasn't done anything wrong. She had a shot of mezcal with him.

Well—two shots. Sippers, though. Not like they were throwing them back. They were savoring the mezcal, taking it slowly.

Taking what slowly? a little voice in her head asks.

She turns around and gives Sid a closed-mouth smile. They cannot make eye contact because she is wearing sunglasses, but she can see his ebony eyes attempting to find hers. She accepts the coconut he's holding out. It has the heft and weight of a bowling ball. To buy time, she takes a long sip through a straw made of paper. A farce, these paper straws. A performance of environmental friendliness that succeeds mainly in making a mess.

"Things are looking up," she says.

"Hey, thanks, man," Sam says, his own coconut in hand. The way he says it and turns around, Sarah can tell that he is trying to tell the manager to get lost. But Sid doesn't move, instead steadies himself against the pale wood pole of their Tucci umbrella.

"Have you thought about that matter I mentioned in the rum hut?" he asks, clearly seeking to speak to Sarah and only Sarah.

"I have." She hesitates. "Actually, we have. We're comparing notes." With her free hand, she holds up the rainbow-swirled notebook.

"My, look at you, so official," Sid says, bemused. "Is this how real reporters work, with candy-colored pads of paper?"

She doesn't mean to laugh, but somehow it slips out. "This was all I had," she says. "Well, I could've gone with the Jala notepad in the room, but that would be less than discreet."

"Fair point," says Sid. "And discretion is of the utmost importance."

"What are you talking about?" Sam asks.

Sarah detects Sid's annoyance at Sam's interruption as he explains his creeping suspicion that Kevin is yet another lawsuit-happy American, the type who probably plants himself at resorts with the intent of finding something wrong, in search of a claim and a payday.

"But he's rich," Sam says. "He owns, like, half of LA. Why would he need to run around suing people?"

"I don't know how rich he is," Sid says, "but I have some fellows in the front office investigating. He booked their stay on a debit card."

"A debit card?" Sarah asks, taken aback.

"No way," Sam says. "Who would book a week at a place like this on a debit card?"

Sarah is not the credit card expert her husband is, but even she knows you do not make major purchases on a debit card if you can help it, you save those for the credit cards that allow you to earn points and miles. The only reason you'd use a debit card is if you had no other option. Or if you had bad credit.

And why would someone who owns half of Los Angeles have bad credit?

"That's wild," she says. "They paid the full amount from their bank account?"

"Not the full amount," says Sid, "just a pre-authorization. As you probably know, the full amount is generally assessed upon checkout. In this situation . . . well, we really don't know what's going to happen, it's unprecedented. Though I must say, things seem to be looking up for Kevin."

He nods across the pool, where Kevin has materialized in his inappropriate pineapple-printed Palm Angels set. He's on a lounger, umbrella-topped drink in hand, chatting up a strawberry blond who looks like Krista minus twenty years.

Sarah can't quite believe her eyes. "That was quick."

"Cady, I believe her name is," Sid says. "Checked in solo. Very likely a pro."

"As in, a prostitute?" Sam chimes in.

Sid shoots him a warning look. "We don't condone such activities in the Maldives, it's strictly illegal. But it's true, some guests have been known to bend the rules, to adjust them to their liking. On her registration form, she said she's a yoga instructor."

"I'll bet," Sam says.

"Not to judge," says Sarah. "Well, okay, maybe to judge—that for sure does not look like a man who lost his wife this morning." In her mind, she pictures disparate pieces coming together from far-flung locales, like the continents reassembling to make Pangea. She was right to question the circumstances surrounding Krista's death. Something about Kevin is not adding up.

Or is it something about Krista and Kevin?

Is Krista a victim? Or was this part of a plan?

As if reading her mind, Sid says, "In any case, there's a lot to unpack and a lot at stake. I'd love to discuss it further with you."

That word out of his mouth, "love." But what is she doing? She doesn't even like this man. And her husband, her well-meaning, try-hard husband, is right here.

"Someplace less public, though," Sid goes on. He looks both ways, as if to ensure no one's within earshot. "What are your plans this evening? Would you like to come to the staff bar?"

"The staff bar?" Sam says, piping up again.

"It's a bit less luxurious than those frequented by guests," Sid says, "but we manage to have our own good time. We'll be able to talk more freely."

"We have a reservation for the omakase," Sam says. Sarah recalls Sam telling her that the omakase at Osaka, Jala's Michelin-starred Japanese restaurant, an amber-lit pagoda on a pier above the water, is seventeen courses and three hours. She detests meals that are seventeen courses and three hours.

"Maybe," she begins, turning to Sam and choosing her words carefully, "we can order some sushi à la carte and head over to the bar?"

He gives her a dead look. "Seriously?"

"We've had such a long day already," she says, "what with this morning. And you know how I get with tasting menus." Recently, she has wriggled out of tasting menus by saying she has lost the patience to appreciate them, that she gets too full, too fast. This isn't exactly true. The fact is that, these days, tasting menus tend to bring out the worst side of Sam, the envious "the things I would do if I had a platform like this" side, and she doesn't want him, or them, to suffer through that.

"It is quite a long one, that omakase," Sid says, which is kind of funny because shouldn't the general manager of a place like this be encouraging guests to go all-in for a meal that costs $400 before the beverage pairing?

But, she thinks again, maybe he does not see her as a typical guest.

"Or you can do it," she tells Sam, striving for geniality. "I don't want to stop you from having the omakase." This is a half-truth. While she will happily eat at a restaurant alone, she knows that Sam, despite his profession, loathes it, likes to have company, feels weird when he's dining solo.

She also knows that he is picking up what Sid is putting down.

Sam inhales sharply. "I'm not doing a three-hour meal by myself," he says. He turns to Sid. "Fine. We'll skip the tasting menu and come to you."

"Excellent," says Sid, though he doesn't look pleased that Sam has accepted an invitation that's clearly directed at Sarah. "I'll liaise with Osaka's chef, perhaps they can put together an express omakase for you, the greatest hits or some such." He turns back to Sarah. "I know I shouldn't say this, but I also can't stand tasting menus. They take too long. Just give me my food and get on with it."

She lets out an amiable little laugh. The guy might be the most outlandish general manager she's ever met.

"What do you like to drink?" he asks. "Besides, of course, top-shelf mezcal."

"Oh, anything's fine," she says.

"Wine," Sam says. "California pinot noir. Russian River Valley, if you have it."

"The staff bar certainly has wine, though it may be of the Yellow Tail variety, if I'm being honest. But perhaps we can procure a special bottle for you from Veranda's cellar."

"That would be nice," says Sam. "You know, considering."

Her husband lets that hang in the air, and she tries to deduce his point. Considering Krista's grisly death? Considering that their vacation has been co-opted by Kevin—slimy, possibly broke Kevin? Considering the official investigation and the vigilante one upon which they've embarked?

Considering that this general manager is clearly hitting on her, a married woman, in front of her husband?

She can feel the gentle tug-of-war between them.

How long has it been since she's felt this kind of attention from two men at once?

Has she ever?

And if she's being honest . . .

She kind of loves it.

TEN

Sam glares at the nigiri before him. Hamachi with a sheen of yuzu, normally right up his alley, but he's having a hard time enjoying it, enjoying any part of this meal, given that it's been co-opted by this ridiculous investigation Sarah is intent on pursuing.

It was supposed to be a romantic dinner. It was supposed to be revelatory, that's what the person on Reddit said, "a revelation, that they can turn out sushi of this quality in the middle of the Indian Ocean."

(Is it a revelation? They're surrounded by fish, aren't they? Are the rose-veiled fairy wrasse doing figure eights in the depths beneath his very seat? He still holds out hope of seeing a rose-veiled fairy wrasse, though the prospect of setting off on another snorkeling jaunt given how the first one went seems ill-advised.)

In any case, Sam would've loved the opportunity to figure it out for himself. He's in the business of restaurants. Can he really be blamed for relishing a tasting menu, for enjoying the pomp and circumstance that seems to so irk Sarah and this wildly inappropriate general manager, Sid?

Yes, he wants the hot towel. Yes, he wants his utensils refreshed after each of seventeen courses. Yes, he wants to take notes on his phone and overhead photographs of his food. He didn't know it was such a cliché, such a *crime*, to relish gastronomy in its highest form. Especially when he's already paid for it.

Well, their credit card points already paid for it. Given that they've been allotted to this meal—one of several add-ons he opted for, including those twin Ayurvedic four-hands massages, which, with his luck, Sid will spoil, too, probably by inserting himself in their treatment room and adding his own hands to the mix—there's no getting them back.

So, no, he does not appreciate Sid's offer of an express omakase "on us, to thank you for your efforts," as the embossed notecard said when they sat down at the bar of Osaka. Couldn't even get a normal two-top, as those are all reserved for the guests doing the full-blown omakase, the one that they were supposed to do.

"Mm, this is incredible," Sarah says beside him, through a mouthful of hamachi nigiri. She reaches up to remove a grain of vinegared rice from her bottom lip. "So much better than Sugarfish."

She knows how much he loves Sugarfish. To kick a man when he's down. What timing.

He reaches for the glass in front of him—a bone-dry Sancerre—his third glass on account of the fact that it's on the house, since Sid and Sarah colluded to ruin his night.

"What do you think, babe?" she asks, turning to him.

He continues staring straight ahead at the bartender pouring a cloudy sake into a ceramic decanter as he sets down his wineglass and uses his chopsticks to pick up his piece of nigiri.

As he lifts it to his mouth, a clump of the vinegared rice falls off the fish, lands in the cloth napkin in his lap.

"Fucking fuck," he says.

"Oh no," Sarah says. Infantilizing, her tone of voice. As if he's a child who's just dropped his ice cream.

He shoves the remainder of the nigiri into his mouth and swallows without chewing it fully. Not exactly savoring this sushi, is he? But how can he, with the anger roiling in his gut, with the hate in his heart? It feels like a boulder crushing him, this ill will. He doesn't want to feel it, but he doesn't know how to shove it off, how to rise above it.

The general manager of the most romantic resort in the world is hitting on his wife, a fact that his wife is either blithely oblivious to—unlikely, she's a smart woman—or, worse, condones. Wants.

It's disgusting. It's despicable. It makes him want to kill Sid, Sarah, and himself, most likely in that order.

In his opinion, he is justified in feeling this way. Even their couples counselor would agree. What husband wouldn't be riled by the threat of adultery, especially when it's happening in front of his face? If he did kill Sid and Sarah, wouldn't he get off scot-free? Would it not be a crime of passion?

Well, it would be a moot point if he were dead, too.

But he doesn't actually want to commit a double murder. He just wants to . . . get back on a plane and fly home. He wants to get out of here.

An hour ago, as Sarah was availing herself of the emerald-tone outdoor shower, he looked at flights, but there is no availability in business class for people who booked on points. He refuses to fly home in economy given that the points he's already spent won't be reinstated. Plus, having experienced Emirates business class, he cannot go back. Not when he knows about the food, the pajamas, the amenity kit, the semicircular bar at the back of the cabin.

This is the problem with flying business class. You do it once, on an airline like Emirates where it's actually worth it, and you're spoiled for life. Once you know how the other half lives, once you get a taste of it, you cannot go back to your gray, drab cog-in-the-wheel existence and feel a semblance of satisfaction. The other half gets technicolor holographic rainbows. How can he be satisfied with his porridge-hued lot, knowing that?

He wonders if he should become a monk. Monks don't seem to have these issues. Wasn't there some Indian banker who became a monk and then became a bestselling author and podcaster, making more than he ever would have in finance alone? Maybe he should do that.

What is he thinking? He's never going to do that. He's never going to do anything but be old B.'s bitch boy. Old B.'s bitch boy and now Sarah's cuck of a husband, the pathetic sap who gets cheated on during the wedding anniversary getaway he has planned and paid for.

He is aware that nothing physical has happened between Sarah and Sid. He would be able to tell if it had. (He thinks.) Sarah is not a great liar; her face says it all. But it's actually the emotional affairs that are more insidious, the ones that start with one party making the other laugh, feel seen in a way that eludes their lawful partner. And once an emotional affair has started, it's hard to roll it back, unless both parties vow to never contact each other, and in this day and age, what with social media and texting and all the rest, that's pretty much impossible.

Add to that the fact that they're on a tropical island the size of a postage stamp. Sid is going to make himself known throughout their time here, whether Sam likes it or not. He wishes there was someone he could complain to. Some higher authority. He wishes he could launch Sid into the ocean with a bowling ball tied to his ankle, let him sink inevitably to the floor of the deep sea. He wonders if Maanav could help with this. Maanav said he could assist with anything. Maybe Maanav and Sharif, given that he only has one guest to attend to now, and Hakim?

Where is Hakim? Sam hasn't seen him around the property since that first night. Wasn't Sid going to wrangle him for questioning?

In any case, short of ending Sid alone or with the help of Sid's employees, who surely hate the guy's guts as much as Sam does, he has little choice but to run out the clock. They have five more nights at Jala. What's the worst that can happen over the course of five nights?

He scoffs at himself for the thought. First a death (or a murder?), now some smarmy GM attempting to woo his wife. Maybe Kevin was right, this place ought to come with a warning label. Maybe Sam should write a review on TripAdvisor.

"I was texting with Sid," Sarah says, "and he said he can try to get us an omakase reservation on our last night, if you still want to do the whole thing."

So now his wife and the GM are texting behind his back. Great. He reaches for his wine, takes another swig. The sake sits beside it, untouched.

"I know you're upset," she adds, placing a hand on his back. It makes him feel about two feet tall, her tone, her whole attitude toward him. "But we're still having sushi, aren't we? It's kind of nice, sitting at the bar, not having to sit through the whole fussy spiel."

Again, she knows that he likes the "fussy spiel." Patronizing him is not the way to his heart.

"I can't read your mind, Sam," she says. Her voice loses its softness, her hand drops. "If you don't use your words, I can't help."

It's "use your words" that sets him off.

"What is there to talk about?" he says. It comes out harsher than he means for it to, but he has lost the ability to modulate. "We're doing what you wanted to do."

"I don't *want* to do this, Sam," she says. "I'm making the best of the situation. You were the one who wanted to come here, to the Maldives."

"Yeah, for a vacation," he says, "not so you can play detective with some shady hotel manager."

"I'm not *playing detective*," she says. Other diners start to turn their heads. The bartender appears absorbed in the cognac glass he's polishing. "Something happened to Krista, and I don't think it's a crime to be curious about the real story. You said you wanted to know what happened, too."

"I only said that because you clearly will not accept no for an answer, just like always," Sam says. "It's your way or the highway. If I don't go along with your plan, you'll start crying and make a scene."

As if on cue, her eyes well.

"I am not *crying*," she says, even as her voice catches.

People are definitely watching them now. He cannot stop the implosion. He is at its center, in a cloud of smoke.

"Sid thinks—" she starts.

The utterance of his name feels like a knife to his gut. Sam whips the cloth napkin from his lap onto his plate, pushes away from the bar, and walks swiftly off.

~

She does not want to cry. Sam does not deserve any more of her tears. But as she stares down at the little blue ceramic dish that previously contained her hamachi nigiri, a single tear rolls down her cheek despite her best efforts.

Then another. She exhales deeply, presses her napkin to her eyes, wills the heat behind their lids to abate.

He is always like this. He is a child. Zero control over his emotions. Actually, he may be even less evolved than a child. She's encountered five-year-olds with more command of their impulses than him. He's a Neanderthal, practically.

It all stems from his father and the anger that Sam carries with him, like one of those hiking backpacks bigger than a torso. He never puts it down, this anger. It's always there, lurking behind them. Even in their best moments, there is the threat that it could all go to hell, because either Sam will start spiraling about his dead-end future in the family business or his dad will actually intervene in the good time they're having, as he did when they were in Italy several summers ago.

The trip had been planned months in advance to Florence and Tuscany, art for her, wine tasting for him, followed by a road trip up north. They were actually in a good place at the time, were thinking they might start trying for children on that very trip. Then, by the pool of Il Sereno, a bowl of spaghetti Bolognese between them and the grandeur of Lake Como beyond, he got a call from his dad. There was a story on some website—Eater, they soon found out—about a bunch of Tiffin's customers reporting debilitating stomach cramps. E. coli in the spinach used to make the restaurant's popular spinach pakoras (as well as several other dishes), but that wasn't the worst of it.

"They're saying we've fallen off," Balraj said. Sam had placed his phone on the chaise lounge and put the call on speaker. His head was in his hands. The glass of Tuscan chardonnay he had ordered twenty minutes prior, when the late-afternoon sun was filtering through the Mediterranean cypress and everything seemed golden and full of hope, sat on the table between them, untouched, a pool of condensation darkening the wood.

"They quote someone saying, 'Tiffin is stuck in the nineties, in the $9.99 lunch buffet era of Indian food.' What's all this about a $9.99 lunch buffet? Our buffet costs $15.99, we'd go bankrupt if it were any less than that."

The problem was not the cost of the lunch buffet, it was the fact that it existed at all. A new breed of American-born Indian chefs had taken the formula cracked by their immigrant parents and run with it, diverting from curry-in-a-hurry fare and delivering fanciful, Indian-inspired dishes with American price points. No member of the demographic Sam wanted to target would trust a $15.99 all-you-can-eat lunch buffet. It signified the restaurant's boomer status, which would've been fine if the food slapped.

But if the food does not slap—even without E. coli in the spinach, Tiffin's chicken tikka masala was a 7 out of 10 at best—you're destined for irrelevance, to descend from hot spot to alternative option to "if we *have* to have Indian" to DoorDash but not even the good kind of DoorDash, because Balraj refused to pay the delivery service the fees that would allow Tiffin into the free-delivery tier. "The customers can pay, nah?" she once overheard him tell Sam at a family dinner at Sam's parents' place, an aging, oft-renovated craftsman in Granada Hills. "Let them deal with the fees if they must order off an app, like some robots."

Balraj believed in obtaining things in person. His favorite place on earth was Costco. Balraj and Chandini went there at least once a week to "get their steps in" if nothing else. (They always got something else.)

Sam drove home from that dinner defeated as usual, his dad having summarily dismissed yet another idea to generate new business—pay a nominal fee to join DoorDash's premium-service-provider tier, reap the benefits of the advertising and promotion that came with it. Riding shotgun, she repeatedly reached out and rubbed his right shoulder, holding space for him to vent. But he kept his eyes stoically on the road, didn't say a word during the twenty-mile drive home to Hollywood.

She sympathized with him. He had been bred to take over Tiffin; he had never had the luxury of dreaming of another line of work, of making something else of his life.

Well—that wasn't true. He had had the idea to start his own restaurant back when they lived in New York. Had come up with a winning concept and a deck for potential investors, even had an ideal space earmarked in the slice of the Lower East Side that would soon become known as Dimes Square.

"Think Balthazar, but Indian," he told Sarah over drinks at Clandestino, the bar next to the space he hoped would soon be rechristened as Daavat Dena, a Hindi expression that translates to "to give a feast."

"It'll be smaller than Balthazar to start, of course," he said excitedly, the flickering candle between them bouncing off his pupils, "but I want that kind of buzzing dining room, that sort of lighting that makes everyone look good, all the dishes you know and love but done right, for people like us, people who appreciate presentation and plating but not at the expense of taste. The type of spot you could go to every week without getting sick of it."

She smiled and nodded, sipped her cocktail, a muddle of gin, elderflower, and mint, and let him go on. It was the height of summer, they had been dating for five months, and she was smitten. She had never seen him so excited about work or really anything, for that matter; she wondered if perhaps he had never been this excited before. It made sense. You would naturally have more enthusiasm for your own vision than someone else's. Sam was the son of an entrepreneur, it followed that he would eventually want to be an entrepreneur himself.

Somehow, Balraj couldn't understand that. Why build a new car when the old Ford runs just fine? And there was only so much Sam could fight. At the end of the day, they were father and son. She couldn't imagine having to go to war with her parents to become who she was.

There was also his inheritance to consider, the trust to which he would one day hold the keys.

When Sam and his father were on the outs, Sarah stuck by Sam's side. She cursed Balraj for not letting Sam spread his own wings in New York or implement the changes that would return the three outposts of Tiffin to their former glory, that would make the collection of restaurants even more glorious. In the privacy of their own home, she was able to say the things Sam would and could not, because he was, at the end of the day, a good Indian boy who obeyed his parents.

Some might have seen this as charming. Sarah saw it as a problem. Because you can't blame your parents forever. At some point, you have to take charge of your own life, and Sam couldn't seem to find it within himself to do that. She told him, several times, that if he wanted to leave the family business, start his own thing, and risk losing his inheritance in the process, she would stand by his side. "You can't be miserable forever," she said. "If we have to sell the house, the cars, if my income has to carry us for a while, it's okay. We'll make it work until you take off."

Did she mean it?

She didn't *not* mean it.

It seemed like the right thing to say, when Sam was all doom and gloom. She wanted him to break off on his own, and she wanted to be supportive. In any case, at the time she made that promise, she also believed that it would never come to that, to her having to carry them on her freelance journalist's income, which was unreliable at best and nonexistent at worst. She also, at that time, felt surer of her talents—maybe she could find work in some other way, maybe if she were forced into the position of provider, she would provide.

But what were the odds of that coming to pass, really? Balraj was, at the end of the day, Sam's father, and he loved his son as best as an Indian man who came of age in the post-partition era could. If Sam has the emotional regulatory system of a toddler, it's because it was passed down to him by his dad, who is similarly prone to outbursts and shutdowns.

Indian moms communicate their love through food. Dads: money and unsolicited advice on how to save and invest it. For men of Balraj's generation, that's just the way it was.

When things were going well in her world, when Sarah allowed herself to dream of a life in which they were both happy, she imagined Sam taking the plunge—breaking away from the family business, forgoing Balraj's financial support. He signed Sam's paychecks, which would come to a halt if Sam quit Tiffin. Back then, Sarah was sure that with her and Sam's combined connections, they could line up investors for his solo project, investors so flush and so willing to give that they'd be able to stay afloat while building out the restaurant. Natalie was always looking for new businesses to back. Alana's boss had an investment fund. There were tons of glittery people in Los Angeles looking to throw money at the next big thing, to plant their flag and say that they recognized genius first.

She and Sam could appeal to the social media Indians, the socialites and Hollywood-adjacent folks that Sarah frequently ran into at events, the type A first generations that escaped their parents' visions of them becoming doctors, lawyers, or engineers and now chronicled their creative careers for all to see, who had legions of followers watching their every move, wanting to be like them.

This is the kind of person Sarah wants to be, perhaps even was, before her fall from grace. These were the people Sarah wanted Sam to socialize with, when she would bring him to events (back when she still got invited to events). Up-and-comers, not just of the South Asian persuasion, but people who had built something from nothing, people who could inspire him.

But reality crept into her imaginings of how things could be, as it always does. The fact is, Sam hates meeting new people. Social anxiety. And back when she was getting invited to events, most of the time, he'd have to go into one of Tiffin's locations to put out some sort of fire, metaphorically and sometimes not. "You go," he'd tell her. "Have a great time. You like those things more than I do, anyway."

It's a problem. If he wants to launch his own restaurant, eventually, he'll have to figure out how to expand his social circle beyond the two dudes he went to high school with who still live in LA—fellow Dodgers fans whom she tolerates on the rare occasions the guys gather to watch a game at their house instead of at the sports bar on Sunset Boulevard. One is an accountant, the other, a dentist. They aren't the type of guys you would call ambitious. They are fine with their lot in life, content. They don't push Sam to be anything he is not. So, like a mouse in a maze, he keeps scurrying along the same, predictable route, hopeful that one day he'll find the cheese, or draining his bank account by placing bets he's so sure will magically unlock a whole trove of cheese, a veritable cheese store.

She realizes these are harsh things to think, given her glaring lack of friends and funds. But her husband *did* just ditch her at dinner.

"May I refresh your sake?" The appearance of the bartender in front of her, frosted black glass bottle held aloft, breaks Sarah out of her spell. "We have a very special Junmai Daiginjo that recently arrived on the island."

Her face must be arranged in a way that suggests she could benefit from a drink, because he doesn't wait for her answer before he begins filling her long-empty cup, ceramic and handmade by the looks of it, blue and black with a delicate fluted lip. "You might taste notes of green apple, peach, and just a hint of white pepper," he says. He places the bottle in front of her and reaches over to pick up her hamachi plate. She looks at the label. Divine Droplets. She takes a sip. The liquid feels silky, sliding down her throat.

"Divine indeed," she says.

"May I offer you anything else to eat?" The concern in his voice is sandwiched by one of the hallmarks of high-end hospitality, the directive to anticipate what your guest wants before they know it themselves. "Perhaps a yellowfin tuna handroll or an order of shiitake gyoza? The gyoza are my personal favorite. The sauce they come with?" He curls one hand into the chef's kiss emoji. "Paired with this sake, you may well see God."

She lets out a little laugh to show that she appreciates his efforts.

Prior to Sam's blowup, she thought that she could use this opportunity, sitting at the bar of Osaka, to ask this bartender about Hakim—surely, all the bartenders knew each other. But now? She is no longer in an inquisitive mood. While she could eat more (she could always eat more), there is no sign that Sam is coming back, nor does she really want him to, and since every person in Osaka is aware of what a horrible evening she's having, she would prefer to close this chapter, move on to the next.

"I think I'm all set, but thank you. Do I have to sign anything?"

The bartender smiles and nods, understanding. "No, ma'am. It's on the house. May I call for a buggy for you?"

"That would be great," she says, stepping down from her high-top chair.

"Back to bungalow no. 7, is it?" the bartender asks, phone in hand.

"Actually," she says, "I think I'll go to the staff bar."

~

Seated in the back of a buggy, Sam finds it weird that, in theory, anyone can go to the staff bar. It's not under lock and key, there's no password to get in. Presumably, the staff know who's been invited and who has not, and maybe that's how they make sure no interlopers crash, though why would there be any interlopers? Management must be aware of everyone on the island, it's not as if a bunch of rogue bandits from elsewhere could roll up by speedboat in the dark of the night (Sam doesn't think).

It's probably also safe to assume that no one paying thousands of dollars per night (or the equivalent in credit card points) wants to drink at a bar in the middle of the island, deep inside the jungle, with no view of the sea, no view of anything at all.

Rumbling down the main path, the buggy cruises past the Ayurvedic spa, from which an older couple, swathed in bathrobes, emerges, arms interlocked at the elbows. They each hold up a hand in greeting, and he waves back, wonders what treatment they just had, wonders whether he will ever see the inside of that spa, whether four hands could relieve him of his current level of stress.

Certainly, four hands wouldn't hurt.

As the buggy turns in from the circular path linking the venues where Jala's guests while away their sun-drenched days and moonlit nights, the uplights between the palm trees and undergrowth grow scanty. The resort's interior is for people who work here, and apparently, they do not get to benefit from romantic lighting or much lighting of any kind at all.

The buggy comes to an abrupt halt in front of a modest two-story compound; the driver announces "Here!" in an overly jaunty way. Sam lurches forward and reflexively grabs the iron bar between him and the driver, nearly snapping the stem of the half-full glass of wine in his hand. Pussy, he thinks to himself, about himself. He needs to be more of a man. Not the man Sarah wants him to be, some two-bit Sherlock Holmes, but more aggressive, more of a no-bullshit type. He feels like he's been accepting a lot of bullshit, more than he deserves.

As if to assert his manhood, he chugs the remainder of the wine in his glass and shoves it into one of the buggy's cupholders. An extra dose of liquid courage can't hurt, but he shouldn't even think of it like that. Liquid ammunition. Like steroids for his personality.

He was in the men's restroom at Osaka when her text message pinged onto his phone.

Going to the staff bar. Good night.

Good night? WTF? Was she going to *sleep* at the staff bar? Was she going to *sleep with* that motherfucking general manager under his goddamn nose?

In the bathroom, where he was, by the way, doing nothing, simply sitting on a Toto toilet and rotting his brain with social media, avoiding his feelings like dirty laundry piled up in a hamper, he decided that he had two choices. Say nothing. Let her go. Silent treatment. Push off the inevitable second, third, fifth chapter of this fight—he's lost count—until later tonight or tomorrow, whenever she decides to return to the bungalow.

Or he could reply and get into it now, commence the firing of vicious missives. He could be all "You're selfish, you don't appreciate anything I do," she could be all "I didn't want to come here, you made me," and that could devolve into a showdown featuring new spins on their greatest hits, because like snowflakes, no two are ever alike. She would bring up his anger issues vis-à-vis his father, something like "It's not my fault you haven't become the man you hoped to be." He would say that she will never understand, à la "You knew my deal when we got married. If you want out, get out, divorce me, leave me alone—I'll probably be happiest that way, alone."

Is that true? He doesn't know. He cannot imagine life without her because she breathed light into his, changed the depth of his shadows, made all the colors shine bright. Letting her go, losing her, would be like shutting off the sun. He can't quite envision who he would be, what would happen.

They cannot keep arguing like this, at least, he cannot. It takes too much out of him, to be at war with his wife as well as his dad. A man can only fight so many battles at once.

He realized, in the bathroom of Osaka, that he had a third option. Say nothing and show up at the staff bar. Even better—say nothing, grab a glass of wine to go (he loves a roadie), *then* show up at the staff bar. Good way to see what's really going on with this general manager, if he was putting the moves on his wife or what.

There was also no way he would be able to sleep at bungalow no. 7 or smoke hookah at Riva—something he had been looking forward to ever since seeing that couple poolside with the pineapple bowl earlier in the afternoon—knowing that she was at the staff bar, canoodling with *him*, that son of a bitch Sid. He wouldn't be able to think of anything else.

Decision made, he stayed on the Toto toilet ten minutes longer, to give her some lead time. How embarrassing it would've been to emerge from the restroom and see her, to have to explain. Better to just roll up, nonchalant, as if this was always the plan—she'd head there first, from Osaka, he'd meet her soon after.

Now, the driver hops out of the buggy and leads him down a walkway fringed by palm fronds. Sam sees, as he gets closer, that what appeared to be one compound is actually two separate buildings, both with long rectangular windows, many of which are illuminated from within. "This is our canteen," the driver says, throwing his hand one way, "and this is our staff gym." He gestures to the other side. Through the glass walls, which are fogged with condensation, Sam is pretty sure he sees the dosa chef from breakfast, in a black T-shirt and basketball shorts, grinding out a set of chest presses.

"I will do my exercise later," the driver says to him, smiling and patting his gently protruding midsection. "I say that every day!" And then he laughs heartily.

Sam's mood lifts a little, thanks to this driver. Maybe it's all in his head, this flirtation between the general manager and his wife. Maybe the guy genuinely wants their help in figuring out what transpired outside of bungalow 17 the other night. Maybe he's not the con artist Sam is almost certain he is.

Maybe he himself has overreacted. Maybe.

The driver leads the way down a zigzagging staircase that opens up to an expansive square patio strung with market lights. On one end is a long bar stocked with well liquor, not the top-shelf stuff that populates the rest of Jala's bars. People are hanging out in threes and fours, lit cigarettes dangling from their fingertips, hands around longnecks of beer and tall cocktail glasses. High-top tables and barstools are scattered about.

"And this here is our staff bar," the driver says with pride. "I recommend the daily special." He pauses; Sam senses the approach of a punch line.

"Drink until you're numb!" The driver throws his head back, cackling.

Sam laughs as well, more at the absurdity of this aging brown uncle advocating that he get blackout drunk than at the joke. If it's even a joke. He'd probably get blackout drunk every day as well if he had to deal with the spoiled jerks who populated Jala.

Overheard at breakfast, a woman in tennis whites badgering a uniformed hostess: "Are you sure there's not *another* breakfast restaurant? An American one with *organic* fruit?"

The hostess had patiently explained that there was a variety of American cuisine on offer at the one and only breakfast restaurant, Veranda, "and all of the fruit we serve is organic—some is grown on property, in fact."

"Well then, why aren't there any organic stickers?" Tennis Whites demanded. "How do I *know* if there's no sticker?"

This is why the rest of the world hates us, Sam thought. Because some Americans would rather have their fruit processed and slapped with plastic than trust what comes off a tree.

"Bottoms up!" the driver says, then turns around.

"Hey, buddy," Sam calls after him, pawing through his pockets. He finds a five-dollar bill. "Thanks for the ride," he says, pressing it into the driver's palm. The driver flashes him a grin.

"Kind sir," he says, "may your every wish come true."

If only, Sam thinks, scanning the crowd. He sees a Veranda breakfast server and a Riva pool attendant, but no Sarah. A housekeeping manager and a reception clerk, but no Sarah.

Finally, he spots her in a corner, in conversation with—who else—the general manger. Whatever fleeting sense he had that Sid might've been a good guy melts like ice on a ledge. The hem of Sarah's silk robe, a beach cover-up she threw on over her jeans and bodysuit, billows in the breeze, gives her away. Sid's back is toward him, so he can't see Sarah's face in full, but he can read her body language, the way she's moving her hands as she speaks, pausing every now and again to touch her neck or tuck a lock of hair behind her ear.

She's having a good time.

He feels the sensation of a stone dropping deep into his center.

Playing on a Bluetooth speaker the size of a soda can is an insufferable EDM remix of a Fleetwood Mac song. It also populates the airwaves back home. Sam hears it all the time when he's driving and can't change the station fast enough. A sudden urge to run overtakes him, an urge to run straight into the ocean and let it subsume him, forget this whole sorry mess of a life, a mess that okay *maybe* he had a hand in making but does not want to now clean up. It's too complicated, it's too fraught, and he feels he's not adequately equipped to handle that task. He needs the emotional equivalent of a hazmat suit.

Sarah's singsong laughter cuts through an auto-tuned Stevie Nicks. He has to go over there. He has to fight for his wife. Or at least for his pride, what shred of it he has left.

He strides purposefully through the fray, nodding at folks here and there, faces he recognizes from around the property but can't hope to place now that they're off the clock and wearing neither their name tags nor their uniforms.

Sid is talking animatedly as Sam approaches, something about someone who insisted on piloting their personal helicopter onto the island, even though it would've been faster to take the Jala plane. "Can you imagine?" Sid is saying. "The idiocy."

Sarah's eyes shift to Sam, but before she can say anything, he slings his arm around Sid's neck, effectively putting him in a headlock.

He's taller than Sid by an inch or two. At least there's that.

"What's up, party people?" Sam says with false enthusiasm. He unfolds his arm and kneads Sid's shoulder, not so much pressing as pinching his flesh. "How's it hanging?" Sarah blinks at him blankly.

Sid wrests himself out of Sam's grip and turns to face him and Sarah, so they form a triangle. "Just regaling Sarah here with tales about some of our high-maintenance guests."

"Is that right? You know, my wife and I—we've been married five years, by the way, we're here for our wedding anniversary, but you already knew that—anyway, my wife and I have seen some *crazy* characters during our travels. Real batshit stuff. Babe, remember that couple in Lake Como, the ones who got drunk and ran their Riva boat into the dock?"

She frowns. "What does that have to do with anything?"

What it has to do with is that we have a rich and textured history, unlike you and this ethically bankrupt hotel manager, Sam thinks. The guy may be in better shape than him, but Sam's got height on his side, and in subcontinental culture, height is very important indeed. He could get in shape if he wanted to. He could get in shape tomorrow.

What's Sid going to do, go to China and get his knees broken and do that experimental surgery where they graft bone onto your femurs? People have died doing that.

It's not a bad idea. Maybe Sam should suggest it to Sid.

He sees that Sarah's holding a glass of something ruby colored.

"Negroni?" he asks.

"Mezcal Negroni," she replies. "Sid brought some of the good stuff from the rum hut."

"I'll try one," Sam says.

"A mezcal Negroni? You hate mezcal and Negronis," Sarah says.

Sam shrugs. "If it's the good stuff, maybe I'll feel different." He looks at the rocks glass in Sid's hand. "What are you drinking, boss?"

"Clase Azul Durango mezcal, neat," he says. "One of one. Gotta stay sharp, what with Kevin on the warpath, seeking vengeance for an accident. As if there's someone to blame."

"Huh," Sam says. "Didn't know that Clase Azul made mezcal."

"You can't be serious," Sarah says. "I wrote that whole story. I went to Oaxaca. They sent me a bottle, and you said it smelled like gasoline, remember?"

"Well, sure, all mezcal smells like gasoline," Sam says, "but I didn't actually taste it." On impulse, he grabs the glass out of Sid's hand and overturns it above his mouth, lets a half shot of the clear liquid slide down his throat. It feels like swallowing one of those sparklers you light on the Fourth of July. Abhorrent.

"Hope you don't mind, bro," Sam says, holding the now-empty glass out for Sid to take. "You just made it sound so good." The words tumble out of his mouth before he really thinks about them. "Why don't we do a shot together? You wanna get this round? I'll get the next."

Sid widens his eyes at him but says nothing. He hears Sarah mutter something to the effect of "What the fuck," but he's not looking at Sarah. He's looking at Sid, who appears to be assessing him in a way he has not before. Making some kind of calculation.

"But of course," Sid finally says, pressing his lips into a tight smile. "May I offer you anything else?"

"Got any snacks? Doritos or something?"

"We may have some nut mix," Sid says. "I'll be back."

"What in the actual hell is wrong with you?" Sarah hisses, once Sid has left.

"What is wrong with *you*?" Sam scoffs. "Leaving dinner like that, forcing me to meet you here?"

"*You* were the one that left dinner to begin with," Sarah retorts, "and no one forced you. I said good night and I meant it. You embarrassed me at the restaurant, and you're embarrassing me now. You're embarrassing yourself."

"Don't talk about who's embarrassing who," Sam shoots back. "Do you know how you look, flirting with this scumbag?" Sam didn't mean to say that Sarah was flirting, but he doesn't know how else to describe it. He sees all the signs—the laughing, the fingers through the hair, the way she bubbles in interactions with Sid, practically effervescent, which is all the more noticeable given that she has all the fizziness of week-old Pepsi whenever she deigns to interact with him.

He doesn't know how to cope with the fear and insecurity that's coursing through him, and now that he and Sarah are firing their opening shots, the rage he felt in the Japanese restaurant has reignited, feels almost hotter, thanks, perhaps, to the wine he drank at dinner and the roadie he took with him on the way to the staff bar and the half shot of mezcal he's had just now.

He hates the stuff, for sure, but the mezcal on top of everything else is fueling the fire inside of him, and he realizes he wants to pour gasoline on top of it, throw caution to the wind. Why not? He is tired of attempting to appease Sarah, make Sarah happy, wondering, What will Sarah think, say? How does Sarah feel? He is sick of trying to save their marriage while she tries to destroy it. If she wants to fight dirty, he will fight dirty.

"I am not *flirting* with him, Sam," she is saying. "I'm sorry that the nuances of adult relationships go over your head. Actually, no, I'm not sorry, because it's not my fault—you don't stand up to your father, you barely stand up to your employees, and you refuse to make new friends or go to any place where that might happen, so I guess you wouldn't know how men and women interact platonically."

"I've got news for you, babe," Sam says, shaking his head and letting out a bitter laugh. "No grown man is friends with a woman that he doesn't want to fuck."

She looks incredulous and says as much.

"Look," Sam says, "if you want to leave me for a hotel manager in the Maldives, go right ahead. I can promise you, though, you won't be happy. Not for one minute. You'll be bored after a week. And broke, too. You want seven-star trips around the world? You're not going to get it from him."

"What are you even saying?" Sarah presses her hand to her forehead, gives him a look of total bewilderment. "I didn't ask for this trip. *You* made us go. And why are you bringing up money? Why is it always about money with you?"

Sam can no longer hear the music. He is dimly aware that heads have turned in their direction. Perhaps all the heads at the staff bar.

"Do you know, Sam, that there's more to life than money?" Sarah goes on. "That's your problem, you're so fixated on how much things *cost*, how much everyone around you is *making*, how much you don't *have*, how much you could make if this team wins by three and that team loses by two and—"

"Earth to Sarah!" His voice is louder than he'd like it to be, but he has lost control. He's like a Bluetooth speaker that's been turned up too high, blaring. Some part of him registers that he's gone to that dark place where nothing good happens, where good things go to die.

"It's *all* about money. The *only thing* that matters is money. You know who really hammered it home to me? Kevin. Good ol' Kevin, the guy you want me to be, because you think that'll save us, if I'm some rich entrepreneur. But news flash—I can't save you, because you have a problem. You're stuck in this fantasy land where all that matters—literally, *all* that matters—is what Natalie thinks, what Alana thinks, what these random women you barely know in real life think about you. And for what? What will their endorsement do? Make you feel like a cool girl? Is that the person you've become? Because the woman I fell in love with didn't need internet strangers for validation, that woman was a badass, but you, you spend all day on your phone doing what? Hoping they'll see you're online and invite you to a party?"

Sarah throws her hand over her mouth, as if to hold back a sob. Talk about dramatic. This is what always happens—he tries to make a point, she starts crying. You can't reason with a woman who's crying.

Is he being too harsh? The alcohol has muddled his mind. Maybe. Possibly. Who's to say?

If he is being too harsh, could it possibly be because she is flirting with someone who is not him?

Even his alcohol-muddled mind can connect those dots.

She is calling him cruel when Sid returns, rushing back; behind him, another staffer carries a tray laden with drinks. Sid plants himself between them, as if to referee. "Please, I know it's been a trying day, but there is no need for all of this."

Sam turns to Sid, the source of his ire. Well, not the full source. A significant part is Sarah. But the way he sees it, through his wine-and-mezcal-tinted glasses, while Sid may have exacerbated a problem that long predates him, he exacerbated it nonetheless, continues to exacerbate it by stealing away, first to the rum hut and now to the staff bar, with Sam's wife and regaling her with stories of asshole oligarchs past.

Sam says nothing, reaches for one of the shot glasses on the tray, and throws it back. An even bigger burn this time; it's like swallowing a flamethrower. Absolutely awful.

He feels the eyes of everyone on the patio. He feels the need to win.

He stares down Sid as he reaches for the mezcal Negroni. He takes a swig and sets it on the high-top behind him.

"You know what?" Sam says, closing the gap between him and Sid.

"What?" Sid replies, taking a step forward.

Sam takes in what happens next in frames, like stills of a film.

His fist hitting Sid's cheek.

Sid's much stronger fist hitting his cheek.

The sound of glass shattering.

A trio of security guards, rushing in from nowhere, dragging him away.

Sarah screaming, "What is *wrong* with you?"

A buggy ride with a bag of ice pressed to his face, the bumps of the boardwalk reverberating through the bones of his cheek.

A guard unlocking the door of bungalow No. 7.

A packet of pills, instructions to swallow them with a glassful of water.

His head on the pillow. A pillow as soft as a cloud.

A dark and dreamless sleep. The kind of sleep from which he might never wake up.

ELEVEN

Sarah heard about Sam's temper back in college. There were stories about him punching holes in walls at parties and getting into drunk fights in front of the late-night pizza place, stories of debatable veracity because the people telling them had also been inebriated, weren't the most trustworthy of sources. Sarah and Sam weren't close back then, but they moved in the same circle of first-generation immigrant kids, and word got around that circle quick. "Did you hear Sam got arrested last night?" "I heard he got his license taken away." "His parents might pull him out of school, how embarrassing, can you even imagine?"

Sarah listened but did not quite believe these stories. Sam remained as constant a presence as ever, tooling around campus in an Audi coupe with California license plates. In her few one-on-one interactions with him, he had struck her as kind and charming, if a bit highfalutin. (He refused to drink anything but Grey Goose, which may have made him the most discerning twenty-one-year-old in the nation.) In another life, had they not already been coupled up with partners who were wary of them hanging out with each other—what did those exes know that Sam and Sarah did not?—she might've been interested in him. Like everyone in their circle, he mellowed after graduation. The real world demanded decorum and consistency. You couldn't go around punching holes in walls (even allegedly) and expect to get anywhere in life. By the time Sarah and Sam reconnected, when she was working as an entertainment journalist and he was at the fancy restaurant in the Time Warner building, feeding her gossip, he seemed to have figured out how to tame whatever fire he contained, how to make it work for him.

Or maybe that's just the story she'd told herself. Because there was, of course, that time at Heathrow where he got so drunk he couldn't board the plane, when he stumbled into the podium at the boarding gate, sending a sheaf of papers flying. A little piece of her died of embarrassment, of being associated with him, in that moment.

Then there was the time in Maui where he got in a fight at the hotel bar with a fellow guest who he claimed had called him something racist.

It ended with Sam being dragged out by hotel security and cut off from ordering alcohol for the remainder of their stay. Sam said he was the victim and expected Sarah to feel sorry for him. She couldn't help but wonder—if Sam was the victim, why was he the one who was dragged out and cut off? Why was she having to order glasses of wine that she then decanted into a S'well bottle from which he swigged from morning until night?

It was mortifying, all of it. Not to mention the fact that she was in Maui for work, to profile a local hotshot chef for *Panache*, and Sam had tagged along. It should've been easy to turn her work trip into a vacation for them, but because he'd acted out on night one, she spent the rest of their stay worrying about what people at the hotel (where the chef worked) thought of her, whether they thought Sam was a crazy drunk. Did they gossip about them? Did they pity her?

That incident was what first drove them to couples therapy. Sam paid out of pocket for three sessions, then stopped, on account of how much it cost and how it took away from time he felt would be better spent at work. Six months ago, after Sarah caught wind of the text messages from Elaine, they began seeing Margaret again.

It occurred to her later that her assignment might've set something off in Sam. The chef was exactly who Sam wanted to be—someone who had taken over a family business and turned it from a tired takeout joint into the hottest table in town. It was very possible Sam was envious and didn't know how to deal, so he drank, and a bottle and a half of Whispering Angel after a five-hour flight succeeded in bringing out his dark side, the side that gets into bar fights and shouting matches with strangers.

But what was she supposed to do? Babysit him? Monitor his intake? Clip her wings so that he could cope?

That was years ago. By now, five years into their marriage, she thought they had turned the page on that chapter of their relationship, the one that appeared airbrushed but was marred with glaringly ugly blemishes—a blowup in the Bahamas, slammed doors in Spain. They were practically middle-aged. They were too old to fight like this.

But once again, she had underestimated his capacity to humiliate her. Decking a general manager was a new low.

Could she be blamed for wanting to leave him? It wasn't easy, being single over a certain age (being single at any age, some might say)—she knew that, but she couldn't stand for his behavior any longer. She had spent so much time thinking she could fix him. Maybe if they went to therapy, maybe if he meditated, maybe if she casually texted him an invitation to this really good meditation app she liked, maybe he would get the hint, maybe his dad would actually give him the business, maybe he would grow up, maybe, maybe, maybe.

Maybe not.

It wasn't her job to form him. To make him conform. To imbue him with manners and a sense of self-worth. To make him feel loved and cared for and worthy.

Well—maybe that was part of her job. As someone who loved him—the person she married, not the monster who drinks beyond his means and goes off the rails. And Sam was right about at least one thing he spewed in that whole, tired tirade. She has a problem, but the problem is being this pillar of support for him when he continues to let her down.

Did she also have a problem with wanting to be liked? Didn't everyone, on some level, want to be liked?

At the staff bar, seated at a high-top table, the tears on her face just about dry, she very briefly closes her eyes. Sam has been carted away; Sid has gone to fetch water. She wants a moment to collect herself, one moment, an interlude of peace to figure out what's next.

"Your favorite." Sid's voice comes to her as if from a dream. She opens her eyes. He's standing beside her with a silver tray, bearing a frosty bottle of Pellegrino. The large size.

"How did you know?" she asks, unscrewing the top and taking a swig out of the bottle. She has never understood why other countries insist on pouring fizzy beverages into glasses. That's how you lose bubbles. And they say Americans are horrible at conservation. Americans swig Budweiser from the bottle, no questions asked.

"It's a GM's job to know what guests order," Sid says, shrugging.

"You guys actually keep track of that?" Sarah says.

"Of course. You're Pellegrino and black coffee, extra strong. And Clase Azul Durango mezcal, of course."

She smiles in spite of herself. "Impressive," she says. She wonders if Sam could recite her favorite beverages with such certainty and accuracy. He probably thinks she drinks skim milk.

Sid looks at her, taking in her puffy eyes, her air of disarray. "Would you like to get out of here?" he says.

She nods. "Very much."

"Come," he says, cocking his head in the direction of the staff quarters. He gave her a brief tour when she arrived at the staff bar, which now feels like a week ago. She follows him, keeping her eyes down, knowing that everyone on the patio is watching them. She wonders if it's against the rules for Sid to be so solicitous with a guest. But, given that there's no person of higher rank on the property, perhaps he gets to make his own rules.

And perhaps, as she's previously suspected, she's not the typical guest.

She follows him up the zigzagging stairs; he holds open the big swinging door to the staff quarters. They climb up a floor and head down a long hallway, all the while silent. It's as if they both know there is something vaguely (or not so vaguely) wrong about them going off together. A violation of the laws that govern guest-staff conduct, a violation of Sarah's marriage.

But is it? It's not like they're *doing* anything. Not like they're having an affair. What physical contact have they had, besides an accidental brush of fingertips? You can't base an affair on an accidental brush of fingertips.

She realizes she has no idea if Sid is married, single, in a relationship, or what. He doesn't wear a wedding band, but then, a lot of men in this part of the world don't, wedding bands being a Western convention that hasn't totally taken hold.

The staff quarters remind her of a college dormitory. Nicer decor—the floor is carpeted in Jala's signature dusty rose; the walls are papered with a texture that evokes rattan—but the quarters are similarly close together. Several doors are thrown open, revealing bunk beds and rooms smaller than the walk-in closet in the bungalow she's sharing with Sam.

Sam. She wonders, in spite of herself, if he made it back to the bungalow okay.

She tells herself not to care. He's hijacked enough of her night, her life.

Eyes look up from devices and books, turning in their direction as they pass. Sid nods curtly every now and again, like a visiting dignitary. She is guessing, from his body language, that he doesn't bring resort guests up here often. He also seems nervous, somewhat ill at ease.

They pass a kitchenette that looks a lot like the one she used in college to warm up Lean Cuisine pizzas and Amy's bean-and-cheese burritos. A staff member she recalls seeing in Veranda is pouring boiling water into a cup of instant noodles. The staffer's eyes flick up as they pass and widen as they meet Sarah's.

It's as if the staffer is issuing a warning, woman to woman.

Does Sid do this often?

Is he nervous because he's going to kill her?

Did he also kill Krista?

The thoughts come to her as if from nowhere. But why would he kill her, and why would he kill Krista? He's the top boss of a resort that, if what Kevin said at breakfast is true, is about to be acquired by Hyland.

Unless Sid is trying to sabotage the acquisition.

Maybe he would've stood to gain had Hyland not swooped in. Maybe he would've been promoted. King of the Maldives, or the hospitality industry equivalent.

But why is her brain going to this place? Isn't it possible that Sid is just a nice guy who got punched in the face by her drunk, out-of-control husband, who could tell that she was reeling? Who wanted to give her a place to gather her thoughts while providing pleasant, platonic company?

She thinks about what Sam said, that no grown man is friends with a woman he doesn't want to fuck.

Was there truth to that?

"Here we are," says Sid. They've reached the end of the hallway. He pulls a brass key with a jagged edge out of his pocket and turns it in the lock of the door. "Welcome to my humble abode."

The room is four times the size of the other quarters. Maybe bigger. It actually looks like bungalow no. 7, except, of course, it's not over the water. There is a canopied queen bed and an en suite bathroom; a sitting area and floor-to-ceiling corner windows that lead to a wraparound terrace furnished with two chairs and a small table. Next to the sitting area is a bar cart identical to the one that's in her room—rose gold, mirrored, only this one is holding full-size bottles instead of the pint-size ones provided by in-room dining.

There's a bag of banana chips on top. Sid ambles over and tears them open, shakes some out into a wooden bowl the size and shape of a cupped palm. He sets it on the coffee table in the sitting area, which is adjacent to what Sarah realizes is a loveseat.

That dreadful word again, "love."

"What can I offer you? Tea, coffee, perhaps some wine? Afraid we don't have the Durango here, but I can certainly call down to the staff bar and have them bring it up if that's what you'd like, it'll only take a moment."

"Tea sounds great," she says, even though she doesn't really like tea. She wants to give him something to do, something to keep him occupied. Something to shut him up, if only for a minute, while she thinks.

"Would you prefer chamomile, English Breakfast, Ceylon, green, Sencha—"

"Chamomile is great," she interrupts. Once again, as when they first discovered that Krista was missing, Sid's solicitousness bothers her. Just get on with it, dude. Or is it a tactic? Is he trying to overwhelm her with minor details so that she won't see the big picture?

But what would that be? Maybe she's just paranoid. The guy's only making tea, after all. How duplicitous can a man in possession of TAZO's entire catalog be?

As Sid empties a bottle of Acqua Panna into one of those electric kettles with the long gooseneck, Sarah privately assesses the contents of his room. There's a record player and a stack of jazz records—Miles Davis, Stan Getz, Charles Mingus. There's a bulletin board on one wall rife with thumbtacked photos; she moves toward it to get a closer look. In one corner, Sid with the Pyramids of Giza; in another, Sid with the Coliseum in Rome. There's a postcard of Capri and another of Big Ben.

Then there's a photo of Sid in a suit, beaming and proud amid other besuited men and one woman. A woman she recognizes as April Hyland. Sarah would know that long blond ponytail anywhere; April was famous for hitting people in the face with it when she would go clubbing in the early aughts. She had been a legendary party girl, and as an entertainment reporter, Sarah had chronicled a lot of her foibles. A wardrobe malfunction here, an over-the-top instance of PDA there. Since then, she had matured into a juggernaut in her own right. April's Hy-Life home goods line was a Target mainstay; Sarah liked her gardenia-scented all-purpose cleaning spray enough that she bought it when the bottle sent by Hy-Life's PR agency ran dry. April had a husband and two children, ages four and two. And with the passing of her father—he'd lived a good life, he was ninety-eight—she now had Hyland. Her younger sister wasn't involved in the family business, busy overseeing a thriving fashion line of her own.

Following her ascension to Hyland's C-suite, *Businessweek* had profiled April, who had spoken about taking the company to new heights.

"Of course, we've always been known as a business traveler's best friend," she had said, "but it's time for us to show what we can do in the world of ultra-luxury resorts." Hyland had new projects underway in Hawaii, Mexico, and the Caribbean, but, April had noted, "we're also shopping. You know how I *love* to shop. There are some pretty spectacular properties in markets where we don't yet operate, and my father taught me that, under the right circumstances, acquiring an existing gem is the smartest thing you can do."

Jala for sure qualified as an existing gem. And this photo all but proved that what Kevin had said at breakfast was true.

"Is that April Hyland?" Sarah asks now.

"Ah, that," says Sid, looking up from his preparation of the tea. "I might've taken that down had I known I'd be having company, given that the news is not yet public. But, yes." He smiles in a self-satisfied way. "As they say, the rumors are true."

"Exciting," Sarah says, without a hint of enthusiasm.

"You know, it is," Sid says, removing the now steaming teakettle from its base. "It's great for Jala, of course, but selfishly, I'm excited about the opportunity to get off this godforsaken island. Transfers will be much easier once we're part of the Hyland portfolio."

"Really?" Sarah is surprised. Island life seems to suit Sid. Big fish, small pond. He seems to like lording over people, tromping around like he owns the place.

"Ten years in the Maldives and you'll tire of the blues, too," says Sid. "I actually dream of London fog, New York snow. Not that I've ever seen snow in New York—I haven't yet made it to the States."

"Then you should know that snow in New York is not at all romantic," she says, and immediately curses herself. Why did she have to say that word, "romantic"?

Does she like him?

He's objectively attractive, for sure. But she realizes now, seeing him in his element, that he's almost too self-assured. Borderline arrogant.

"Is that right?" he says. Snow, right, they're talking about snow in New York. He keeps his eyes on the tea bag he's dunking over and over again in a porcelain cup identical to the ones in the guest rooms, one that looks fit for a dollhouse.

"It's gross," she goes on. "It's pretty when it's coming down, initially, but then it piles up on the sides of the road and turns black and melts into slush that gets into your boots, no matter how high and waterproof they are."

"Well, perhaps I can be lucky enough to witness the pretty part," he says, approaching her now with the cup and saucer.

Saucers. She doesn't get them. Like fancy coasters, only heavier and laden with spoons that always end up falling off, clattering to the floor.

"Do you have plans to go to New York?" she asks, accepting the cup and saucer, not knowing how to refuse the latter.

"Once the ink is dry on the deal, yes," he says. He turns around, fetches his own cup and saucer, and comes back to face her. "Might I meet you there?"

He takes a sip from his cup, his eyes watching hers over the rim. "Might I meet you there?" Is he asking her out? Is he testing the waters, seeing how far he can go?

Doesn't he know she lives in Los Angeles? But everyone outside of the US, especially those who've never been, thinks that it's easy to go between New York and Los Angeles and Dallas and Phoenix and all the rest. These people and their cute little countries, with their government-funded railways and dinky border crossings. They have no idea how big and messy America is, what a clusterfuck it contains.

And anyway, that's not the detail to fixate on.

The detail to fixate on, she realizes as she meets Sid's eyes, is that he wants her. Quite clearly.

Does she want him?

What does she want?

"I don't," she begins, not sure where she's going.

He takes a step closer to her.

"I," she starts again.

He takes another step.

Suddenly, a clatter. Her teacup falls sideways, spilling hot liquid all over her hands. The saucer falls to the floor, as she always knew it would.

A mess. She's suddenly made a very big mess.

~

The pounding in his head feels like a jackhammer pulverizing cement. Attempting to pulverize, more accurately, because if the pounding had actually done what a jackhammer could do, he would be blissfully unconscious, no longer able to feel pain, which sounds pretty appealing right about now at, what—he turns over his phone, bashes his thumb against the screen so he can check the time—6:07 a.m.

He has no idea what time he came back to the bungalow. He has no memory of returning. Seeing a torn-open pill packet next to a half-drunk bottle of Acqua Panna, it starts coming back to him. The buggy ride, the security guards.

The punch.

The punch . . . es? Plural?

Oh God, the punches.

Fucking roided-up hotel manager. But even as he thinks it, he knows it wasn't entirely Sid's fault. Sid never would have clocked him if Sam hadn't hit him first, but what else could Sam do? How else to assert his manhood, the fact that Sid had intruded on his territory. And yes, he knew that Sarah was not a piece of *land*, she was not property to be *owned*, but was it not true that Sarah was *his*, in the sense of . . . proprietary-ness, or something?

His brain isn't working.

Worse than the pain in his face is the tightness in his chest. Anxiety. He knows this feeling all too well, the morning-after panic, the price one pays for the dopamine spike brought on by a proper night out.

Except last night wasn't a proper night out. It was the worst kind of night, filled with fights of all kinds and forcible removal. And mezcal—damn that fucking mezcal, damn it to hell. *That's* why he got so heated, he realizes now, it was that wretched lighter fluid masquerading as liquor. He never acts like this when he sticks to wine. He should just stick to wine.

Or cut it all out. Because he is sick of waking up consumed with regret. Even the finest bottle of Bordeaux is not worth it if it unlocks this ugly, evil side of him, someone who hurts the ones he loves and injures himself in the process.

His mouth feels dry and parched, craggy like the inside of a rock. He wants his electrolyte drink. He wants Sarah to make him his electrolyte drink. He knows that he is wrong to want this, given that he has likely made her madder than she has ever been at him, but this is the nature of love and marriage. It often doesn't make sense.

People who hadn't been married thought that marriage was about the big wedding, but it's really about all the other moments, from the mundane to the tear-your-hair-out frustrating. It's about all the times you want to leave but don't, about seeing the worst in your other half and sticking by their side despite what you've witnessed.

The electrolyte packages are somewhere. What about her?

He knows in his heart she hasn't texted, but he picks up his phone and looks anyway, just in case.

Heart, one. Head, zero.

He crumples back under the covers, defeated, slides down so that the duvet reaches the bottom of his eyes. He lets his phone drop to the floor. He doesn't need it. The only thing he needs, the only *person* he needs, is the one person he's pushed away, who is, for all he knows, in the arms of the general manager of the most romantic resort in the world, a general manager who should *definitely* be fired, if not crucified or shot.

Sam would like to ruin Sid's life. Short of murder, he wonders how he can do this. If this Hyland acquisition is for real, can he file an anonymous complaint?

But why anonymous? Why not say it with his chest?

Because he's embarrassed. Because then he'll have to admit that he let his wife get scooped up by this island schmuck.

But who pays attention to anonymous complaints? Who would care?

Can you sue someone for sexual harassment in the Maldives?

But if Sarah wanted it, was it sexual harassment?

His stomach curls at the thought. His head can't handle this. He wishes he could go back to sleep and wake up and be in Los Angeles, before they set off on this whole sorry trip. Had he known what would happen, he never would've gone, never would have suggested that they come here. People should be warned about the Maldives. This resort. The things that can happen. Crazy Kevin may have been on to something, once again.

Maybe he should text her. They've always been better at communicating over text than in person. No surprise on her end, given that she's a writer. But for him, text messaging provides an extra layer of comfort, like a pair of cushioned socks, especially when he feels bruised. Over text, he can say how he really feels, he can be cute or raw or—in this case—apologetic without feeling like a loser.

He can send blue bubble after blue bubble and not wonder if he's being too much. This is his wife, after all, the woman with whom he exchanged matching rose gold wedding bands at a winery in Napa. A rose gold wedding band has got to count for something, right?

Right?

Good morning.

How are you?

I'd like to apologize for my behavior last night. I know violence is never the answer. That being said, I was very upset.

He reads back the last message only after he's sent it. "Violence is never the answer"? "That being said"? Did the circuit between his mind and his thumbs snap? He tries to unsend the message, but that doesn't work.

Forget what I said. I'M SORRY. I MESSED UP. BADLY. Where are you? Are you okay? Please call me?

He patiently waits for gray dots to materialize from her side.

One minute passes, then another.

Where *is* she?

He tries calling. Her phone goes straight to voicemail.

Beneath the blackout blinds, he can see edges of light.

It doesn't seem plausible that she's with the manager. She wouldn't do that. She wouldn't cheat on him. Not under his nose. Not like this. Not at the resort where they were supposed to be reconnecting, working on their marriage. Only a sociopath would do that. His wife is not a sociopath. Is she?

He calls again. Straight to voicemail again.

What if this was what she wanted all along? Did she come here with the intent of meeting someone else, losing Sam in the process? Has she *been* cheating on him? Is Sid the latest in a long line of notches on her belt?

The least you could do is reply.

Let me know that you're okay.

Seriously?

Another call, another lack of response.

I can't imagine what you see in that manager, but whatever you want, I will support.
I just want you to be happy, Sarah.
If you want to leave me, I'll make it easy for you.

Seventeen minutes since his first message, and still, no sign of life from his wife.

No sign of life . . .

She couldn't be. She had to be *fine*, right? His messages are all coming up blue. The calls are connecting, if only to voicemail. If something were wrong, if her phone had, like, sunk in the water because *she* was in the water, they would be green. There would be an automated message: "This call could not be completed as dialed."

He realizes how flawed this logic is as he thinks it. Whether his messages are coming up as green or blue or purple only indicates the status of Sarah's phone, not Sarah herself. She could be in pieces for all he knows. Fish food.

He springs out of bed, hitting the button by the headboard to raise the blinds. He stumbles up to the floor-to-ceiling windows that lead to the private pool and terrace and throws open the sheers and the sliding glass door and then rushes out onto the deck. He needs to get a lay of the land, see what's out there. If there were a body in the water, the search and rescue team would be assessing the situation in the early morning light, the authorities might be with them as well.

But there is nothing. Just wave after placid wave, glinting coral under the rising sun.

No, wait, there is something in the water, something flapping, radiating ripples. It's probably not a hand—please, God, don't let it be her hand—but he needs to get a closer look. The binoculars—where are those binoculars that Maanav pointed out the first day, meant for close-up viewing of fish and dolphins and birds and whales?

He runs back into the bungalow, nearly tripping over the frame of the sliding glass door, and spies them on the mantel below the flat-screen television, on top of a book about indoor-outdoor living.

Back on the terrace, the rubber shield of the eyepiece firmly planted to his face, he identifies the source of the flapping: a black-naped tern. Not a hand. Not her hand. Phew.

Across the lagoon, he sees two figures on the terrace of an overwater bungalow at the Four Seasons. They seem to be doing the same thing as him, surveying the early morning scene. Well—probably not the same thing, given that there are two of them. Presumably one has not absconded with the hotel manager of the Four Seasons. Fuck, he should've just stayed at the Four Seasons. Nothing ever goes wrong at the Four Seasons. This would never happen at a resort governed by a North American entity with North American rules and regulatory practices—Kevin was right.

The woman places a hand above her forehead and leans on the railing of their terrace, as if to get a closer look at him. Why does she look familiar? He doesn't know anyone in the Maldives outside of this resort, certainly not this woman in a black bikini and billowy white cover-up who's now all but horizontal across the railing, peering at him.

She rights herself and takes a clip out of her hair.

Her long, strawberry blond hair.

The light catches something on her neck.

Is that a heart-shaped locket that goes for the cost of their monthly mortgage on Goop? (Sarah once texted it to him, hopeful for an anniversary present that they could in no way afford.)

It's not possible. He must be seeing things. Hallucinating, for sure.

He removes the binoculars from his face and readjusts them, like that might clear the mirage. When he lifts them up again, he sees that the woman has turned her back to him, crouching down and gathering what appears to be a bong from the terrace floor. The waves falling around her head—very Krista coded. She's put on a banded straw hat that he does not remember Krista wearing, but it also seems like something that would be at home in her walk-in closet, in her aluminum Rimowa.

The woman turns, keeping her head down, revealing her knee.

Her knee with a scar like the island of Madagascar.

"No fucking way," he says, and repeats. This can't be any woman *but* Krista. But who is this man with her? He shifts his gaze. Definitely not Kevin.

He might get canceled for saying this, but if he had to bet—and he is a betting man—he would say the guy is gay. The black muscle tank, for one—he doesn't know any straight men who wear muscle tanks, though maybe they exist in Europe. He's also wearing a collection of silver necklaces and black combat boots, of all things, along with a black hat that's a cross between a cowboy and fedora. There's probably some name for it. Bolero? He's not sure.

His ears are pierced and he's making a great variety of jazzy gestures with his hands in a way that feels foreign to Sam, hetero cisgender male that he is. Sam has no idea who this guy could be. Kevin and Krista never mentioned anyone else in their party. Could it be their son, Connor? But—and again, he's not trying to be offensive—this guy doesn't look like a Connor. He doesn't look like he could be the biological child of Kevin and Krista; he looks vaguely North African, maybe Egyptian. Kevin and Krista are purebred, *Mayflower*-type whites.

He would think they would've mentioned if Connor was adopted. But this is all beside the point—how is Krista *alive*?

And if Krista is alive, who did they pull from the water twenty-four hours ago?

Now that he thinks about it, there was no way the body that came out of the water could've been Krista's. He only got a glimpse while attempting to comfort Sarah, but he remembers thinking that the physique was different. Not quite as muscular. And the hair was all off. It was a grayish blond, the color of hay. But he didn't get a close look, and he has no idea how untold hours in the water could change one's hair and body. It certainly seemed *plausible* that it was

Krista's; how many dead blondish women were found floating in the Indian Ocean every day?

Now, on the terrace of the Four Seasons, Krista—he's just going to call it like he sees it—is saying something to her sidekick while pointing at Sam, jabbing her finger in the precise direction of him and his binoculars.

Panic spears him. He knew something about Kevin and Krista was off. He did not think it was that they were . . . well, he doesn't know *what* they are, they could still very well be swingers, but they are also something else, something perhaps much more dangerous.

He blithely wonders if Krista wants to kill him. If she's telling her minion—the guy has minion energy—to hunt him down and end him, once and for all.

Has he seen too much?

He needs to get out of here. He needs to find his wife. He . . . doesn't *really* want to know what's going on, but he has a feeling that he's going to have no choice but to find out before he gets off this island, which now feels like something he has to do—*they* have to do, he and Sarah—as soon as humanly possible, even if they have to fly back in economy.

(Do they *have* to fly back in economy? Maybe some availability's opened up in business.)

Later! He can check on that later. Now he has to shower and find her. Find his wife. Happy wife, happy life, like Kevin said, like untold numbers of husbands have reminded themselves since the dawn of time or at least the dawn of marriage. He should get it tattooed on his forehead so he never forgets. Or maybe the inside of his wrist. Easier to see the inside of his wrist than his forehead.

She still hasn't texted back, but his previous enmity toward her has transformed into something else: a sense of urgency, a mission.

He can be the hero. He can get them out of this wretched place. He just has to find her, and she just has to give him one more chance.

TWELVE

Knock-knock-knock-knock-knock.

Through the haze of a deep sleep, Sarah can hear someone at a door. She mumbles something incomprehensible into the velvety cotton surrounding her face. "Come back later" is what she means, but it's unlikely that those words can traverse the distance between wherever she is and wherever they are.

The knocking stops. She opens her eyes. They feel heavy, like twin weighted blankets.

This is not her bed. This is not the bed of bungalow no. 7.

That's when she remembers Aimy and what transpired in Sid's suite.

Sarah let out a yelp as the hot tea hit her hand, and while Sid thought he had closed his door, it had a tendency to open on its own if it wasn't latched. Hearing the sound of a woman in distress, Aimy, who was eating ramen noodles in the kitchenette and had seen Sarah and Sid walk past, came running in.

"Is everything all right?" Aimy said.

"Fine, just a spill," Sid said, paper towels in hand, annoyed at Aimy's interruption or Sarah's clumsiness or both.

Aimy shot Sarah a look again, the kind that women shoot each other all the time, the one that says, "Are you really okay? Do you need help? Do you need me to save you? Doesn't it suck sometimes, being a woman, having to defend ourselves against these men with questionable morals, men who want, want, want, everything under the sun except to hear the word 'no'?"

This time, Sarah held her gaze. This time, Sarah silently said yes.

"You may have sustained a burn," Aimy said, picking up Sarah's left wrist and assessing it. Sarah knew it wasn't that serious, but she was happy to play along. "Let's get you to the medical clinic, apply some cream."

"What nonsense are you talking?" Sid scoffed. "The tea wasn't even that hot."

"Come," Aimy said to Sarah, ignoring her boss. "You can follow me."

"You don't have to go with her," Sid said. "I have some Neosporin here, if that's what you're really concerned about."

"It's okay," Sarah said, turning to him. "I should probably go, anyway."

"Back to your dear husband?" A sneer played at Sid's lips.

"Back to a place that's not this room," Sarah said. She was not the perfect wife, no, and Sam was not the perfect husband, but this general manager had no right to mock them. What was she thinking, coming back here with him? It's not like she was in love with Sid. She hardly knew the guy. He was a distraction, something to shift her focus from the weightier problems that hounded her: What was she going to do about her marriage? Her career? Her life?

"He does this all the time, you know," Aimy said once they were outside the staff quarters. "Zeroes in on a female guest he thinks he can bed, then turns on the charm, takes them to the rum hut, brings them back here or to an unoccupied room, has his way. It's quite sick, really."

They had reached a row of buggies plugged into electric chargers. Aimy slid into one of them; Sarah hesitated a moment before getting in next to her, on the passenger side. It would've been rude to ride in the back seat, given the circumstances: Aimy saving her from herself, from lecherous Sid.

"I feel awful," Sarah said.

"Don't," said Aimy. "Of everyone at this resort, you should feel the least awful of all. The day you've had!" She turned a key in the ignition and reversed, throwing her arm over the bench seat as she backed out of the parking strip and onto the main path. "Most people would've had a nervous breakdown by now." She threw a sideways glance at Sarah. "You're not about to have a nervous breakdown, are you?"

"Not that I know of," Sarah said, looking up at the palm fronds rushing past in the starry sky, "but the night is young."

"You know what you need?" said Aimy, in a way that indicated she wouldn't wait for an answer. "Rest. Good, solid rest. Without all these annoying men asking for this and that, buzzing about like flies. I have an idea."

"Oh?" Sarah said. Sleep would be nice. Sleep without the interruption of Sam's snoring, although as soon as she thought of his snoring, she also imagined the feel of his heavy arm over her torso and the way that, had this whole sorry night not happened, she might have taken comfort under that heft.

As things stood, though, she did not want to slink back into their bungalow, try to be quiet, even though it was pretty much impossible to be quiet when you were navigating inky-black dark studded with heavy, oddly shaped, unfamiliar modern furniture. She did not want to hear his tearful apology that wouldn't really be an apology, that would be a sort of justification for why he acted the way he had. As if he had no choice but to punch Sid. Yes, Sarah taking Sid's bait was foolish, but what Sam did was much worse, and she wanted him to own up to it. To say "sorry" and mean it. Given how rarely it happened, you'd think it was the hardest thing for a man to do, to say those two syllables, no caveat. Herculean effort, it must take.

Granted, she ought to apologize, too. Come clean. It dawned on her that she had adopted this cynical view of marriage as a battle in which someone always had the upper hand. But Sam was not her adversary, Sam was her partner. You couldn't "win" a marriage. What was she trying to prove?

"Here we are," Aimy said. Sarah must've drifted off without realizing it, because the buggy had come to a stop in front of a smaller footpath that had sand on both sides. At the end of the path was a house. More than a house—a two-story villa, it looked like, lit up on the outside with lanterns. Crickets chirped. Close by, waves lapped against and receded from the shore at a lulling rhythm.

"What is this?" Sarah asked.

"Beach villa no. 6," Aimy said. "I call it the pearl, because the headboard of the bed in the primary suite reminds me of an oyster. It's yours for the night. Actually—it's yours for the rest of your stay, should you want or need it."

Aimy led the way to the front door despite Sarah's protestations. "Everything works just as it does in your overwater bungalow, except there's a full chef's kitchen, a swimming pool, Jacuzzi, a private beach, two additional bedrooms upstairs, and a private gym and sauna on the ground level," Aimy said.

"I couldn't," Sarah stammered. "Don't you need this for another guest?"

"Not anymore," Aimy said, shrugging. "The Beijing billionaires who had booked this for the week canceled at the last minute. They had paid in full, and we can't resell it at this late stage. Well—maybe we could, maybe there's some oligarch somewhere who would bite, but as the director of rooms, I get to decide what's available for booking and what's not." She winked at Sarah as she hovered a key card over the lock and pushed down the handle. Sarah followed her into a foyer that looked like the Guggenheim, all curves and light and money.

"Welcome to your new home," Aimy said, handing her a packet that contained two key cards. "The Beijing billionaires opted for the deluxe welcome snack basket, which you'll find in the kitchen. Help yourself to whatever you'd like. Or would you like me to ring room service and order you a real meal? You must be hungry."

Speechless at this show of generosity, Sarah threw her arms around Aimy. Tears welled in her eyes.

"Oh, there's no need for that," Aimy said, patting her back in a soothing way. "It will all be fine, you'll see." She pulled back from Sarah. "Do you know what saved my marriage?"

Sarah sniveled.

"Long distance. He works at another resort. We see each other on weekends and holidays. He comes to my place, I go to his, or we pick a spot on the map and meet there."

"Sounds romantic," Sarah said, wiping away tears she didn't realize had fallen.

Aimy smiled and shrugged. "It works for us, for now. You never know what turns your marriage will take. It's quite the ride." She appraised Sarah and seemed to conclude that her work here was done. "Here's my WhatsApp," she said, taking out her phone and revealing a QR code for Sarah to scan. "Please reach out if you need anything at all."

She pressed her palms together at her heart, briefly bowed her head, and saw herself out.

Now, in the creamy morning light leaking through the slit beneath the shades, Sarah thanks whatever powers that be for Aimy. For women in general. Of course it would take a woman to save the day. These idiotic men can't tell their heads from their asses.

Sid. She can't believe Sid. Worse than Sid is the fact that his schtick almost worked on her. Guy presents her with a glass of mezcal—a bottle of which she owns, not as if she's never had the stuff before—and she thinks he knows her better than her damn husband, practically falls into his lap.

Is she really that desperate for attention? Does she need it so badly that she'll lap it up from the general manager of what's supposedly the most romantic resort in the world?

It's sickening, the person she's become. Worse still, she realizes, as she slides up in bed and props herself against the oyster-shaped headboard with one of the fourteen pillows she unceremoniously shoved off the duvet when she flopped onto it the previous night—it's not Sam's fault that she ended up like this, needy and desperate and never not feeling sorry for herself.

It's hers. It's her fault.

She let herself be defined by her professional wins and losses, by the number of followers she had on social media, by the parties she got invited to and the PR agency gifts she received. But none of that was what made her *her*.

She lost sight of why she wanted to become a journalist to begin with. She was curious. She wanted to learn. She wanted to see parts of the world that would not have been open to her had she not been a journalist asking questions.

And somehow, she got caught in the rat race of getting ahead, in a popularity contest in which there were no winners because once you attained a certain level of popularity, the people rose up to tear you down, went through your old posts, found something questionable by contemporary, changed standards, held it up for everyone to see, and cackled with glee as you were stoned in the town square. "She had it coming." "She flew too close to the sun." "She thought she was one of them, a star, but she was wrong, she's just like us. She's nothing."

In light of this realization, sinking in in the curtained confines of beach villa no. 6, she feels newly awful about what she did to Natalie. The way she parlayed Natalie's vulnerability to elevate her own status, to make a buck. What a horrible thing to do to someone she genuinely considered a friend. Friends don't artfully arrange themselves on a couch and pretend to like natural wine so as to solicit confessions that might come in handy later. Friends don't share each other's secrets, even under the couching of "sources." Friends don't seek opportunities to gain from each other's pain.

She had done all of the above.

She can't call Natalie. Besides the fact that it's late in Los Angeles, given that Natalie blocked Sarah on all forms of social media, Natalie has probably blocked her number as well. In any case, this isn't the sort of apology one can issue over the phone. Sarah will have to do the work in person, maybe start with a handwritten card or letter and a bouquet of flowers, a proper arrangement, not one of those sad, grocery store bundles.

She must own up to how horribly she fucked up, without blaming her editor, without blaming the pressure on her to come up with an ever more relevant story. *You don't know how hard it is, being a freelance journalist.* The nerve she had. Does anyone know how hard it is being any other thing at all?

She reaches for her phone. She sees a string of missed calls and texts from Sam. He must be worried, wondering where she is, but she's not ready to face him, yet.

They also location share. If he were really *that* worried, he could find her. But he always forgets that they location share and forgets how to use it, so.

She opens up her most-used social media app, sees a post from Alana. It's Alana and her daughter again, at the Beverly Hills Hotel, this time, at a tea party sponsored by Chanel. They're dressed in the label, head to toe. The four-year-old even has appropriately sized Mary Janes with interlocking *C*s and a mini quilted cross-body purse.

For the longest time—actually, probably for the entire time they've known each other, even though she never admitted it to herself—Sarah has envied Alana. The feelings that Alana's apparent joy brought up for Sarah—they were ugly. They were gunky, gross feelings the color of sludge. A resonant thump of "Why can't that be me?"

But maybe it's the clarity brought on by an uninterrupted night of sleep on three-thousand-thread-count sheets or the Maldivian breezes or the chaos of the past twenty-four, forty-eight—how long has it been now?—seventy-two hours, she realizes now that Alana's joy does not have to be to her detriment. Why should the happiness of another woman—another brown woman, another brown woman who made the same cross-country move, who carved out a career in the same general industry, and in this situation, what they have in common has a lot to do with it—hurt Sarah? Alana has worked for everything she has. Sarah respects Alana; Sarah wants to *be* Alana. That's not Alana's fault. Again, it's Sarah's, for projecting her insecurities onto someone else, for thinking that there's some finite pile of joy somewhere, and every woman only gets so much. (Brown women get even less.)

It's probably a vestige of how first-generation children of immigrants, like her, were brought up, pitted against their cousins and family friends: "Vidya got an A+ in chemistry and you only got an A-. What's wrong with you? Did you not study hard enough? What happens when Vidya gets into Harvard and you don't? What will you do then? You'll be a failure, you'll embarrass us, we're getting you a tutor. No more going out with friends. Study, study, study—beat Vidya." Et cetera.

She's stopping this cycle now.

First, she likes the photo. She rarely likes Alana's photos under the justification that Alana gets enough likes; she doesn't need one from Sarah. This, Sarah realizes, is flawed. If you like it, you like it. What's the point of doling out your affection in carefully measured teaspoons? Heap it on, why not, life is short.

Then, she taps on the button to direct message Alana.

Motherhood looks good on you! Happy to see you thriving ❤

She sends the message before she can think too much about it. Immediately, gray bubbles appear.

LOL currently covered in vomit
Rose overdid it on the pastries
So much for my vintage Chanel
Spent a whole afternoon in Paris shopping for that set and she has the nerve to throw up all over it
How are you????? Maldives looks amaze

Sarah forgot that she posted a photo of the sunset the other night, their first night at Jala, when Krista was still alive. Ancient history, it feels like. If Alana only knew, she thinks.

And then she realizes this must be how Alana feels all the time. This must be how so many women feel all the time, after posting a photo of themselves glowing on social media. Sure, for one moment, everything aligned, and they managed to get their angles right and the light hit just so, but behind the scenes? Girl, if you only knew what it took to get here. She starts typing.

It's . . . a TRIP. Would love to catch up when I'm back.

She wants to say more. She wonders if it's too much. But what's the worst that can happen?

Lunch?

For a few moments, there are no gray bubbles. Sarah wonders if she overstepped. Maybe Alana was just being polite. Maybe Alana still hates her because of that profile of her Grammy-winning singer boss from way back when. Maybe Alana never liked her at all.

Then a message appears.

Would love that. Will have my assistant reach out to get it scheduled. Gnight from here! Have a cocktail for me xx

Sarah collapses against the pillow-padded headboard; the hand that's been clutching her phone goes limp. She lets out a little laugh of disbelief. So that was all it took. All along, Alana was there, a flesh-and-blood person with her own problems, neither Sarah's best friend nor her worst enemy, just another woman in Los Angeles who liked her well enough to consent to lunch.

(Consenting to lunch was one thing; having it, actually sitting down and breaking bread, gluten-free or what have you—totally different. Sarah was fully prepared for this lunch to be rescheduled thrice and then canceled in favor of a get-together at an undefined later time. That wasn't personal. That was just LA.)

Unfathomable, the way that we can build people up in our minds without their knowledge. It's the kind of construction that ought to be illegal, that should at least require some permitting.

Sam. She remembers Sam. Perhaps she's made him squirm long enough. She looks at her phone and the string of messages from him. She doesn't have the energy to scroll up and read them all—or listen to a voice note that is two minutes and eight seconds long—and she's not quite ready to call him.

She recalls what Aimy said about beach villa no. 6's private pool and private beach. Perhaps a baptism of sorts is in order. A ritual cleansing to rid her of the bad vibes from last night—grade F awful, those vibes—and imbue her with the good faith to move forward as a new person, or at least, a better person. A person with better intentions.

She hits the button next to the bedside to raise the shades. It appears to be a perfect Maldivian day: full sun, blue skies, popcorn clouds on the horizon.

She is naked because all of her clothes (besides the ones she wore last night) are in overwater bungalow no. 7, but since all of this prime Jala acreage is private, she has no qualms kicking off the bedding, searching through her purse for her sunglasses—please tell her that she remembered her sunglasses, *yes*, here they are—putting them on, floating to the sliding glass doors separating the primary bedroom from the pool area, and going right in.

The water is divine.

She perches her sunglasses on the far edge of the pool, the edge that faces the beach, which is just visible through a low row of hedges, and submerges her head beneath the surface, savors the momentary pause for her senses. This is what they should be doing. Enjoying the water. Not investigating the accidental death of a woman who—Sam is right—was a stranger to them mere days ago.

As she comes back up above water, she's dimly aware of a knocking at the door.

Again?

Probably in-room dining, wondering if they can refill the minibar. They always came at the most inconvenient times.

She grabs a towel from one of the chaise lounge chairs positioned by the pool, hastily wraps it around herself, slides her feet into a set of fluffy slippers, and pads to the door.

"It's okay, I haven't even touched the minibar, I've still got this snack basket to get through," she's saying as she flings the door open. "Sam?"

She's surprised by several things, but mostly by the fact that he's clean-shaven and wearing something besides swim trunks or basketball shorts. He's in neatly pressed white chinos and a summery patterned button-down shirt that suits him, a riot of beige-and-cream-colored swirls. She recalls judging all the shirts he packed as garish, but were they? Or was that just another instance of her wanting to find fault with him, looking for something to get mad about when she was really mad at herself?

He's holding a cup of something steaming as he strides in purposefully, a man with a plan. "Did you listen to my voice note?"

"How did you know I was here?" she asks.

"Location sharing," he says, matter-of-factly. "Though I thought maybe it was inaccurate because I knocked earlier and you didn't answer. But then Aimy sent me a message."

So Sam knows how to use location sharing. Huh.

"She said you were probably still asleep, given how late it was when she brought you here. So I went over to the coffee shop by Veranda and got you this—extra-dark-roast Italian, black, just the way you like." He hands her the cup.

"Oh." Tech savvy and considerate? She needs caffeine to process this.

"By the way," he says, and she can predict what's coming, "I am really, truly sorry. There is no excuse for the way I acted. None at all."

She waits for the justification, for the "but."

But nothing comes. Sam is just standing there, in the foyer, holding her gaze as surely as she's holding the towel around her torso.

"Sarah," he says, reaching out for her free hand, which she offers, gingerly, aware that if her upper arms stray too far from her torso, her towel might fall to the ground, "I know you rearranged your life to be with me. I know things haven't been easy. But I want you to know how committed I am to you, to us. You are my entire world. Sun, moon, and stars. I will do anything in my power to make you happy.

"I'm going to work on myself," he goes on. "Seriously, I'm looking into therapists. I know you wanted that, but I want it for me, too. The sports betting app? I deleted it. Same with the bookies' numbers—all of them. And the drinking—I know it's gotten out of control, and I know I need to do something about it. I want to be the best man I can be, not just for you but for myself. For us."

She lets out a little sound of disbelief.

She is not so naive as to think that sheer will is all it will take for Sam to change. She knows how easy it is to lose yourself in an app—she does it every day, for hours at a time. And she knows how tempting it is to quiet the voices in your head by reaching for a glass of something, how it can be so much easier to lean into oblivion than to do the hard work of getting to the root of why you want to tune out.

But he's never voiced a desire to change before.

That's something. More than something. It's huge. It almost makes her want to cry.

But he deserves more than that.

"Sam, I'm sorry," she blurts. "I'm sorry for taking my frustrations with work out on you, for thinking that a general manager was worth an ounce of attention, for letting social media determine how I feel about my life, how I feel about *us*, for latching onto Krista when I should've been connecting with you, for—"

"Wait, did you listen to my voice note?"

"What?" Sarah assumed the voice note was a version of the apology Sam just delivered.

"Krista's *alive*."

Sarah feels the ground shift beneath her feet.

Sam explains what he saw: the woman with strawberry blond waves on the deck of the Four Seasons, the dead giveaways of the necklace and the scar on her knee, the minion by her side, the way she clocked Sam and stared him down.

"That's . . . How . . ." She cannot put these pieces together. So Krista was not who Sarah thought she was at all. Krista is something else entirely. Most importantly: Krista is *alive* and knows that Sam knows. What does that mean for the two of them?

"We've got to get out of here," she says. She doesn't know what's going on, but the fact that they're a mere lagoon away from a woman who faked her own death—if that's what happened?—and knows way too much about their lives is deeply unsettling. The way she mourned Krista. She could kick herself.

"Pronto," says Sam. "But the next flight doesn't leave Malé until 11:00 p.m. tonight."

"And we'll have to take the seaplane to get there."

"I've already talked to Maanav," Sam says. "It'll be six hours before a seaplane can get here."

"So we should lay low."

"Ideally without them having eyes on us. They have no idea we have access to a beach villa."

Good thing the Beijing billionaires didn't show. For the first time in a long time, Sarah can disagree with nothing Sam's said. He's thought this through. Her knight in shining . . .

"Is your shirt Casablanca?" she asks, running her hand down its silky sleeve.

Sam nods. "Thought I should spring for the good stuff for this trip."

"You thought of everything," she says with a little laugh.

"So, what do you want to do?" he says, placing his hands on her shoulders.

What they should do, she thinks, is call security. Tell them what Sam saw. Let them deal with it. Reclaim the romantic vacation they were supposed to have.

But they can do that in a little while. Because right now, given this reprieve, this bed, this beach villa all to themselves and their self-imposed directive to hide from prying eyes, there are other things she'd like to do.

She unfurls the hand that's been holding the towel tight to her torso.

The towel falls to the floor.

She sees exactly where his eyes go, and for the first time in a long time, she does not mind it at all. Quite the opposite.

She paws at the buttons on his shirt, tugs at the zip of his chinos. She wraps her legs around him as he picks her up and carries her to the bed, and when she comes, she says his name. His full name.

And then she asks him, very sweetly, to please do it again.

~

Had he known that a Casablanca shirt and ironed pants was all it would take to get Sarah to want to have sex with him, he would have bought into this $460 made-in-India scam *years* ago. Jesus, he'd have an entire Casablanca wardrobe if it meant *this*. Morning sex with his wife!

Forget the award-winning spa, the outposts of Michelin-lauded restaurants, the magazine accolades, and the TripAdvisor ratings—morning sex was why people went on vacation, why anyone went anywhere, certainly, why anyone crossed an ocean to come here! The prospect of it! The ability to engage in it without a care in the world about your calendar, about what's going on eight thousand miles away!

Can they do this every day? Can they pull this off back home? Maybe if they wake up early enough?

But even in his postcoital haze, Sam is not so deluded as to think that the Casablanca shirt and J.Crew chinos were all it took (nor does he genuinely believe that morning sex would be achievable on a regular basis with a nine-to-five that in his case is more of a nine-to-nine). He knows that it was more than the set and setting, although it certainly helps to have ocean views and a king-size bed clad in the softest sheets possible at your disposal.

He knows that his apology meant everything to Sarah, and he meant every word of it. He knows that he has to work on himself if he's ever going to get anywhere, if he's ever going to get out from under the hold his father has on him, and that frenzied parlays that occupy more of his brain space than he would like will get him nowhere in the long run.

He also—though he hasn't said it, may, in fact, never say it—hopes that his being open to therapy compels Sarah to seek out a therapist of her own, because *not that he's in a position to judge* but she could certainly benefit from it.

She had apologized as well. Admitted that she was the person she was truly mad at, that her own internal spiraling about motherhood—whether she could handle it, whether they were fit to be parents—had overwhelmed her to the degree that she'd taken her frustration out on him, which wasn't fair. Deep down, he might've known all along, but it was nice to hear her say the words, own up to it.

"I get what you were trying to do with this trip," she said, tracing circles on his bare chest. "I'm sorry that it went sideways, but at least it put us back on the same page."

Amen to that.

Now, blinking up at the sloping ceiling, he thinks about how he'd like to start their trip over, run it back to when they got to LAX, do everything differently, with clearer eyes and fuller hearts now that they've finally had an honest conversation that should've happened a long time ago.

They won't get those days back, but at least they have each other. And four more days at Jala, which, in some fantasy land, if they could avail themselves of this beach villa and avoid Sid, Kevin, and Krista, would be pretty swell indeed. Do they have to leave? Could they stay? Sam wonders if there's a chance in hell they could make it work. Room service for every meal. A barbecue on their private beach; he had seen that offering on the in-room iPad. Daily massages, hourly dips in the pool and the ocean, alternating between the two.

He's dimly aware of his phone ringing.

"Do you want to get that?" Sarah asks, dozing on his chest.

It's the middle of the night in Los Angeles. No one from home could be calling him. He reaches for his phone, turns it over.

Kevin. Of course it's Kevin. Kevin has texted him twice, asked if he wanted to have breakfast with him and this "great gal" he met by the pool: Think you and the wife would love her, she's a hoot. What kind of man picks up a prostitute the day after losing his wife?

But then, of course, Kevin has not actually lost his wife. Kevin has quite possibly lost his *mind*, but that is not Sam's concern. Sam does not care. Let Kevin and Krista play their weird sex-slash-true-crime games—remember those sex toys on the bed, a spread worthy of a suburban shopping mall Spencer's circa 1997? Sam wants nothing to do with it. Sarah, it seems, wants nothing to do with it. Either they'll hide out here for four days or get on the next flight home—availability opened up in business! And heck, maybe he *will* take this up with Amex, try to get some points back. Surely they'll take pity on him after hearing that the general manager of Jala clocked him in the face. Maybe he should sue Sid. Or Jala? Or both?

All of this is ancillary to his main achievement: his wife back in his arms, and Krista and Kevin out of the picture, twin tumors excised.

He lowers the volume on his phone and flips it face down.

It stops for a moment, then resumes ringing.

Seriously? He thought he silenced the damn thing. He turns it over.

Sid?

That motherfucker?

Sam can't resist. He got the girl; he *always* had the girl. He feels the need to gloat, if only to himself.

"What do you want?" he says, holding the phone to his ear.

"Presume I'm the last person you want to hear from," Sid says, "but you need to come to the staff quarters. Your lives are at stake."

THIRTEEN

"Where are they?"

No answer.

"Ali? *Ali?*

"Fucking fuckity fuck," she mutters, storming down the length of the wraparound terrace of their sunrise overwater villa at the Four Seasons Resort Maldives at Voavah, Baa Atoll. She wanted a sunset villa—who wouldn't pick sunset over sunrise, given the option?—but Kevin, fucking *Kevin*, said sunrise was cheaper, so sunrise it was.

Kevin had initially wanted to put her at the W Maldives. A *Bonvoy* property. Over her dead body.

Ali is not on the terrace at all. He was supposed to be at the eastern end, binoculars in hand, affixed to his face, patrolling. She finds him instead inside, at the minibar of the one bedroom they're sharing, jabbing at the Illy espresso machine.

"It's not *working*," he whines. "Where does the capsule go?"

"For Christ's sake," she says. She has to do everything around here. She grabs a capsule, pops it into the portafilter that Ali seems to think is just for decoration—it's heavy, it has the look and feel of a wrench, it could come in handy later, she makes a mental note—wedges it into place on the underside of the machine, and presses the button for a lungo.

"There," she says, as the machine whirs to life.

"Thanks, Mom," Ali says, stamping his feet and clapping.

"Don't call me that," Krista snaps. Ali is not her son. Ali is her ne'er-do-well gay best friend, someone she should replace because of the whole ne'er-do-well thing. Ali is great for a Parisian shopping spree or midnight rave in Marrakech, but he could not find his way out of a cardboard box, lacking, as he is, in situational appropriateness, in common sense. He brought Tom Ford combat boots to the Maldives. Who brings Tom Ford combat boots to the Maldives?

"I thought you were on watch duty," Krista tells Ali, admonishingly. "Have you seen them?"

"The Indian couple?" Ali asks, tearing open a packet of sugar. "I haven't." He shrugs. "Maybe they're asleep?"

"They are not *asleep*," Krista says. "They know. They saw me. That guy—what's his name? Samir. You saw him, too. He's probably gone to tell his miserable journalist wife, and *she's* probably putting the pieces together, as miserable fucking journalists do, scum of the earth, those people." Just her luck that the girl ended up being a journalist. Freelance, though, and one of those "generalists" who doesn't specialize in any one subject, probably because she's flaky, probably because she lacks the wherewithal to commit.

Unlike Krista. She commits, she commits so hard that she'll get a replica of a Foundrae heart pendant made and throw it in the water along with a beach cruiser, she'll train and lift and swim lap after lap at the Burbank YMCA so that when she has to dive into the deepest ocean in the world in the dark of night, she'll be able to reach her new home away from home without a hitch. "Home" is a generous way to put it. She is pacing now, pacing the length of the space between the minibar and the far wall of the suite, which is not far enough, not compared to Jala.

She misses her room at Jala. "Room," what a quaint way to put it. It was an overwater mansion. And just her luck that she lost the coin toss with Kevin the last and final time they run this scam. Ali had been dispatched to collect her things, the clothes and purses and needlepointed works in progress that would keep her company while she whiled away the time between "dying" and Kevin inking a settlement, but she had a bad feeling from the moment she left Jala. She'd barely made progress on her latest project, an eyeglass case that reads "I see through you."

She's getting too old for this. She wants to take her cut and go far, far away, somewhere they'll never find her, to a beach house in a country that does not have a set-in-stone extradition treaty with the US. Montenegro, maybe, or Vietnam or Cambodia. All fine options. New name, new passport, new backstory.

Her dollars would go further in Southeast Asia, but Montenegro has the advantage of feeling like the coast of southern Italy or Spain while harboring criminals like only an Eastern European country could. Which is to say, in style. Her designer wardrobe would not go unnoticed.

But she's thinking too far ahead. They're not free and clear. Not yet.

They *had* to smoke this morning. Ali *had* to forget the vapes. What kind of gay best friend forgets the vapes but remembers the bong and the weed, all expertly disguised and compartmentalized so as not to alert the authorities? You know what you don't have to disguise *or* compartmentalize? A vape! A finger-sized vape.

If she didn't know any better, she would think that Ali was trying to sabotage her, making her go outside to smoke because God forbid they set off the in-room smoke detectors, which for some reason can't be removed from the ceiling or the walls. Fucking Four Seasons and their airtight alarm system.

Is he trying to sabotage her?

Is he working for Kevin?!

She turns around, takes a good, long look at him. In his Alo shorts, black bolero, and Tom Ford combat boots, he looks positively ridiculous, like he fell off the back of the truck to Burning Man. But Ali is more than meets the eye, she knows that. She's seen him shoplift from the shiniest facades of Fifth Avenue and Rodeo Drive; it's how they became friends, running small-time scams like stealing a Bottega bag from the boutique and selling it at cost on the RealReal.

It's always easier to be a con artist when you have company. Hence, incidentals. It was her and Kevin's thing. Latching onto a couple at whatever resort they were trying to rob made them less suspicious, made them seem more like normal vacationers, the kind who socialize and make friends they exchange numbers with but know they'll never see again, because you can't really base a friendship on a week you spent poolside with umbrella drinks. Real friendships tend to require more of a foundation than that.

Of course, in Kevin and Krista's case, they'd never see the incidentals again because they would change their phone numbers and never return to the resort where they met the fools in the first place.

That was the first mistake that bald guy made in *The White Lotus*—find another luxury resort brand to patronize, bro! Kevin and Krista had watched the season set in Thailand—separately, in their own homes, they never hung out unless they had to—and laughed and laughed. They would never be so stupid.

She would never step foot in Thailand again, not after what they did in Phuket. (Kevin sustained a "traumatic brain injury" from "falling down the stairs"—they left $2 million richer.) Nor did she have any desire to go back to Puglia after what they pulled at Borgo Fasano and the very real scar on her knee that resulted from chasing after the whore Kevin got on some cheapo site, the whore who did not want to die, so Krista had to swallow a nearly fatal dose of poisonous mushrooms and get her stomach pumped *and then* find the energy to accuse the Italian luxury resort that was about to be acquired by Marriott of gross negligence in the culinary department.

Or whatever it was on paper. Whatever the lawyers called it. In any case, they left Italy $1 million richer.

And she thought $1.5 million—her cut of those two scams—plus her side gigs, slip and falls here, looting and reselling there, would be enough to keep her going for a while. But spend too much time in luxury resorts and you start to think that you belong in them. That this is the life for you.

And your one-bedroom in Toluca Lake begins to lose its luster, not that it contained much to begin with, sandwiched between the 134 and the 101 and the parking lots of the studios that reject you time and time again, no audition of yours good enough for them. It's hard to be satisfied with the cozy little life that is for sure an upgrade from the way you were living in boring and barren Bakersfield but is not . . . the Four Seasons. It's not Jala. It's not even close.

Can anyone blame her for wanting one more score? One more to catapult her out of LA and into a new life? Maybe she'll take up yoga. Maybe she'll find God. Maybe she'll find a genuine husband, although she's all but convinced that all men suck. Good for attention, good for a night of fun, if you're lucky, little else. They tried with that bartender, Hakim. Tried to have a threesome. He freaked out when he saw the sex toys, said he couldn't do it. "These are illegal in the Maldives, don't you know?" No, of course they didn't know. They didn't read up on the laws of this backward island nation, why would they, when Jala would soon be an American entity, governed by the legislative system they knew and loved to evade?

Or would Jala be subject to Maldivian law regardless? In any case, it wasn't Krista's job to know. It was Krista's job to execute, and she had done so with flying colors until that so-called chef locked eyes with her across the lagoon. The guy's dad opened a couple of curry-in-a-hurry joints, and he goes around calling himself a chef. The audacity!

"Okay, we need to find them," Krista says now, clapping her hands. "Find them and pay them off or kill them off or *something*—I'm not letting them get in the way of my bag."

"What's that, babe?" Ali is sipping his coffee and scrolling on his phone. "What bag, the Bottega?"

"The *money*, Ali. Can you please keep up? The money that you're going to get a cut of?"

Ali looks up from his phone and rolls his eyes dramatically. "Money, money, money—you do know there's more to life, sweetie? *That's* why you're still single. All you care about is money!"

~

Kevin knows the right thing to do is abide by the plan that he and Krista agreed upon. But the thing with this line of work is that nothing's ever set in stone. There are no contracts to sign, you never want a paper trail. Even their text messages—this latest string of text messages, with these particular 310 numbers—never stray from logistics, sweet nothings, and passive-aggressive nags, the type typical between man and wife.

Although she shouldn't be texting him now, given that she's supposed to be dead.

Hi babe, all good over there?

It's like she knows he's got a wandering eye, even though they're not, in fact, man and wife, and his eye can wander wherever the heck it wants. Kevin has never been the marrying kind. His one true love is money. Well—sex and money. Which brings him to Cady.

Cady is just like Krista, only twenty years younger. Lither. More flexible. She is a genuine yoga instructor! But a yoga instructor with a heart of . . . gold vermeil. Markedly different from actual gold.

Cady is impressionable enough that Kevin can shape her into the new Krista, because let's face it, after that spill she took at Borgo Fasano, Krista's age has started to show. The crow's feet. The frequency of her hair appointments. She can't even stick to the same strawberry blond shade—it's always a little too red or a little too yellow, a little too much like straw. She has the money to spend on a decent colorist, she really doesn't have an excuse. And she can't even keep the stories of their supposed kids straight! The only reason they have kids—fake kids, that is—is because it makes them seem more innocuous, like the mom and dad next door. Even though he considers himself a daddy.

He needs a partner who's sharper. Someone with more skin in the game. Someone with more skin of the plump, youthful variety.

The best thing he can do is not respond to Krista's message. If their phone records are subpoenaed later, he can say that this was a message that was drafted on Krista's iPad, which died and was later brought back to life. Or something. He's not going to be done in by a rogue text message.

But if she refuses to play dead? Well. It wouldn't be his first time killing someone. And he's got all this ocean water at his disposal, all this deep, salty ocean water in which bodies can mysteriously float away never to be found, though thankfully not in the case of the woman he bought on the dark web off that body broker site, an intermediary between morgues with unclaimed corpses and people who, well, need a body. He made damn sure they'd find the body and ID it as Krista's. You can pick them out by height and weight and face and build. There's a site that's like Build-A-Bear for this kind of thing, if you have enough cryptocurrency and you know where to look.

Is his line of work sad and dark? Morally reprehensible? Welcome to capitalism. The sooner you realize that everyone's morals are fungible, that everyone and everything has a price, the better you'll do.

He paid off the search and rescue team. He paid off Jala's security staff. He paid off Hakim, who ferried the body over in the middle of the night, in a soundless electric speedboat for which he also had to pay, and which Krista insisted on jumping in to get to her hideout even though she'd said she could swim the distance (which meant he'd had to pay even more). The charges associated with this gambit had accrued to the point that he felt emboldened to do *whatever* he wanted, now that the charade was over with. Well, almost over.

Now, in the confines of the primary suite of bungalow no. 17, with Cady in the bath and Sam—his buddy Sam, he really likes Sam!—not texting back, he figures he'll order breakfast in. Why not? Per his source at the white-shoe law firm in New York, the firm he used to work for out of their Los Angeles office, it'll be about forty-eight hours before the ink on Hyland's acquisition of Jala is dry, before his lawyers (at the white-shoe law firm, of course) can get to work. Five million, his source told him. Five million to walk away from this "wrongful death" with a signed NDA and a promise to never return to Jala again. Don't have to tell him twice! He can't stand the beach. Much prefers the mountains. Aspen is way more his style.

He's supposed to split it with Krista, half and half. If she wants to give a cut to her sidekick, that's her business. He said he would carve off a little for the source at the white-shoe law firm, but the source is a trust fund nepo baby who pisses away several grand every time she goes for "drinks with the girls," which is all she seems to do. He knows this because she told him as much when they were doing cocaine in a senior partner's bathroom. It was the offense that got him fired, as if the senior partner had never made a bad call. This was the partner that brought in the nepo baby! Surely, he could've predicted what would happen.

All of which is to say—he could cut Krista out of it. He could go all-in with Cady. Take her under his wing.

Would Krista come after him? For sure. But he can take her. She talks a big game, but she's a lightweight in real life. The way she howled when she hit her knee on the stone stairs of Borgo Fasano. He could end her with one hand tied behind his back and a leg in arabesque (Cady has educated him on the finer points of arabesque).

"Babe?" Cady's voice. Closer than the en suite bath. He looks up from his phone and sees her before him, at the entrance to the bedroom, in a bikini of bath bubbles, like the girl in *Varsity Blues* but better, because who can eat all that whipped cream?

"I put too many bubbles in the bath," she says in a little-girl voice. She puts the tip of one finger in her mouth, between her full, glossy lips.

"Bad girl," he says, shaking his head. "What are we going to do with you?"

He flings his phone to the far end of the bed as she steps closer. He doesn't need to reply to Krista. He doesn't need to tell her anything at all.

He does want to do one thing. He rings up Sharif. (Another person he paid off to keep quiet—so many incidentals on this trip, a whole army of them.)

"Hey, bro, do me a favor," he says, as Cady climbs on top of him. "Take down the flag? Thanks a bunch."

~

"Something's off." Krista is still pacing, phone in hand, fingernails in mouth. "Kevin's not answering." Gone is the American flag outside the bungalow—their signal to each other, visible across the lagoon, that all is going according to plan. The lack of it flapping in the wind, combined with Kevin's lack of response, means that something is seriously wrong. On top of that, she's unsettled by the fact that Sam and Sarah have not shown their faces since Sam spotted her and Ali early that morning.

"Girl, you texted Kevin?" Ali asks. "Aren't you supposed to be dead?"

She groans with frustration. Ali doesn't understand anything. "They're not going to *ask* for our phone records, they don't have that kind of time. This will settle out of court, within the week, no question."

She and Kevin have the same source at the white-shoe New York law firm. First-year associate. They had a threesome last spring, which is when the associate gave them the heads-up about Hyland's acquisition of Jala. It's why they picked this godforsaken place in the middle of the ocean. Krista would never come here otherwise. Being surrounded by water, frankly, creeps her out. All that deep, dark sea, the depths still unplumbed.

They had planned to find incidentals once they got to the property. Sarah and Sam were dumb luck. Krista saw them fighting in the Emirates Lounge and figured out, through some stealthy drive-bys during which she glanced at their boarding passes, that they were on the same flight. They were giving last-chance-at-romance energy. Desperate people made the best incidentals. Desperate people were up for anything, by definition.

"Let's go over there," she says. She's stopped pacing. She's just tapping one foot, maniacally, all her outrage seeking some sort of outlet. "I'm not letting him do this to me. I'm not letting him cut me out."

"*What?*" Ali drops his phone face down on the bed. "Babe, what part of 'play dead' do you not understand?"

"Don't *you* tell me what to do," she says, snatching up the drawstring linen pants that go with her blousy white tunic from Toteme. She pulls them on violently. "Go to the marina, get a Jet Ski, pick me up, let's go. We'll do circles around the island until they come out."

"Until who comes out? The Indians?"

"The Indians, Kevin and his new girl—I'm *sure* that's what's going on, there's no way he would cut me out if he weren't distracted by some pretty young thing, some 'new me' he thinks he can groom. But he can't. He can't! There is only one Krista King, and he's fucked with her for the final time."

"Isn't your real name Lana?"

"*Not the point*, Ali. Is that even your real name? Who the fuck cares? Go!" She shoos him, like a mosquito. "Get the Jet Ski! Now!"

He consents, whining again as he laces up his Tom Ford combat boots. Idiots. She's surrounded by idiots. A whole sea of them.

~

Sam refuses. Outright refuses to go slinking back to the staff quarters, to hide in Sid's room. Of all people! The man he punched just yesterday—the man who punched him and tried to seduce his wife! It sounds like Sid's plotting to kill him, if he's being honest. He won't stand for it.

"Should we go?" Sarah asks.

"They don't know that we're here," he says. "They think that we're in our original room, bungalow no. 7."

"Right," Sarah says, though he can hear the trepidation in her voice.

She is scared, he can tell. He wants to protect her, really, he does, but he doesn't think that Sid's room is safe, *genuinely* safe. Maybe it's safe from Krista and her minion—it doesn't sound like Kevin is part of her rogue plan—but it's not safe from Sid, the slimiest, scummiest general manager on God's green earth.

Who knew what Sid's motives were? What if he was working with them? Sam flashes back to how calm Sid was when he first informed Sam that Krista was "missing"—did he know more than he let on?

"I'll protect you," Sam says. Sarah's in bed, clutching the sheets to her chest. She needs clothes. He jumps out, goes to the en suite.

"Here," he says, throwing her one of Jala's branded silk robes as he finds his boxers, his now-creased chinos and shirt. "Better than nothing."

She shrugs on the robe, ties it tight around her waist. "But how are you going to protect us? Krista is a madwoman. Who knows what she's capable of?"

Sam shrugs, as if the prospect of a very likely unhinged woman who faked her own death doesn't concern him. He has no idea what he's going to do, but he knows one thing—he's more of a man than Sid, more of a man than he's been these past many months, and he's going to prove it to Sarah once and for all.

~

Sarah trusts Sam. She can't remember the last time she felt this way. But more than Sam, she trusts *them*. The two of them. It's the sort of blind faith that she's read about, the notion that you should trust your gut, trust your intuition, trust in . . . the powers that be that things will work out the way they should. She hates when people say "Everything happens for a reason" because god-awful things happen all over the world every day, and what can be the reason for all that strife and loss?

She doesn't know, but she knows that if this is it, if this is where it all ends, she wants it to end with him, on their terms, not in the middle of the jungle, hiding in the room of a man who tried to get in her pants the previous night. In the room of a man who did not respect the bounds of her marriage, and let's face it, neither did she in the moment, but she's seen the light, she knows things can be better, things *will* be better. She'll work on herself, too. She and Sam will be stronger than ever if they ever make it out of the Maldives.

An increasingly unlikely possibility, as they wait like sitting ducks, listening to the whirring of a Jet Ski doing lap after lap, evading Jala security, which is on Jet Skis of their own, doing jumps and flips. For a guy in Tom Ford combat boots, Krista's minion knows his way around one of these things. It's kind of impressive.

The whirring stops.

The lack of it—eerie.

Beyond the pool, Sarah spies a Jet Ski, bobbing in the water in front of their private beach.

Her sunglasses.

She left her sunglasses on the edge of the pool.

The pool that faces the beach.

Krista had complimented those sunglasses. "Ooh, Celine, I have that pair too, I think I brought them. We should wear them at the same time—twins!"

And now, Sarah sees, Krista is wearing those same Celines, all-black Wayfarer frames, timeless, really, they go with everything, especially this flowy white almost see-through linen set Krista is wearing over her black bikini. If circumstances were different, Sarah would ask where she got it from, but given the current circumstances, wherein Krista throws what appears to be the portafilter of an Illy espresso machine through the plate glass door, which shatters to pieces, inquiring as to the provenance of her outfit seems . . . inappropriate.

What it is appropriate to do: run, scream, hide.

"Follow me," Sam shouts, and she does, embarking on what is effectively a top-to-tail tour of beach villa no. 6, tearing through the private workout room, where she picks up a black matte kettlebell and flings it back at Krista, narrowly missing her bare foot; then they're pounding up the stairs, past the secondary bedrooms, into the primary, where Sam grabs the Dyson hairdryer out of its holster and hurls it at the minion, hitting the minion's shoulder and causing him to stumble backward, into Krista, knocking the two of them into a heap.

"Come on," Sarah says, racing back down the stairs but to where? Out the door? Should they leave? But what if Kevin's out there, and who knows what role Sid has played in all of this? Who can they trust? What can they do?

They pause in the kitchen, panting, calculating. It's a true chef's kitchen, with a Sub-Zero painted the same dusty rose shade as the cabinets, a fact that Sarah realizes at the same time as the door hits the side of her head. Did Krista catapult down here from the top of the staircase? How did she not hear? How did Sam not hear? No time to worry about that because now Krista has gotten hold of the kitchen's array of Christofle utensils—very nice utensils, high quality, sharp. They make high-pitched pinging noises as they bounce off Sarah's limbs and clatter to the floor and walls, and speaking of clattering, talk about the china, Versace, with gilt edges, shattering into shards as she and Sam fling plate after plate at Krista and her minion, never quite hitting their targets.

And then there's the knife block.

Wüsthof. The chef's series.

She remembers Sam talking about the Wüsthof, how he wanted to get it for Tiffin. "Top of the line, sharper than anything, could probably cut through steel if you tried hard enough."

If a Wüsthof could probably cut through steel, it can certainly cut through her.

Cleanly.

Might even be quick and painless.

But it would take an expert to know what to do, where to drive in the tip of the blade.

Someone who's butchered before.

Someone who staged at a very expensive French restaurant in New York, one with three Michelin stars.

Someone who said they would save the day.

EPILOGUE

One Year Later

The velvet booths have been brushed, the candles have been lit, the bulbs in the brass sconces have been dimmed to a level that ensures everyone will look good in their glow.

He is almost certain. He fiddles with the dial that controls the lights once more.

"I think it was good the other way, boss," Steve says.

"You're right." Sam takes his hand off the knob, shoves it into the pocket of his suit pants. Not too long ago, this would be the time that he would go on his phone. On the app. Searching for "sure things," "no way not to win," the type of bets that made you think there was a trove of gold coins in some other dimension, and you were leaving money on the table if you didn't buy in.

Now, thanks to the meditation program he's enrolled in—at the suggestion of his therapist, it involves guided meditations that are emailed to him each morning—when he finds himself in situations such as these, itching to calm his nerves, he performs what is known as a "physiological sigh." Inhale deeply through the nose, pause. Inhale just a little bit more. Pause. Exhale out the mouth. Repeat thrice.

From what he understands, the physiological sigh increases the intake of oxygen and removes carbon dioxide more efficiently than regular breathing, which, he has to admit, he never thought much about before taking up meditation. This activates his parasympathetic nervous system, which is a fancy way of saying that it calms him down. In theory. Sometimes in practice. But today, ahead of the reopening of Tiffin West Hollywood, his pet project, his pièce de résistance, even the physiological sigh cannot fully settle his pitter-pattering heart. Perhaps he ought to accept this and roll with it. After all, this isn't the most nerve-racking situation he's ever been in, is it? It's a different kind of bet. A more substantial one, with a greater upside, and sure, bigger risk.

He also has Steve to thank. There was a reason that bookie Steve connected him to never wrote back—the bookie didn't exist. Steve had given him a nonworking number. Exactly the sort of referral Sam needed, though he didn't know it at the time.

He pushes through a glass door to Tiffin West Hollywood's terrace. The bistro tables are set, a fireplace roars, the hedges have been trimmed to look well-kept but not *too* perfect. The new location—fourteen stories above Sunset Boulevard, Sam convinced his dad to give up the old outpost on Fairfax Avenue, start fresh—feels like Chateau Marmont meets the Taj Mahal, regal as well as (artfully) run-down. Well. Sam never would've described it in such glowing terms. That comparison came courtesy of Eater, which, after a media preview, bestowed the "new and improved" restaurant with a 9.1 rating, "reigning over the competition in its new location in the strip of West Hollywood that bleeds into Beverly Hills."

That line gave Sam pause. The thought of blood still turns his stomach, just a little. He needs to get over it. He's a chef, for Christ's sake—blood and guts are part of the job. The whole job, if you think about it.

And yet, even though he was never at fault, even though he was lauded by Jala and Hyland and especially the FBI, of all entities, for doing what he did—apparently the FBI had been on the hunt for Krista and Kevin for years, on account of their ritzy and diverse array of scams—it will never sit right with him, the fact that he had to kill one woman to save another. To save himself.

Sure, Krista was crazy, but did she deserve to die? All she wanted was money in the bank and a roof over her head and a taste of the good life, now and again. Same as him.

Kevin and Ali had absconded, though where to was anyone's guess. The FBI was continuing their investigation, and crucially, Hakim and the electric speedboat Kevin paid for had also gone missing. Maybe they'd started a bro compound on some deserted island. Maybe Sid joined them—Hyland had fired him on account of his illustrious record of wooing and bedding guests, a violation of a whole host of company policies, human resources and otherwise. Maanav and Sharif actually came out ahead. Just before Krista and Ali stormed the shores of Jala, Sharif had come clean to Aimy, which allowed her to assemble troops—fellow staffers, including the two butlers who knew all the parties involved best—who would've apprehended Krista had Sam not finished the job. Maanav and Sharif were promoted from the jadugar roster and were now running the Rum Hut, which had been turned into an on-property nightclub, complete with a disco ball hanging from its wooden rafters. Good for them, in Sam's book. Whatever was going on in those crystalline waters, it wasn't his problem anymore.

"Hey, boss." Steve materializes by his side on the terrace with a small plate. "Anand wants you to taste the pakoras."

He takes a bite. Shatteringly crisp on the outside, steamy and savory within.

"That's a killer," he says to Steve, handing back the plate. Had he known how readily Anand would take to hot yoga—as reliable a way to meet women as barhopping, if not more so—he would've suggested a class a long time ago. His head chef no longer calls out sick on account of hangovers, though now he wanted two weeks off to attend an Ashtanga retreat in Mallorca.

Sam initially thought of doing a Tiffin pop-up at the Soho House—the West Hollywood location of the private members club was just down the street. But then he thought, why give them a cut? Why define his success by what the old guard thinks? Why not carve out his own fortune, be the type of man Sarah can be proud of, that their future child can be proud of?

Not that children are proud of their parents, necessarily, and certainly, it will take at least eighteen years before their unborn child is nice to him, maybe more like thirty, but he likes to think that one day he'll be able to take his son or daughter to this very terrace and tell them, "You know when the business turned around? When I opened this restaurant. Wasn't easy, convincing your granddad, but it was worth it, because look at what we have now."

Now, if the establishment came to him? He'd happily open the door. Michelin stars, the World's 50 Best list, he'd be a fool to turn them down. If Erewhon wanted a line of microwaveable meals? Sure. If Emirates Airlines asked for an in-flight menu? Heck, yes.

But on his terms, not on his dad's, not on the Joneses'. Or the Kings', if he's being specific. Those conniving Kings. He knew something was up. No one wants to be vacation friends *that* badly.

"First guests are coming in," Steve says to him now.

Sam nods. "It's showtime."

~

Sarah will never get over the way Los Angeles unfolds from the rooftop terrace of Tiffin, the 360-degree view. From the skyscrapers of downtown to the manicured lawns of Beverly Hills, seen from this perspective, fourteen stories up, she can trick herself into feeling privileged for calling this place home.

Well, it's not exactly a trick, is it? She *is* privileged, of course, but it's easy to get lost in the traffic and the isolation and the vapidness and the way that people say yes to your face but something else behind your back and the traffic and the parking and the property taxes and the taxes in general and the traffic and the lawlessness and the way no one really stops at stop signs and the traffic.

And forget that you live in one of the greatest cities on earth.

This terrace reminds her of that. Sam reminds her of that. Their unborn child, kicking now in her belly, reminds her of how lucky she is, really and truly, to get to call this place home, to be alive at all.

As she ascends the staircase to the rooftop dining room, she puts a hand on her midsection, grounding herself. She didn't need a fairy godmother to get here, to save her marriage, to fix her life, but she did find a mentor, of sorts, in her new boss, who is texting her now.

CHECK THIS OUT!!!!

And then there's a link.

April loves to text. All the livelong day. Sarah has had to exercise boundaries, has had to learn how to not reply immediately, how to manage her time and do a decent job but find satisfaction from things beyond her career, has rediscovered hobbies like painting and sketching and tennis—she plays doubles every Monday, in a group that includes Alana—things she does for the pure joy of doing them (and frequent frustration, her serve being what it is), not for money, not for accolades, because if you stake your happiness on money and accolades alone, you're setting yourself up to fail. (She also downloaded one of those apps that limits your time on social media. At first, she thought it was juvenile, locking herself out of her own account, but oh, the hours she's gained.)

After learning how Sarah and Sam saved Jala and thereby Hyland from going up in flames—in legal terms, if not literally—April offered Sarah a job. She offered Sam a job, too—a Tiffin outpost in Hyland's tony Wilshire Boulevard hotel, though he turned it down in favor of going all-in on the new West Hollywood restaurant—but what she proposed for Sarah was game-changing in that, for the first time in a long time, it allowed Sarah to go to work, do the job, and call it a day. As Hyland's director of brand expansion, all she needed was a curious mind and an internet connection. If April had it her way, she'd be in Hyland's Beverly Hills headquarters every day, but one of Sarah's conditions of accepting the job was the ability to work from wherever she pleased. Boundaries!

It also allowed her time to work on a novel. A new one. About a couple who cons luxury resorts.

Through the glass doors separating the terrace from the main restaurant, she can hear beautiful people drifting in, flocking to the bar. Sam did well, sprung for the gleaming brass accents and emerald-tone marble. Enticing, this bar, as well as what's behind it, and she still has to figure out her relationship to all of that.

She stopped drinking after returning from the Maldives. What started as a one-week cleanse turned into a month-long streak turned into an abstention of indeterminate length, depending on what happens after the baby is born. It's not that she doesn't want a martini—or a Negroni, or a glass of rosé. It's that, for a long time, she didn't know when to stop, and the decisions she made when she was under the influence were not good decisions at all. She got tired of being tired, effectively asleep at the wheel of her own life. It's a wonderful life! One for which she ought to be present.

Her phone buzzes again. Should she check April's text before heading into the dining room to meet Sam?

Might as well. Doesn't want to have it niggling in the back of her mind. Don't need to reply right now, well past normal business hours, 7:00 p.m. on a Friday. Just see what it is.

Sarah clicks on the link. It goes to the homepage of a luxury wine resort in Napa Valley, Kismet.

April has sent another message.

Grisly past but tons of potential. Owned by Anjali Sharma and Rachel Venkataraman.

She shrugs. It looks nice. She likes wine country. Sam likes wine. (In moderation. He's held up that part of the bargain.)

She doesn't need to reply, but it's easy enough. All that business about boundaries—true! But boundaries can be flexible.

Sure.

Why not?

What's the worst that could happen?

ACKNOWLEDGMENTS

Thank you to my agent, Claire Friedman, for cheering me through the many versions of this book. Thank you to my publishing team, Carmen Johnson, Sangeeta Mehta, and everyone at Amazon Publishing, for asking the necessary questions and guiding these characters to the truest versions of themselves. Thank you to the fellow authors who helped me wrap my mind around this story, read early drafts, and offered invaluable advice: Amy Chozick, Avery Carpenter Forrey, Colleen McKeegan, Amanda Montell, and Lina Patton.

Thank you to the many hotels and resorts around the world that have let me take a peek behind the curtain. Thank you especially to Joali Maldives, which served as an inspiration for Jala and boasts some of the most hospitable staffers in the archipelago and beyond (Sid wouldn't last a day there).

Thank you to the friends and family who are steadfast in their support: Amrutha Jindal, Aishwarya Iyer, Ashley Aull, Ritu Lal, Halsey Harper, Ankur Dalal, Michelle Lam, Ameya Pendse, Khushbu Shah, Zain Ahmad, Diana Myint, Aditya Bhatia, Vanisha Raval, and Alexander Ali, who could make Tom Ford work anywhere, even the Maldives. Thank you to my mother, Padma Marikar, for inspiring my own sense of adventure, and for going on so many with me.

Thank you, finally, to Nikhil Lal, the best partner in travel and in life.

ABOUT THE AUTHOR

Photo © Will Tee Yang

Sheila Yasmin Marikar is the author of *Friends in Napa* and *The Goddess Effect*. Her work has been published in *The New Yorker*, *The New York Times*, *The Economist*, *Fortune*, *Bloomberg Businessweek*, *Vogue*, and many other publications. She lives in Los Angeles with her husband. For more information, visit www.sheilayasminmarikar.com.

Praise for *Incidentals*

"*Incidentals* is a deeply nuanced, heartfelt, and hilarious portrait of a marriage—disguised as a delicious true crime story and set against the shimmering backdrop of the kind of Maldivian resort we all fantasize about escaping to. Sheila Yasmin Marikar writes with such wit and empathy, you don't know whether to laugh, gasp, or highlight every line. I didn't want this novel to end."
—Amy Chozick, *New York Times* bestselling author of *Chasing Hillary*

"*Incidentals* filled the *White Lotus*–shaped hole in my heart. With an exotic setting in the Maldives, the most luxurious amenities you can imagine, and drama for days, it is truly the perfect escape (minus the murder, of course). Clever, snarky, and edge-of-your-seat entertaining, *Incidentals* is one of those books that I didn't want to end! I can't wait to see what Marikar does next."

—Sara Ochs, author of *The Resort*

"A one-way ticket to the Maldives, full of vacation fizz and irresistible views, plus marital struggles and a mysterious death. Break out the minibar popcorn—no one does rich people behaving badly with as much intelligence, wit, and heart as Sheila Yasmin Marikar."

—Avery Carpenter Forrey, author of *Social Engagement*

"A couple on the brink of marital collapse embarks on a luxe anniversary trip to the Maldives in an attempt to reconnect and rekindle their romance, only to have a murder thwart their plans. Marikar vividly evokes the postcard setting, from sherbet sunsets to the Indian Ocean's ombré hues—a stark contrast to the sinister events that transpire on the island. *Incidentals* is a thrilling, deliciously entertaining read that pulls back the curtain on privilege and marriage."

—Kristin Vuković, author of *The Cheesemaker's Daughter*

"Sheila Yasmin Marikar is the go-to author for stories that provide the perfect escape. *Incidentals* explores the complicated ways we navigate the relationships with our loved ones, our inspirations, and ultimately, ourselves. This propulsive story is perfect for fans of *The White Lotus*. Readers everywhere will relish this intriguing mix of marriage and mystery."

—Saumya Dave, author of *The Guilt Pill*

"A novel that flies first-class in wit and glitz yet lands firmly in heart. At once a hilarious commentary on luxury travel and a deft exploration of marriage and self-worth."

—Lina Patton, author of *The Lake Club*